HOW TO KILL A KINGPIN

HOW TO KILL A KINGPIN

THE EX-WHISPERER FILES #2

GABRIELLE ST. GEORGE

LEVEL
BEST BOOKS

First published by Level Best Books 2022

Copyright © 2022 by Gabrielle St. George

First edition

ISBN: 978-1-68512-212-6

Cover art by Level Best Designs

This book was professionally typeset on Reedsy.
Find out more at reedsy.com

To my mercurial mother, Olive Merle (Orser) George. We definitely didn't have an Ozzie and Harriet home life, but you sure gave me loads of fodder for my writing. Being your daughter was a never-ending roller coaster ride of highs and lows, but I held on tight and never doubted that you loved me hard and true. Thank you for doing your best mom, I have always loved you and I always will.

Praise for the Ex-Whisperer Mysteries

"Clever Gina is bound to win the hearts of readers, who will look forward to her further adventures."—*Publishers Weekly*

"Gabrielle St. George mixes razor-sharp wit with a healthy dose of edge-of-your-seat suspense to give us a page-turner thrill ride. Who knew being an advice columnist could be so deadly...or so wickedly funny?"—Annette Dashofy, *USA Today* bestselling author of the Zoe Chambers Mysteries

"Gabrielle St. George brings a fresh voice to Canadian crime writing which is simultaneously chipper yet chilling, and she introduces us to characters who are simultaneously engaging yet alarming—a perfect combination for a writer of psychologically suspenseful stories which are also fun to read."—Cathy Ace, award-winning and Amazon #1 bestselling author of the Cait Morgan Mysteries

"... a fun, whimsical, laugh out loud ride... and Gina Malone, one part Stephanie Plum one part Dear Sugar, is the kind of character you can't get enough of! Loved it!"—Danielle Girard, *USA Today* and #1 Amazon bestselling author of *Far Gone*

"... written from the heart. Gabrielle St. George draws from her own considerable experience to create a fun and intricate story with terrific characters and a surprising twist at the end."—Authorlink.com

"Fun, clever, and suspenseful... a feel-good mystery featuring a protagonist I instantly wanted to be friends with. Gina Malone and her loving, hilarious crew of family and friends set out to protect her and catch the criminals. With a touch of romance, delicious food, adorable dogs, and a superbly fluid voice fizzing with perfectly timed wit, this novel will make you laugh out loud and give you the ideal escape."—Samantha M. Bailey, *USA Today* and #1 national bestselling author of *Woman on the Edge*

Chapter One

TOP 9 REASONS TO SKIP YOUR HIGH SCHOOL REUNION

1. High school was not the highlight of your life. In fact, it sucked.
2. You already know everything you want to/need to know about your former classmates from social media.
3. Some people peaked in high school and then failed to launch. You're afraid you may be one of them.
4. Old exes/old crushes.
5. Having to watch your old exes/old crushes dad dance.
6. Mean girls/popular girls.
7. Still not being invited to sit at the cafeteria tables with the mean girls/popular girls.
8. The dude who will relentlessly try to sign you up as a client/involve you in his pyramid scheme.
9. Someone could get murdered, and you might be next.

T rue story—I'm currently being emotionally accosted on all fronts while trying my best not to burden anyone. If therapists weren't so damn expensive, I'd be on the couch on the daily right now. Cue the violins.

I just bid an extremely teary and snotty farewell (I said I was trying not to be a burden; I never said I was succeeding) to my four children at Toronto Pearson International Airport. They're heading back to Europe and their uni studies after spending a blissful week on the beach with their martyr of a mom, for which I am eternally grateful, and if I did my job correctly, they feel eternally guilty for leaving me, once again.

Bad news: I turned fifty a week ago. Good news: it really doesn't feel any different.

Bad news: my old high school is having a reunion in my little hometown, which I just moved back to six weeks ago. More bad news: the festivities start the day after tomorrow and I need to lose eight pounds by then. Good news: I'm driving from the airport to Toronto's West End to pick up a couple of new outfits for the homecoming celebrations, so I probably shouldn't lose the eight pounds, or the new clothes I'm about to purchase may not fit by the weekend. Strategy redirect: hunt for slimming silhouettes.

Good or bad news: depending on how you look at it, I may decide to hole up in a hotel room in the city for the weekend and forgo the inevitable drama and potential trauma that high school reunions are bound to bring.

So many dilemmas, but short of having a shrink on speed dial, nothing a large latte and a bowl of spicy noodles won't cure. I hop off the highway before the Harbourfront and head north through the Trinity-Bellwoods neighborhood into Koreatown. God, I missed the sights and smells but mostly the choices in the city. I am spoiled for them when it comes to food in Toronto, the most multicultural metropolis in the world.

It takes all my strength to resist stopping at the fabulous Buko Shack for Filipino ginataang gulay (vegetables in coconut milk) or the multitude of amazing Caribbean and Mexican eateries sprinkled throughout the neighborhood. I grip the steering wheel tightly to keep myself from veering west into Little Tibet for momos stuffed with fresh ginger and garlicky cabbage. Just a few blocks north, Little Portugal beckons with warm custard tarts. A right turn, and I'd be in Chinatown for veggie gyoza and fiery dragon noodles. It takes superhuman strength to get through Little Italy without pulling over for literally everything. Are you considered a foodie if you're obsessed with eating but not so big on cooking? Final bit of good news, the mystery of how the extra eight pounds appeared has been solved.

At last, I reach Bloor Street, and I'm tempted to stop for Salvadoran tacos, but a parking space magically opens up before me, and I effortlessly slide into a spot right across from Ma Boo Korean Kitchen.

It's always busy at lunch hour, but I snag a tiny wooden corner booth built for two next to the sparkling clean window, and the friendly waitstaff pours me a steaming cup of bori-cha (roasted barley tea). As fast as I drain it, my glass tumbler is refilled, and I'm certain I can feel the health-giving properties of the golden liquid rebuilding my cells as it permeates my body. For starters, I order the vegan japchae (Korean stir-fried glass noodles made from sweet potatoes) with an assortment of brightly colored, thinly sliced veggies and juicy shiitake mushrooms. Chef's kiss.

While I slurp my slippery carbs and sip my barley tea, I look onto the street teeming with pedestrians and diligently attempt to take as many mental snapshots as I can of the busy bodies scurrying past me. Toronto never disappoints when it comes to variety. People of every imaginable shape, size, and color enthrall with a full spectrum of fashion, style, and attitude. It's also Halloween in a few days' time, so the flamboyance dial is turned way up. Every bit of it fascinates me, and after a while, exhausts me, which is why I no longer live in an urban center, but for now, I'm pumped to connect with the vibrant energy of this cosmopolitan city. Soon enough, I'll be back in my tiny new/old hometown on the deserted sandy beach alone with the seagulls and sailboats.

My phone buzzes in my bag, yet another email. I pull it out to check my inbox while I savor the aromatic japchae and am met with loads of unopened messages. They can wait until tomorrow. I scroll through Insta and check out the latest tweets while I wait for the main event, bibimbap, a hot stone pot of crunchy rice topped with veggies and tofu mixed with sesame oil and red pepper paste.

The pungent scent of the bibimbap wafts across the dining area, announcing the arrival of the steaming entrée before it reaches my table and is set down reverently before me. The dish is believed to harmonize nature with the human body, and I'm in desperate need of harmony, so I chow down guiltlessly. Cheaper and infinitely more satisfying than a life coach.

Another ping, another letter to me, The Ex-Whisperer, who has fallen down on the job while I have entertained and been entertained by my four fabulous offspring for the past eight days. I pick my phone up again, my old bestie, guilt, takes over, and I click on an email to read it while I eat.

Dear Ex-Whisperer,

I remember you and your friends from Sunset Beach High like it was yesterday. You were one of the pretty girls who never talked to me. In fact, I don't think most of your stuck-up cheerleader girl gang even knew I existed. But in senior year, one of you vacuous pom-poms slipped a note in my locker telling me I should do the world a favor and hurry up and die. I considered taking the advice but decided that maybe it should be one of the Barbie Brigade who snuffs it instead. Can't wait to see you all again this weekend for hellos and maybe a couple of goodbyes. I wasn't invited to prom, but I wouldn't miss this reunion Halloween costume dance for anything. Give me an R, give me an E, give me a V, give me an E, give me an N, give me a G, give me an E! Gooooooo Whitecaps!

See you there,
Team Outcast

Holy crap, I'm a freak magnet. Pretty sure no therapist can help me with that. It would probably require the services of a past-life regressionist or perhaps an exorcist. I have no idea who this person could be. I'm terrible with faces and worse with names, which will likely make me extremely unpopular at my high school reunion, proving only that not much has changed in thirty-odd years.

I'm at a loss. I don't even remember hearing rumors about anyone in my high school treating someone like that. There were bullies, of course; they're everywhere, but this is extreme. I can't imagine any of the kids I knew being that cruel. So disturbing. I don't even know whether the writer is male or female. Team Outcast's message is cryptic, but it certainly sounds as if they're threatening to do terrible things in retaliation for the perceived wrongs against them. Or maybe there were actual wrongs, and maybe I was

4

more of a self-involved and oblivious teenager than I recall.

You can hardly blame a person for carrying a grudge if they were treated that awfully, but none of what Team Outcast is intimating here is okay. A couple of goodbyes? Does that mean *goodbye* as in peacing out or snuffing out? Other alumni are coming to the high school reunion for the food and the beer. This person is coming for revenge. Or maybe naming it and venting through my column will be enough for them. Most people talk about acting way more than they act, and that would be a very good thing in this instance. I was dreading the stupid reunion before I read this letter. Now my stress hormones are replicating at warp speed. Even the harmonizing bibimbap can't combat my sky-high cortisol levels. I pop a CBD gummy. I need to chill out big time.

I can honestly say I don't think I was ever mean to anyone in high school on purpose. This letter writer certainly has me pegged wrong. I was a floater, had friends in every group, and basically got along with everyone, but I wasn't in the popular girl clique—the drawbridge to that gatehouse was shut tight. Can't say I didn't give trying to join the populars my best shot, but they wouldn't have me. By the time I got to college, I knew I'd dodged a thousand bullets by not being in the cool girl circle, but at the time, the rejection felt totally traumatic.

I tried out for the cheerleading team and made it to the final audition but got cut when Sissy Greensplat, the head cheer flyer, found out her boyfriend, Russ Carney, captain of the Whitecaps wrestling team, had asked me to go to the movies with him. I turned him down, of course (saying yes would have been reputation liquidation), but Sissy blamed me anyway, so the whole cheer squad blamed me—for the entirety of the following four years. Oh God, please don't let Sissy or Russ be at the reunion. Two more reasons for me to hole up in the city for the weekend and skip the Sunset Beach High drama club.

Sometimes it seemed as if the popular girls' mission was to destroy the nerds and weird kids and, anyone else they had deemed misfits. I guess they succeeded in destroying Team Outcast, whoever they are. So sad. Maybe the nasties deserve to be taught a lesson, but Sunset Beach was a very small pond, so I'm betting adult life knocked them off their pedestals pretty quickly and provided them with more than enough reality checks once they left for the big, bad, outside world.

Everyone knows the real reason high school reunions exist is so people can show up and prove that the predictions about them were wrong—that they turned out to be more successful in life than their classmates expected. That would be the best revenge for Team Outcast.

My reply:

> Dear Team Outcast,
>
> I am so very sorry that horrific thing happened to you. I will never get used to humans' capacity for cruelty. Bullying is unacceptable and inexcusable and the opposite of cool. Trust me, mean girls don't make it in the world after high school. You don't have to concern yourself with trying to exact revenge on those harpies who hurt you—the boxing ring of life will have had those lightweights on the ropes over and over again. I know that being treated so terribly creates scars that sometimes can't heal with time alone. I hope you have someone to talk to about what happened to you. In case you don't, I'm listing some links to counselors below, and I hope you will reach out to them.
>
> PS I actually never made the cheer squad, so I never was part of the Barbie Brigade. Let's hope everyone has grown up and grown kinder.
>
> Affectionately yours,
>   The Ex-Whisperer

I hit Post.

Every word I wrote to Team Outcast is the truth. I hope they believe me because I genuinely hate to be thought of as mean (although I have no problem being unpleasant or even aggressive when circumstances call for it). Also, I really don't want to be on the bad side of a person like him or her. I'm not that brave, and I don't want to throw my hat in the ring. I'm feeling fresh out of fight at the moment.

When I look up from my phone, I see that a lunchtime line-up has formed out the door of the restaurant now. An early Halloween partygoer dressed as SpongeBob SquarePants scowls at me for obliviously lingering at my table for an inconsiderate length of time. Ugh. I only moved up north a month and a half ago, and I'm already emanating country bumpkin vibes. I catch the waitstaff's eye, and the bill is on my table in seconds. I'm on the street and in my car a minute later, but on my way out the door, I make it a point to give SpongeBob my best Krabby-Patty death stare.

My Korean lunch was delicious, but I've got a stomach ache from my reading material. Overall, I'm feeling pretty crummy between saying so long to my four beautiful babies and racking my brain to figure out who my vengeful reunion letter writer might be. And now I have to hunt for chic outfits that look effortlessly put together and make a statement without trying too hard and also make me look eight pounds slimmer. My initial eagerness for clothes shopping has waned, and I haven't stepped inside a store yet. I might end up rocking my authentic self and sporting faded Levi's and white T-shirts with my Docs for the whole reunion weekend. That's if I attend at all. The chances of me going are shrinking by the minute.

Despite my now dampened enthusiasm to try on toggery, I park in a lot on Queen Street West near a bevy of beautiful vintage shops. To fortify my resolve, I first line up for a latte at a fave café. Me and my good buddy Procrastination go way back.

The aroma of the percolating coffee beans instantly lifts my spirits. Shopping for clothes always entails a lengthy warm-up period for me. When it comes to trying on bathing suits, it can take years of prep. My phone dings sweetly with texts from my kids telling me they're boarding their plane now and that they'll message when they're all safe and sound in their various European flats. A new email catches my eye, and I open it.

Dear Ex-Whisperer,

Sounds like you're telling me I should just take it on the chin and throw in the towel. I think you must be punch-drunk. Your memory has faded. No worries, though, I'll help jog it for you. Let's catch up at the reunion costume party. You'll find me easy enough. I'll be dressed as the Grim Reaper.

Team Outcast

Chapter Two

Yeah, so not planning on replying to that creepy message. Not interested in hanging with the Grim Reaper—get back to me in forty years on that one. Also not shopping for new outfits because now I am definitely not going to any of the Sunset Beach High reunion festivities, so my afternoon just opened right up, and I'm going to spend it at the art gallery followed by dinner at whatever all-you-can-eat place I can find (what eight pounds?). I could grab a hotel room for the night and enjoy a luxurious morning brunch complete with a chocolate fountain (what eight pounds?). I just need to arrange for someone to take care of my fur babies, Zoe and Spook.

Hugh will be at my place, working on putting the new roof on the bunkie until five, and he's going to let Zoe out to piddle before he leaves. I originally planned to be back at my cottage by eleven tonight. I don't want to ask Florrie to pick up my pup for the evening because, of course, my Energizer Bunny cousin is on the high school reunion decorating committee, and she'll be up to her eyeballs in crepe paper streamers and disco balls for the next four days.

I guess I'm going to have to drive back up to Sunset Beach tonight to take care of my dog and cat myself. Plan A: me hiding out in the city until the reunion is over is not going to pan out because, pets. I'm going to have to spring into action on plan B: me holing up at my cottage with the lights out for as much of the weekend as I can manage so that no one from the camera club, school newspaper, or anyone I practiced the awkward art of kissing on finds me there. Chances of success: extremely low.

The multitude of mental lists I carry around in my head run in a loop pretty much nonstop. Currently playing is *List of Commitments for This Weekend That I Cannot Squirm Out Of*—I agreed to record an episode of my *Ex-Whisperer Files* podcast on Friday night with an old school friend guesting who is a super-successful Instagram influencer. But she doesn't have to know where I'm zooming from, so that could still work in with my clandestine plan.

I also promised Cordelia, my grade school girlfriend turned head librarian (and anonymous best-selling novelist who writes erotica under the pseudonym Primrose Wilding), that I would do a reading from my latest book, *The Gal Guide to Navigating Narcissism*, on Sunday afternoon in the library lobby. I love libraries, but I hate doing appearances. All the pressure to have a successful reading revolves around people showing up, and that's one of the few things the author can't control. Oftentimes, attendance numbers can be humbling, and reading a chapter of your book to rows of empty chairs while pretending you don't care that no one came to hear you because nobody has any interest whatsoever in you or your book is humiliating.

At least in Sunset Beach, I know I can fill the seats with the warm bodies of my immediate family members, even if a few of them are likely to doze off or chat to each other nonstop and loudly, possibly in Italian. I know Cordelia planned the reading as part of the reunion festivities. Our little town doesn't have that many published authors. She has to fly under the radar in her genre, and as far as I know, I'm the only other bestselling one, but even so, I will ask her if I can postpone.

I also promised my eccentric twin Italian aunts that I would use my jeep to transport their portable tarot-card-reading booth to the school gymnasium and help them set it up for the Halloween dance. They're running a two-for-one divination special for alumni, but they've doubled their price on the first reading. They're Calabrese. What are you gonna do?

I'm going to have to figure out a strategy to bail on these events and promises because there's no way I'm chilling with Team Outcast. I suppose I should warn the cheerleaders about the dude in the Grim Reaper duds who literally wants to gag them with a spoon. Then again…maybe I do have a couple of mean bones in my body after all.

I toss my empty coffee cup in the compost bin, then leave the café to put another ten bucks on the parking meter. I can walk to the art gallery from here, and I don't want to take a chance on finding a parking spot closer to it—they're hard to come by in this bumping city. The parking gods were good to me today. I don't want to push my luck. Also, could stand to burn off a few calories—I. Am. Stuffed. Ugh. I may be up another eight pounds after today. Luckily, I still haven't unpacked all the boxes from my move last month, and my weigh scale is MIA, so this hypothesis cannot be proven. I won't unpack any more boxes until my skinny jeans are no longer digging into my fleshy waist. Note to self: get back to the gym.

I never have managed to figure out the connection between satiation and eating, however, I do have a thorough understanding of food for comfort and food for love and food for sorrow, and food for celebration. Eat when one is hungry, and stop eating before one feels full? Sorry? Pardon me? Say what? I don't get it. If Malcolm Gladwell is right, and ten thousand hours of doing any one thing makes a person an expert at that thing, then I am definitely an expert on eating one's feelings. Does this expertise qualify me as a foodie? I aspire to that title.

I need to escape myself for a while, and the incredible art I feast on in the AGO does the trick. I am quickly lost in the inspirational energy of the gallery, and my soul swells with the painted visions of Emily Carr. I'm blinded by the brilliance of astounding Indigenous artists like Norval Morrisseau. As soon as Hugh has my bunkie renovation finished, I'm filling it with my brushes and canvasses, and I can't wait to get back to painting again.

The blissful bubble of my artist's date is periodically punctured by invasive thoughts of Team Outcast and his not-so-veiled threats. I push him out of my head as best I can with the engrossing works of Tom Thomson, Lawren Harris, and the rest of the Group of Seven, but the creepy letter writer slithers back inside my brain at every opportunity. The two-hour art gallery visit I planned stretches into four. I never visit the city without stopping by my BFF Siobhan's gravesite for a chat—I'm going to have to haul ass to squeeze that in now. It's dark by the time I finally make my way outside, and I battle a biting October wind back to my car.

Time to say so long to the city and make the return trek to Sunset Beach to rescue my dog and cat. I'm caught in the tail end of Toronto's rush hour traffic, and for all the crowd of populated vehicles that surround me, I suddenly feel very alone. I spent a lovely afternoon solo in the city, but now it's just me, my thoughts, and a very long drive ahead with no convenient distractions like prodigious paintings to ogle and worldly cuisine to consume.

Now in the quietude, I can't help but relive the bittersweet goodbyes I bid my four amazingly perfect children only hours earlier. I'm recalling the delicious scent of their skin and hair and how it felt to hold them in my arms for that heartrending farewell hug and, worse, the wrenching feeling of having to let go of that last embrace. It hurts so bad.

Miles of glowing red brake lights, stretch out before me like winding serpents, and I wonder how many thousands of my fellow drivers also feel forlorn and lonely right now. It's one thing to be alone, but it's worse to physically be with someone and still feel that way. That's how it used to be for me in the last years of my marriage. Heartache can be so debilitating. At least I don't exist in that particular painful space anymore. It's been replaced with other painful spaces—ah, the plight of the human condition. There's no escaping it.

I think going home, to my pets tonight was the right decision after all. I need some loving cuddles, especially from a couple of beings I adore and who worship me right back. Every kind of true love is healing. Zoe and Spook are the medicine I need tonight for my emotional ails.

I pull off the highway to swing through my old town and pay a quick visit to my girl Siobhan. I miss her every minute of every day. Cancer is a thief that steals forever the bodies of the ill and the joy of their loved ones. It's late and pitch black out, and I've got to get home to my dog soon, but I can't not stop in to say hey to my better half. I park and jog across the lawn of the cemetery to Siobhan's spot. I'm the only living one haunting the place tonight. We have a quick chat, and I press my forehead against the cold granite of her tomb to connect with her and tell her how much harder and crummier life is without her in it. "I love you, gal." I know she says it back to me, and then I'm sprinting to my car, trying not to trip over the fresh mounds of loose soil.

The drive takes twice as long in the heavy traffic, but once I'm outside the city limits, everything simmers down. It's late on a Tuesday night, so the roads heading north are mostly empty except for me and the odd trucker or tractor—the farmers work through the nights at this time of year, hurrying to get the final cuts off their crops before the winter weather sets in.

My car headlights swim in a sea of blackness, the dotted yellow line on the asphalt my North Star to follow. Orphan lampposts periodically illuminate my path to assist my navigation like lighthouse beacons directing my way in the dark. I actually don't mind the empty roads, but the silence is starting to weigh on me, encouraging my mind to go places I'd rather not. I'm thinking of my vengeful letter writer Team Outcast now and wondering how far they might be willing to go to obtain the justice they believe they're owed. I've known people who would go to any lengths to get what they wanted—including my ex-husband. That's almost never a good thing. When what they're seeking is revenge, it's always disastrous, for them and for their intended targets.

No guiding streetlights anymore along my journey, only vast acreages of slumbering fields and darkened farmhouses. When I approach the quaint community of Harriston and drive along the main street, it seems the whole place has retired for the evening, doors shut tight and the blue light from big screen TVs spilling out living room windows onto the sidewalks.

I pull over at a twenty-four-hour gas station to fuel up. I'm the only car at the tanks. I hop out, prepay, and pump as quickly as possible so as not to let my takeaway coffee cool. It's dark as pitch beyond the perimeter of the garage, and it's grown colder and quieter, and eerier since I started my drive home. I shiver for no reason at all and can't stop looking over my shoulder at the sinister shadows behind me. That damn wild imagination of mine never fails to mess with my psyche and fire up my nerves at the most inopportune times.

I hang the nozzle back in its slot at thirty bucks instead of the fifty I planned to purchase because this fraidy-cat is in a hurry to get out of this deserted station and back on the deserted road. I jump inside my jeep like a dumbass who knows perfectly well there are no serial killers lurking in the lot but has worked herself into a full-on fright anyway. No more scary books or movies for me. Oh wait, Halloween is right around the corner. Okay, maybe a few scary movies, but no more conjuring up imaginary monsters lying under the bed or phantasmic slashers crouching behind gas pumps.

I lock the car doors, buckle up, and take a few deep breaths. Since the limbic system in my brain, has no way to know that the fearfulness I'm experiencing has zero facts to support it, my poor body is involuntarily flooded with adrenaline, and my hands shake on the steering wheel. I pull out my phone to check my messages before I start driving. No texts from the kids yet; they'd still be in the air. But there is a letter to my blog from the very last person I wanted to hear from right now.

> Dear Ex-Whisperer,
>
> I stopped by and dropped a little something off at your home tonight. Sorry I missed you. I was looking forward to a catch-up chat. I sure hope you haven't decided to skip the reunion this weekend. That would screw up all my homecoming plans, and then I would be very, very angry.
>
> Team Outcast

Chapter Three

So perhaps I need to take back what I just told myself. Maybe my brain hasn't been flooding my body with fear hormones based on the reality I was experiencing, but it wasn't just my imagination running amok, either. Looks more like my intuition was sounding the alarm bells. My gut was warning me to stay sharp, a primordial, protective premonition desperately trying to keep me safe. Thanks, psychic ability or watchful ancestors or whatever else is responsible for putting me on the alert.

I'm not usually a speeder, but I do at least thirty over the limit for the rest of the drive back. I'm not sure what sort of surprise Team Outcast has left on my doorstep, but I'm willing to bet it's a gift I'd prefer not to receive. I just want to get home to my pets and make sure they're both safe and sound. Zoe would know if anyone was anywhere near our property, and if somebody was skulking around, she'd be hugely distressed and might be barking even still. I wish now that I hadn't stayed so late in the city. Then again, I'm kind of relieved I wasn't at home when my peeved peer came knocking.

My emotional right brain engages in its regularly scheduled tennis match with my rational left hemisphere. What if Team Outcast is still there when I pull up? What if they come back later tonight? Should I call Florrie and ask her to meet me at the cottage when I arrive, so I'm not there alone? No, I can't do that. I know she's exhausted between her volunteering to organize half of the reunion festivities and running her bakery while having to make extra batches of absolutely everything because, of course, every visitor in town will be lining up around the block for Florrie's fabulous food. I could go to Florrie's apartment and crash there for the night. I'd rather return to my cottage in the daylight, to be sure, but that doesn't help my neglected pet situation. I have to get home to let my Giant Schnauzer out and feed my perpetually ravenous feline. It will be close to midnight when I arrive. There's no one I would bother at that time. I've got dozens of family members I could ring for support, but a phone call to one of them at this late hour would set the sirens off and have them all raised in a mob and swarming my place with pitchforks and scythes. Gotta love my family—they're always there to back me up and also to gather as much gossip as they possibly can.

I've reduced my options to one: I go home alone. This option presents two possible outcomes. One: I pull up at my cottage, high beams on, take a few moments to scan the scene. If Zoe is barking, it means a stranger is still present on the property, and I backtrack full tilt and head into town to gather recruits, despite the late hour. Two: I pull up at my cottage, high beams on, take a few moments to scan the scene. Zoe might whine excitedly, but she won't bark if she knows it's me driving up, so if she's silent, that will mean the coast is clear, no visitors in the vicinity. In which case, I jump out of my car, run to the door hell-bent for leather, and release the hound, letting my giant protectress relieve herself and keep guard over me before we both hurry back inside our home and seal it up lock, stock, and barrel for the night.

That too familiar hormone, adrenaline, has returned with a vengeance to course through my veins and tie my neck muscles in knots. Can't wait to hit my bed. It's going to feel amazing tonight, if I make it there in one piece.

If the roads were dark earlier in my drive, they're black-hole black now. An hour later, I'm approaching Sunset Beach. It's a relief to finally drive along the familiar streets, and I'm surprised that this tiny town of only seven thousand residents, already feels like home to me even though I only moved back here a month and a half ago. I turn onto High Street, which is well lit as always by its lovely vintage lampposts and the soft glow of the night lights emanating from pretty paned storefront windows, every one of which has strung up banners, flags, and blue-and-white team pennants exalting the old school spirit. I'm sure the entirety of the townsfolk, have exhausted themselves with the excitement and preparations for the big reunion that's been years in the planning.

There are no signs of life at this hour, not a soul out on the streets. I turn onto the Coastline Trail and drive the ten minutes to my cottage. Every home I pass by is in total darkness. The sky and the lake are the same inky color, and they meld into one, disappearing in the bleakness where the horizon usually hovers. A person wouldn't know how near or far the water was from them if it weren't for the loud and rhythmic sound of the waves crashing against the empty sand beach.

My heart begins racing, my hands shaking once again as I approach my little cabin in the woods, which makes me feel like a traitor to my sweet home. I love it dearly, and I totally resent having been coerced into feeling scared to return to it. I'm sick to my stomach when I think that someone has stolen the joy of my going home and replaced it with fright and loathing. My fear is morphing into anger, and maybe that's a good thing. I hope it will serve me if I do have an unwelcome visitor and need to kick their ass off my property. Yeah, it's a lot better to be angry than afraid. I'm going to go along with the rage welling up inside of me. It feels way more empowering than fear, even if it may be less wise.

High beams on, I pull up onto the scrubby, sandy lawn that is my front yard and my driveway. My car lights flood the entire face of my cute little cabin. I scan the grounds. It's very dark. And very quiet. No signs of any visitors. I listen hard. No sounds of anyone nearby. No barking from my guard dog. Only the noise of waves and faint whip-poor-will calls floating on the air. It's a little late in the year to hear chants from whip-poor-wills, and my superstitious aunts have always told me that when those birds sing close to your house, it means death, or at least bad luck is on the way. I'm usually adept at ignoring the aunts' nonsense. Tonight, not so much.

According to my left brain, the fact that my dog is silent should mean that I have permission to proceed, that there is no threatening former schoolmate lurking in the woods, waiting to pounce, and I am safe to exit my vehicle, unlock the door of my cottage, and take my time enjoying the brisk night breeze while my pup sniffs around in the grass looking for her favourite piddle spot.

Unfortunately, as per usual, my right brain is at the helm, and fantastical imaginings are at full throttle. The dog isn't barking because . . . No, I can't even allow the thought. The shadow beside the woodpile isn't being thrown by the creaking silver birch standing next to it. It's not the silver birch doing the creaking. The cedar branches rustling nearby aren't being disturbed by a rapacious raccoon. It must be a serial killer in the bush, behind the tree, waiting for me to climb out of my car and step into his zip ties and duct tape gag.

Oh, for God's sake, being me is fricking torturous. The worst-case scenario is my default and go-to twenty-four-seven. I exhaust myself, and I need a vacation from me.

I'm calling on you, left brain. Let's do this, whip-poor-wills or no.

And we do. I take the key out of the ignition, find the house key. The headlights will stay on for another minute. One deep breath, and I push my driver's door open. My hormones haven't yet received the message that I'm not supposed to be afraid, so I'm still shaking and breathing unevenly, but I move with long, swift strides across the lawn and up the few steps to the front door of my little clapboard cottage, house key in hand.

House key out of hand. Damn it, I've dropped them. My car headlights choose now to auto extinguish, plunging me into a murky dimness. The coach light over the cottage entry throws a small circle of yellow on the porch floor, and I drop down to my knees to hunt for my keys. My eyes haven't adjusted yet to the lessened light, so it seems darker than it actually is. Zoe stirs on the other side of the door (thank God for that). I try to reassure her. "Good girl, Zoe. Hang on one minute. Be right there." I pull out my phone to use the flashlight, which falls out of my hand, too, and clatters on the deck.

Okay, got 'em. Keys and phone. I stand up, fumble with the lock and...

"Gina?"

I scream. And leap out of my skin. And scream again. And drop my keys and phone again. Zoe goes off the rails, barking frantically. I whirl around to face my killer.

She stands there before me, all silvery shimmer in the moonlight. "I'm sorry; I didn't mean to startle you."

I can barely hear her for the banging of my heart between my ears. "What the—?" I'm definitely hyperventilating. "You're Team Outcast?"

"What? No, it's Vivi. Vivi Murphy. What's Team Outcast?"

"Vivi? You scared me half to death." I see metal glinting in the light by my feet and bend down to snatch up the house key and my phone once again. My hands vibrate as I struggle to unlock the door while taking purposefully calming, deep breaths.

Zoe bounds outside, still barking. She sniffs Vivi up and down, rules her out as a threat, then hightails it to the tall grass to relieve herself, finally. Poor thing.

Vivi's voice is soft. "I'm so sorry. I know it's late."

I'm just regaining enough composure to be pissed off at my old friend. Pissed off because she scared the crap out of me and also because she looks frigging amazing. "Yeah, it is late. Is this an emergency? Because if it's not, then it's really weird of you to pop by at midnight. It's a high school reunion, but we're not in high school anymore. What were you going to do, throw pebbles at my window to wake me up so we could sneak out to a beach party with the seniors?" I probably don't have to be quite so snarky, but she does look aggravatingly attractive.

Zoe is back and at my side, wanting attention. I rub her scruffy head. The physical contact helps both of us settle down. I try to take in Vivi carefully now, read the distress I can see in her pretty face.

Vivi is anxious and speaks quickly. "I am really sorry. I got into town late last night. I'm staying at my parents' old cottage up the road. I popped in to say hi to you today, but there was no one home. About an hour ago, I couldn't sleep, so I went for a walk and passed by here. There was a car out in front, and I figured it was yours, but then I saw someone walk around from the lakeside, and I could tell it wasn't you. The person kept pacing back and forth past your door. They seemed really agitated, and I could hear your dog going crazy inside the cottage. It didn't seem right, so I just hung back in the shadows for a while and watched them."

My old best school friend just dumped a whole lot of information on my doorstep. Maybe a few too many details, the way people who are lying tend to do. I wrote an entire book on this topic, which may or may not make me an expert, but regardless, it makes me suspicious. "Did the person see you?"

"No. After a while, they got in their car and drove off. I didn't have your cell number, so I couldn't call, but I emailed you to tell you I was here. And give you a heads up that someone else was here, too."

I check my phone and see that Vivi did send me an email half an hour ago saying exactly that. It's going to take some time for all my vital signs to come back into normal range. "You want to come in for an herbal tea? I don't expect I'll be relaxed enough to fall asleep for quite a while."

"Sure, I don't think I'll be nodding off anytime soon, either."

Vivi follows a happy Zoe and me inside the cottage. I turn on all the lights and put the kettle on.

"Take a seat. I just have to feed the pets." My cat Spook has clearly missed me, or at least missed his meal. He rubs against my ankles while I dish out his grub, but then he punishes me for being gone so long by ignoring me and lavishing all his feline attention on our guest.

Vivi looks closely at the old prints hanging on the walls that have literally been there forever. I put out kibble and treats for the dog and cat.

"Wow, this sweet place looks exactly like I remember it. So many good times here." Vivi runs her hand along the edge of the speckled Arborite countertop and the backs of the painted wooden chairs, touching memories. She takes some photos with her phone. "Do you mind?"

"No, go ahead. It's like a museum, but some things need to be updated since I'm living here now. I'm having it renovated over the next year." I put out a plate of plain biscuits and a dish of blueberries for us. "Chamomile or Lavender Lemon Balm?"

"Chamomile would be lovely, thank you." Vivi pulls out a chair and sits down at the kitchen table.

"So, who was the person skulking around my place? Did you recognize them?"

Vivi shakes her head. "It was really hard to get a good look. I took a few shots on my phone. Obviously, I couldn't use the flash, but they're way too dark to make out any details."

Vivi holds her phone out for me to have a look. "I can't even tell if they're male or female. It's just shadows."

Vivi shakes her head again. "They had a loose hoodie pulled up over their head. Average height and kind of beefy."

I rack my brain, trying to figure out who it could be. My cousin Florrie knows what rock I hide the spare key under, so she wouldn't be waiting outside for me. My contractor, Hugh, has his own key in case he needs to get inside to shut the water or power off or on when he's working here, so not him, either. "What kind of car were they driving?"

"A small dark one, like a little hatchback. I didn't want them to see me, so I stayed on the other side of the road in the bush."

"Someone I don't know sent me a message tonight saying they stopped by and left something here for me, but I didn't see anything on the doorstep when we came in."

"They did leave something on your front porch. I picked it up."

"Why would you do that?"

"I didn't want you to find it if you came home alone and felt nervous."

Vivi is making me more nervous than Team Outcast managed to with their cryptic emails. "Why would it make me nervous? I don't understand. What was it? Where is it?"

Vivi reaches into a deep pocket in her jacket and pulls out some photographs. She looks reluctant as she passes them to me. The snapshots are old, as in three decades old. High school pictures. Cheerleader tryouts. Football game days. A bonfire party on the beach. I'm in all of them along with bunches of my old girlfriends. Florrie is in them, too. I recognize her, and Vivi, and our friend Cordelia. I can't tell who all the other ones are because, in every single photo, all the girls' faces have been angrily scratched out with red pen.

Chapter Four

"This is beyond creepy." I scan the photos for clues. "Who would do this?"

"Someone who really didn't like our girl group."

Of course, my mind has jumped to Team Outcast, but I decide to keep that to myself for now. "Our group was made up of all the good girls. This person has got it all wrong."

The whistling kettle makes me jump. I pour the herbal tea for Vivi and me then sit down across from my old gal pal. "How did you know that what the person left at my door was something you'd feel compelled to intervene with? What made you go and look at what the person left for me in the first place? Didn't you think it might be private business of mine? It's kind of weird that you decided to check out what the person left for me." It's really bothering me that Vivi took it upon herself to take the photos off my porch. Something doesn't feel right. But maybe it's me. I don't completely trust anyone anymore after the events of the last few weeks. Correction, the last few years.

"I just figured it was something...I don't know, not nice."

"But you were across the road. In the dark. How could you possibly know?"

Vivi shrugs. "It was just my intuition. A bad feeling. The person looked agitated and out of place."

Vivi and I were the best of friends all through school. She came from a high drama home, but she wasn't like the rest of her family. She was sweet and kind. She's a super successful interior designer in Toronto now, but she didn't start her career until after she left her husband eight years ago. She wasn't allowed to work when she was married to a mob boss. I have to hand it to her—it's not easy to extricate yourself from a relationship like that, especially since they were high school sweethearts. But in the last two years, she's become a bit of a celebrity for a different reason.

Vivi let her silver hair grow in and documented her progress on Instagram. Two million followers later, Vivi is a pro-aging poster girl, collaborating on endorsements with clothing, cosmetics, and all manner of wellness companies. I follow her page, *Silver Lining*, with total fascination, and she looks even more serenely attractive in real life than she does on her filtered reels. Her silver hair looks like a crown, and she glows beneath it.

But something's off in Vivi's manner. It feels as if we could easily pick up right where we left off, as if twenty years didn't just slip away with only sporadic contact between us. But at the same time, she has me on my guard, and I'm not exactly sure why. Maybe it's just that I'm not sure I want to become entangled with whatever complications she's got going on. I'm definitely sensing trouble.

Is there another way to live when you've been married to the mob? Probably not, and it's not her fault, and I'm aware that I sound like a super crummy gal pal, but I don't think I have the bandwidth to deal with anyone else's issues right now. I've got so many of my own to sort through. To top it off, I'm emotionally and physically exhausted. Also, just downright cranky because I'm tired from a lack of sleep and cranky because I'm tired of trouble like Team Outcast coming at me.

I'd invited Vivi to guest on my *Ex-Whisperer Files* podcast because I like to interview older women who are slaying it. I'm supposed to host it live from the reunion this weekend. I suppose if Team Outcast has their way, instead of me being the host for a guest who's slaying it, maybe there'll be a twist, and I could be the host who gets slayed. There's that trusty wild imagination of mine kicking in once again, luring me into worst-case scenarios at every turn. I need to dial all this tension back for now and try to let the sleepy-time tea kick in so that, at some point tonight, I'm actually relaxed enough to catch some z's.

"I'm exhausted. Maybe we should change the subject, deal with these unsettling photos tomorrow."

Vivi nods. "I agree. How are your kids?"

"Perfect. They left to return to their studies in Europe today. I'm already missing them so much. Saying goodbye never gets any easier. They'll be back home for Christmas, though, and I'll go there in the spring. How are your two doing?"

"They're amazing. One's in school in California, one's in Vancouver. They're not big on the snow unless they're skiing in it. And our divorce was so messy, and Sal made it so difficult that they wanted to get as far away from the drama as they could. I don't blame them. I miss them, but we talk almost every day."

"Sounds a lot like my kids." I top up our teacups. "Divorce sucks but staying in a bad marriage sucks harder."

Vivi smiles wryly. "I agree. I didn't know if I'd survive the divorce. Sal's not the kind of guy you break up with unless you want to end up sleeping with the fishes, but I knew I wouldn't survive the marriage, so it was kind of a toss-up."

"Is Sal still a pro bowler?"

Vivi shakes her head. "His *Bowling for Dollars* days are over."

I can't help it; I shudder. Bowling is just not my jam. I think it's the whole sharing shoes thing that makes it seem so icky. Also, the shirts—not my style and not a style I want to see on anyone else, either. "So, he hung up his wingtip shoes and shelved the antifungal odor spray?"

Vivi winces, too. "Not quite. He doesn't bowl pro anymore, but he's got a regulation size four-lane bowling alley in the basement of his McMansion. It was our McMansion, but I always hated it. It's so embarrassingly over the top. I was happy to let him have it in the divorce settlement. I got my parents' cottage, which is what I wanted."

"Oh wow, that's great to hear."

"I'm going to start trying to spend more time up here, far away from Sal. He spends all his leisure hours in his basement, knocking down tenpins and knocking around his crew of goodfellas."

"He's a true kingpin."

Vivi nods. "You've got that right. He's the Black Hand in bowling and in business. I guess you and I didn't make the greatest choices in marriage partners."

"But we got the greatest kids."

"True, and we were young. What did we know? But still, you married a dick, and I married a bowler who ended up a wiseguy."

I'm perplexed. "Is bowling a sport? And, are bowlers athletes?" I'd truly like to get to the bottom of this age-old question.

Vivi's lips curl. "If it is, it's got to be the least sexy sport on the planet."

"Followed by curling."

"Followed by golf."

"Sumo wrestling."

"Race walking."

And just like that, we are laughing like two silly high school girls, and the distance, of our decades apart dissolves. We smile at each other, and cross a bridge of understanding. I know Vivi is hurting, and she'll talk to me about it when she's ready.

"Does Dick have a new woman in his life?"

"Yes, Rochelle. But you can call her the cockroach, I do. Sal?"

Vivi nods. "Tiffany, but you can call her a child, I do. She's twenty-three."

"Oh my God. Maybe she's into antifungal odor spray, who knows with kids these days. Sal won't have the nerve to come to the reunion, will he?"

"Sal didn't do very well in school. Remember he got voted most likely to wind up in jail? The yearbook committee was right about that prediction, but Sal wants to show those people up, and parading a twenty-three-year-old Instagram model around on his arm will be a good start."

"Oh no, poor you."

"I'm going to spend most of my time trying not to run into them. They've rented the Steller Estate by the flagpole for the weekend."

I'm impressed because I can be shallow sometimes, too. "Wow. I saw it on Airbnb. It's got like fifteen bedrooms and goes for twenty thousand a week."

"Sal's got his problems, but money isn't one of them. They don't call Sal

Richie Rich for nothing. He likes to splash his cash around."

"Hmm, maybe bowling can be sexy after all." Very shallow indeed.

Vivi cringes. "Nothing sexy about Sal anymore, including his money." Vivi gets up from the table. "It's so late. I'd better get back to the cottage. Festivities start tomorrow, and it seems like we're going to need to be on our A-game for so many reasons." She winks and crosses to the door.

"All of them exhausting." I confess, "I'm planning on skipping pretty much everything."

Vivi looks skeptical. "I don't think Florrie's going to let you get away with that."

"Florrie is my greatest obstacle to hermithood." I follow Vivi. "I don't know how safe it is for you to be out there alone now with that weirdo creeping around. You can sleep here for the night if you want. I've got an extra bedroom, and the bed's made up because Florrie stays here a lot."

Vivi smiles appreciatively. "It's not necessary. I'm fine, really. I've done this walk a million times."

"We both have." I'm not comfortable with her leaving alone. "I'll take Zoe and escort you halfway to your cottage."

"So we're both unsafe?" Vivi laughs. "I was out for a stroll in the dark on my own tonight when I came across your visitor, remember? I love walking around here in the night and hearing the waves. I've been doing it for nearly fifty years. And anyway, that weirdo didn't call on me. You're the one they want to connect with."

Maybe Vivi's had more sleep than me. She seems so strong and calm, although I think, after thirty years with Sal, she's finely honed the skill of staying centered or perhaps mastered the trick of masking all emotions. I'm nowhere in the vicinity of strong and calm. I shudder involuntarily. "Yeah, but all of us are in the freaky photos."

Vivi waves me off assuredly. "Along with most of our graduating class, so whatever. This person has got to be some bitter, washed-up loser who gets off on frightening people and probably doesn't have the guts to actually confront any of us. I bet they're just hoping to get revenge for whatever they think we did to them thirty-three years ago by ruining the reunion for all of us instead."

I hadn't thought of that, but it makes sense. "Actually, you're probably right about that. And what this person is doing would be a brilliant way to accomplish that. Florrie has done so much work getting this whole weekend organized. I don't want it to crash and burn for her. I don't think I'm going to mention any of this to her, at least not yet."

Vivi nods. "Sure, I get that. You know, I've never once felt scared in this sweet little town in fifty years, and I'm sure as heck not going to start now."

"I like your attitude. I'm going to try to ride your coattails and pretend I'm brave, too." I pick up my cell phone and dial Vivi's number. Her cell rings in her purse. She answers it. "Let's stay on the line until you get to your cottage."

"Okay, that works." Vivi heads out the door.

I stand on my porch, watching her go while Zoe does her bedtime potty, but Vivi disappears into the darkness in a few short moments.

We continue chatting on our cell phones for the next five minutes until Vivi reaches her old family cottage.

"I read your new book on narcissists. It was really great."

"After thirty years with Sal, you must be an expert yourself."

"More like a survivor."

"That makes two of us."

"I'm at the cottage now. Nobody around but me and the raccoons. I'm unlocking the door. And...I am inside, safe and sound. Thanks for keeping me company on the walk home."

I lock my own little cottage up tight. Zoe and Spook have already tucked themselves in for the night. I take a look at the defaced photos one more time and shiver despite my proclamations of bravery. Team Outcast has got a serious chip on their shoulder. Maybe more like a boulder. Hopefully, Vivi's theory is right, and their only aim is to scare us all and wreck our reunion weekend. For my part, I can't wait until Monday when this is all over.

So far, ninety-five reasons to hide out in my cottage. Zero reasons to attend the reunion.

The more I think about it, the more I'm convinced the situation is exactly as Vivi suggested—Team Outcast is probably just some bitter person who hated high school, like half the world did, and is disappointed in their adult life, like more than half the world is. I place a call to the Sunset Beach police chiefs, Floyd and Lloyd, to inform them anyway. I only get through to the stationhouse voicemail, and the message I leave is more apologetic than a request for assistance. Receiving nasty emails from trolls and weird things in the mail is literally part of my job description—I don't even know why I'm reporting it. I do know the police are busy with the reunion crowds streaming into town, and I'm sure my garbled, shrinking message will be low on their list of priorities.

I wash up, strip down, and am out cold within minutes.

My cell vibrates at three o'clock in the morning, and my heart stops cold. No one calls with good news in the middle of the night. As long as my kids are safe and healthy, I can cope with any other announcement that accosts me. No Caller ID. That could be the police, maybe calling about an accident, oh no. I fumble for the phone, hit the green button, hold my breath.

"Gina? It's Dick. I'm in trouble, and I need your help." My ex-husband's voice trembles, his breathing wheezy.

Dick hasn't called me in years. Hearing his voice on the line is so shocking it adds to my half-asleep confusion. "Are you hurt?" Why do I care? I remind my groggy self that I do not.

"I will be soon. More likely dead." Dick's signature dramatics have clearly not toned down with time.

I give my head a shake, turn on my bedside lamp to orient myself. I take a few deep breaths and recall that Dick is a dick, but he's not my dick anymore. "You've called the wrong number. We're divorced, remember? I'm not your next of kin. I'm not anything to you. I can't help you. I'm hanging up."

Dick pleads, "Gina, please don't hang up. I've got nobody else to turn to. I need you."

"No, Dick. No. I'm not available for you. I don't want anything to do with you. Don't call me again. Get in touch with one of your many therapists or

28

your girlfriend, the cockroach."

His voice cracks. "Gina, there are people after me, and they mean business. They're going to kill me. Please. You've got to help me."

The slippery slope appears, and I proceed to slide down it. "Who's going to kill you?"

He hesitates. "I can't say. Some very bad men." There it is, his customary caginess.

Sliding, sliding…. Stop. I cannot go there. Never again for any reason. I save myself.

"Goodbye, Dick. Don't call me again." I disconnect the call. Callous? No, cautious. I know firsthand that involving myself in any way with Dick is courting disaster. Also, melodramatic does not even begin to describe Dick. These very bad men may just as soon have threatened to turn off his electricity for not paying his bill, as murder him.

Life is just all too much right now, and I find myself thinking of alternatives, and that is a danger zone that is not safe for me to enter.

I. Need. Sleep.

Chapter Five

Morning comes way too soon. My alarm clock is the scream of a skill saw, the squeal of a power drill, and Hugh hammering away on my bunkie. It's a rude awakening, but at least somebody around here is working, and it sure isn't me.

I. Need. Coffee.

The weekend is off to a roaring start. So far, I'm up against a disturbed former classmate who's looking to rub out my old gal pals and me, an old gal pal with a disturbed mafioso ex who's looking to rub in his new infantile arm candy, and my disturbed ex who's afraid, possibly paranoid, that he's about to be rubbed out by heinous henchmen. I have convinced myself that none of these things is particularly foreboding—there is a simple solution to all, and I have formulated a plan to deal with the lot. I may be suffering from delusion, but my strategy is to remain positive, to detach, and to avoid excessive worry, despite all evidence to the contrary that I should do so.

After three strong cups of life-giving caffeine and a hot shower, I'm grounded enough to know that I'm definitely spending the next four days hiding out in my cottage until the reunion has wrapped. No way am I venturing into the shark-infested waters of Sunset Beach High. Problems solved—I shall bury my head in the sand until the coast is clear and leave everyone to work out their own affairs without the benefit of my involvement.

Ostrich syndrome sounds extremely convenient, but I am aware that at some point, a non-avian has got to come up for wine, at the very least.

I've put off checking my phone for the whole morning because I don't want to see the dozen missed calls I'm sure I've received from No Caller ID. Or the profusion of texts I'm certain my twin Italian aunts have sent me reminding me that I volunteered to transport their portable tarot-card-reading booth to the school and set it up for them today.

I swallow hard, turn on my cell. Check, check, and double-check. Exactly twelve missed calls from a frantic Dick. He's filled up my voicemail, hogging space for messages from people who aren't about to be executed and are asking me to save their life. I delete all Dick's messages without listening to his pleas for help. Really, in what capacity, in what world, would I be capable of doing anything to save his life from mysterious murderers? My sharpshooting skills are a little rusty, and if I had access to a gun, I might use it on Dick.

Also, many, many texts from the aunts wondering *dove diavolo sei stato* (where the hell I've been). They're ticked that they haven't heard from me and also want to know what I've eaten in the past two days. The commitment I made to help the aunts is not one I'm going to be able to wiggle out of. Sunglasses and a baseball cap will hopefully conceal my identity, keeping me under the radar for the fortune-telling booth set up in the high school gymnasium. If I go early enough, maybe nobody I know will be there. A lot of people coming to the reunion won't roll into town until tonight or tomorrow.

There are also numerous messages from my cousin Florrie, who is freaking out because I haven't shown up to help blow up party balloons for the welcome-back ice-breaker slideshow event she's organizing, and she's wondering whether I'd like to be Ginger to her Mary Ann, Veronica to her Betty, or Daphne to her Velma for the costume dance. She also wants to know what I've eaten in the past two days. Our family is food driven.

I check my work emails.

Dear Ex-Whisperer,

I'm sure you've been receiving loads of letters from high school alumni who are excited about attending the Sunset Beach High reunion. I'm one of them, and I've been waiting for and dreaming of this weekend for twenty-five years. I really need your advice, so I don't blow my one big chance. My old crush will be there, and I've never gotten over him. We're both married to other people, but our kids are off to college now, so I figure it's the perfect time for us to reunite. We were always meant to be together, but he was just too young to realize it at the time. We haven't kept in touch, but I've followed him on social media for years, and I know everything about him. In prep for the reunion, I've been on a physician-supervised liquid diet for the past two months, and I've lost sixty pounds, yay me! (Gained back four yesterday when I started eating solids again to try to stop the fainting spells.) I also had a brow lift and lip implants. I did this all for him because I'd do anything for him. At forty-nine, I think I look better than I did at seventeen when we broke up. I'm ready to throw my family and everything else in my life away for him. I love him that much. My question for you is what's the best way for me to break this fabulous news to him? I was thinking of making a surprise announcement, kind of like a gender reveal, maybe on the football field scoreboard or over the microphone at the gala costume dance. Or do you think I should let him know in private that we're going to be together at last? So excited to finally start living my best life with the love of my life. I have all your Gal Guide books, and I hope you'll sign them for me on the weekend.

Still Crazy After All These Years

Honestly, I think there were fewer obsessive people back in high school when everyone was riding an out-of-control hormonal roller coaster of estrogen and testosterone than there are now. I'll chalk it up to peri and full-blown menopause and andropause, but come on, people, get your shit together and stop living in the freaking past. It wasn't actually all that great back in the day. We're just getting too old to remember properly. This temporary suspension of reality is another reason I hate reunions.

Dear Still Crazy After All These Years,

Yes, you are.

I couldn't even be arsed to purchase a new dress for this reunion, and you've bought yourself a whole new face and body. You win. Might I suggest that rather than spending all that money on plastic surgery, you invest it instead in having your brain tweaked and tucked. First off, no reasonable man in his late forties wants the first girl he mortifyingly figured out the mechanics of boffing with as a teenager back in his life. I'm quite certain that, by now, he considers himself a mature, experienced, world-class boffer. You found him on social media. If he wanted to find you, he would have. Also, move on, girl! You've lost three decades looking in the rearview mirror. And I promise you, no matter how much money a person spends, no one looks better at forty-nine than they did at seventeen, nor does anybody need to. But alas, that is not the point. The point is that you are delusional, and if your husband has put up with you for all these years, he sounds like a pretty standup guy to me. Also, eat real food. Being skinny is overrated.

Affectionately yours,

The Ex-Whisperer

I hit Delete. I do not want to post this but feel better for having vented. Rewrite.

Dear Still Crazy After All These Years,

Please, do not, I repeat, do not, 'throw your family and everything else in your life away' for a pimply teenage boy who I can almost guarantee barely remembers anything about his high school years, including you. He's lived a dozen lifetimes since then, as have the rest of us, except, it seems, you. The high school kid you dream of doesn't exist anymore, and he probably never did—you created the fantasy of a young boy, and you projected him thirty years into the future and aged him exactly as you wished. You haven't lived your life fully because you've been holding on so tightly to the past. Sadly, that's prevented you from being present in the potentially beautiful life you and your husband have built over the past twenty-five years—the life you're willing to toss into the trash compactor now. Please don't suicide bomb your personal life or this other unsuspecting person's. Maybe you're unhappy with your marriage partner, or yourself, or your children, or your work, but for the purposes of this letter, I'm going to assume that you're unhappy in your marriage. My best advice is always to love your partner exactly the way you want to be loved. If you want more affection, be more affectionate. If you want more intimate talks, speak more openly. If you want more sex, initiate sex more often. If you feel unloved, give more love. Your partner will either rise to the occasion to meet you in that more loving space, or if they're not capable of leveling up, then they'll fall away, and you will find the love you desire in another partner. Either way, you win with this method. Everybody wins with this method.

PS It's more important to feel great than to look great (although the good news is that when you feel great, you almost always look great, too). Please do not starve yourself for anyone ever. And only make alterations to your body to please yourself, never for someone else.

Affectionately yours,
    The Ex-Whisperer

I hit Post.

That was unfortunate, but most unfortunate of all, there's another letter to my blog…

Dear Ex-Whisperer,

34

Hope you liked the school spirit pics I dropped off for you. Those were the good old days when you and the Barbie Brigade were the reigning queens. Sorry about the damage to the photos, but I just couldn't stand to look at your pretty baby faces for a moment longer. I'll be sure to deliver your next present to you in person.

Team Outcast

Is Team Outcast just your typical troll, a coward with a computer? A virtual bully who gets off on scaring people online? Would that act be enough to satisfy their hunger for revenge? It's probable. Still, because I am me, I take the next hour to sit and stare and elude life. My strategy of staying positive and avoiding excessive worry has vaporized. If I keep my head buried in the sand, chances are I won't see Team Outcast coming for me, so I'm thinking I need a new approach. Moving back to the city, changing my name, deleting all my social media accounts, and giving up my career is the only game plan I can come up with presently. It would be kind of like going into witness protection without the protection part.

Before I ditch my entire identity, I suppose I will have to venture into town and do my aunts' bidding. No one has ever successfully said no to the aunts and lived to tell the tale. Plus, I'm starving; wallowing in worry is not getting me anywhere, and distractions from my problems work like magic for me. Even when those problems are life and death, actually, especially when they're life and death. The aunts are sure to feed me, and good food is the answer to many a mortal's dilemma. Like I said, I've basically got a Ph.D. in eating my emotions. Bon appétit.

There's a knock at the door. I consider diving under the bed with the cat, but instead, I peek out a side window and see a major distraction. Hugh is leaning against the porch railing. I'm surprised to realize that the sight of him lifts my spirits.

He looks ridiculously handsome, even with his dirt-blackened hands, which are large, square, and probably the strongest-looking mitts I've ever seen. Note to self—I am letting things cool off with Hugh because life is overwhelming at the moment and rushing into a relationship with someone who is working for me is not a wise thing to do, and I need to wax my legs, and I am possibly an idiot who is blowing off a great guy.

I open the door, attempt to look nonchalant. And maybe even a little sexy—femme fatales like me can't help it. "Good morning."

Hugh looks at me, concerned. "Morning. You okay? You look a little frazzled."

Failed majorly at the sexy thing, no surprise. "How about nonchalant?"

Hugh looks puzzled now. He's getting used to not being able to make sense of most of what I say. I should come with subtitles. Hugh's thick eyebrows knit together endearingly above piercing blue eyes. I am also failing miserably at the cooling-off thing.

My traitor of a dog, Zoe, rushes to greet her favorite person. Hugh ruffles her huge ears.

"Did your kids get off okay at the airport yesterday?"

"Damn, was that only yesterday? Yes, they did, thanks."

"You must miss them already." Does this guy ever say the wrong thing?

"I do." I wonder whether this is the only context in which I will ever say these words to this man. God, somebody shoot me. Where are the murderers chasing Dick? I need their services right now.

"You heading into town to help with the reunion prep?" Hugh pushes up the sleeves of his sweatshirt, exposing his ropy forearms. He's crushing the sexy, nonchalant vibe.

"Yes, but against my better judgment. Will you be attending the festivities?" I cleverly conceal any traces of hope in my voice.

Hugh laughs loudly. "No way. I didn't go to Sunset Beach High, so I have no reason to join the trip back to the future, nor any desire to."

"Where did you go to high school?" I lean against the door jamb, tilt my head. *How about this? Does this pose look sexy?* I guess not. He's inspecting a leak in the porch roof.

"My uncle had cancer and couldn't run his farm on his own anymore, so I had to move out to Walkerton to live with him. Took care of the farm and my uncle for four years and went to high school there. After he died, I came

36

back to Sunset Beach."

"Oh, I'm sorry to hear that. That must have been so difficult for you."

"I was bummed about leaving my friends when I first moved in with him." Hugh shrugs. "I was a teenager. But in the end, I was glad that I could do what needed to be done to help out. And I was happy to have the time with my uncle. He was a great old guy." Hugh's sky-colored eyes look as if they might be misting up.

Based on the fact that he pulls a very quick retreat back to his sawhorse, I think that's exactly what is happening. Handsome, self-sacrificing, sentimental, the list goes on. It's confirmed—I am an idiot to let this one get away. Then again, he hasn't seemed to notice my attempts at seduction, so maybe it's not just me who's doing the stepping back.

I follow Hugh to the construction zone he has set up in the side yard, so he can show me a selection of wood siding samples that he's milled up for the bunkie while Zoe runs around happily outside. His man Ryan waves, then takes Hugh's truck to head into town to pick up supplies.

Hugh holds the various pieces of siding against the exterior wall of the bunkie one at a time, and I stand back and consider each option carefully. I try to focus on the lengths of wood with their minuscule differences in profile, but there in my face are Hugh's damn bulging biceps straining against the rolled-up sleeves of his sweatshirt and his still-tanned, flexing forearms rippling in the sunlight that would distract a flipping Benedictine nun. His salt-and-pepper hair skims the back of his thick neck and blends perfectly into his short but unconsciously stylish scruffy beard.

If the Universe didn't want me to make a fool of myself, why did it send me a Jeffrey Dean Morgan look-alike for a contractor? My Venus in Aries, an aspect in my Natal Chart that I share with Marilyn Monroe, which explains a lot, I tell myself, must be being triggered by transiting Uranus, or the recent Taurus eclipse, or a perimenopausal estrogen spike because what other explanation can there possibly be for what I do next?

I literally dive headlong, I mean throw myself at, I mean jump the bones of, I mean take a massive, totally uncalculated risk and plant my lips on Hugh's. I just outright make his hotline bling, and lucky for me, he answers the call. Hugh responds by pushing me up against the wall of the bunkie, grabbing the sides of my face in his rough, massive hands, and shoving his long fingers into the tangle of my hair, holding the wavy strands tightly, making it impossible for me to slip away. Not that I want to. Ever.

Chapter Six

I think we make out for hours, but when I do the math after I leave and check the time on my phone, I realize it was seven minutes. But I mean, come on. I can't remember the last time I French kissed nonstop for seven minutes. My lips are perfectly bee-stung, and I can't stop looking at them in my rear-view mirror on my drive into town. It was so great, so cool, so hot, and I am so not thinking straight. The man is working for me; I am in no shape mentally to enter into a relationship, and I clearly have serious issues with impulse control. But also, it was so great, so cool, so hot. Note to self: just because a man doesn't reject you when you throw yourself at them doesn't mean they're looking to enter into a relationship with you.

It's warm enough that I'm able to roll my window halfway down for the drive into town, which is good because I need to chill out.

Sunset Beach is bumping. Early October is a busy time in this neck of the woods, with cottages, campsites, and motels booked solid for Canadian Thanksgiving and the annual Pumpkinfest celebration the following week-end. There are actually fall foliage traffic jams, and even parking spaces in Tobermory, at the most northern tip of the Bruce Peninsula, have to be reserved weeks in advance by hikers heading out to the breathtakingly beautiful provincial park trails. But after all the trees have released their vibrantly colored flora, and the leaves, which were Instagram darlings mere days earlier, litter the ground in offensive piles of wet brown muck, the tide turns, and the city folk disappear with the last warm rays of autumn.

The tourists desert their summer playground, and the sidewalks are rolled up until spring. The cottagers board up windows and barricade doors to protect their beachfront holiday homes from the battery of fierce winter storms that Lake Huron is famous for.

This is the time of year when the locals get their town back all to themselves, and it is a sweet six months indeed. To be sure, many of them depend on the summer tourist dollars to earn their livings, but all the same, it's nice not to have line-ups at the restaurants and shops for a change and to be the only person on the beach for miles even if the winds off the lake are brisk and sometimes gale-force in the fall. But this year is different.

The sidewalks haven't been rolled up; in fact, red carpets have been unfurled everywhere. For the 150th anniversary of Sunset Beach High School, generations of former students spanning six decades of graduating classes have flooded the tiny town wearing the blue-and-white team colors of the Sunset Beach Whitecaps. It's a very big deal for a very small town, and there will be no shortage of pride and nostalgia, and partying. And maybe no shortage of danger if Team Outcast has their way, or at least fear if they're all talk.

The Victorian-era town of Sunset Beach is steeped in its marine history. There's not a shop on the High Street from which the endless waves crashing against the golden sand beaches cannot be heard. When storms rage, as they often do, the winds off the lake at the foot of the commercial street force shoppers to take refuge in the grand, yellow brick buildings housing cozy cafés and diners, and quaint shops selling gourmet goods and handcrafted local fare. It's impossible to forget that this town was born where the mouth of the Saugeen River meets the Great Lake Huron, the third-largest freshwater lake in the world, that, with its seemingly infinite abundance of fish and fertile soil, sustained the early settlers and the Indigenous peoples before them. For nearly two centuries, the deep-water port has welcomed and bid farewell to countless ships carrying precious cargo throughout the country. Many of those vessels were never to be seen again when their hulls met with the jagged, granite shoals of the churning inland sea. Thousands of shipwrecks, and tens of thousands of lost sailors, rest submerged in watery graves, most of them still undiscovered today. It's a haunted town, for sure. I often sit by the weather-beaten lighthouse that keeps guard at the foot of High Street, and on days when the lake is calm, I'm certain I can hear the swishing of petticoats, heavily laden with lake spray and rain and the mournful keening of heartbroken widows—the ghosts of mariner's wives trudging back and forth, back and forth, waiting for the unforgiving waters to return their husbands to them. I sit there and cry about the opposite—wishing something would show up and take my ex-husband away.

I park on High Street in front of Happily Napoli, my aunts' Italian eatery, and don my disguise of a baseball cap and dark sunglasses. Before I'm out of my vehicle, my squat twin zias are out of their restaurant and on the sidewalk dragging a plastic table and chairs, a tacky purple cardboard fortune-teller booth with moons and stars cut out of the sides that they ordered off Amazon and a lunch cooler on wheels filled with enough bread and pasta to feed the Foreign Legion. They've insisted on setting up at the high school a day earlier than necessary because they're anticipating a cooking marathon with line-ups for their restaurant all weekend long—that I don't doubt.

My old aunts eye me up and down with their usual look of loving disapproval.

"Whatsamatter with your lips?"

Cripes, these old birds miss nothing ever. "Nothing's the matter with my lips."

Their gaze zones in on my mouth.

Zia Angela is concerned. "They're swollen. You got the food allergies? Or the hay fever?"

I shake my head no, but I can feel my cheeks flushing.

Zia Rosa yells at her sister. It's how they communicate. "She's been kissing, *un bacio.* How you not know that? You too old already?"

Argument is the aunts' first language. Then profanity. Then Italian. Then English.

Angela throws her hand up *fungula* style. "I knew it. I didn't want to say it."

Rosa is always loud and brusque. "You didn't know it! You thought it was

41

the shellfish."

Thankfully, it's easy for me to ignore the aunts now and to be ignored, because they're all wrapped up in their squabble. I help myself to a delicious basil, tomato, and mozzarella sandwich from their lunch cooler while I struggle to load all their equipment into the trunk of my jeep.

By the time I'm done with packing, the aunts have turned their attention back to me and proceed to yell at me in Italian for being late and for being *stupida* and for starving myself in the seventy-two hours since I last saw them, which is evidenced by the fact that, according to them, I look *"come uno scheletro,"* like a skeleton. They also kiss both my cheeks and tell me I am *bella*.

Surprisingly, the high school parking lot is mostly empty at the moment, thank God. Incognito in my cap and shades, I muscle the aunts' divining paraphernalia into the school gymnasium while my zias trail behind me, pulling their picnic cooler while nonstop nattering at me.

"Why you wear this hat?" Zia Rosa.

"You a movie star now? Why you got the sunglasses on inside? You famous, Gina, but you not that famous." Zia Angela, keeping me grounded.

"Whatsa matter for you?" The both of them in unison.

I scan the dim gym before stepping inside, but through the lenses of my dark Ray-Bans, it's not easy to make out all the shapes with the profusion of rented tables and rows of folding chairs. There are boxes everywhere, but I'm looking for human silhouettes. I think the coast is clear, but before I can make sure, the aunts are hurriedly pushing me through the doors from behind.

"Sbrigati!" Hurry up.

The impatient old biddies point to a darkened corner at the back of the gymnasium, and keeping my head down, I trail behind them to the space. I follow their instructions for the psychic booth setup, zip-tying the sides of the kiosk to the front facade. I rig up a heavy curtain on a wire to enclose the back of the cubicle, and at the front, place the aunts' crystal ball on their vintage 60s fiberglass folding TV tray table. My zias focus on setting out a nine-course lunch for the three of us.

The main door smashes open, and my heart stops at the flurry of motion coming straight at me as someone charges into the gym and bolts down the length of it as if they're rushing for a touchdown.

The aunts yell in surprise, "Madonna!"

They clutch their rosaries. *"Rallenta!"* Slow down, they scold.

It's my cousin Florrie. She's wild-eyed, out of breath, and hits her brakes a mere two inches from my face.

I catch my own breath, dreading whatever news she's about to spill all over me.

Florrie gasps. "You need to sit down. I need to sit down."

"Who died?" The aunts always leap to the absolute worst possible conclusion in any situation, a family trait I learned at my zias' knees. The aunts make the sign of the cross and kiss the gold Jesuses dangling around their necks for protection.

"It's Dick." Frantic Florrie is trying to calm her breathing.

"Dick died?" I am shocked. I shouldn't be. He told me he was about to die, that someone was going to kill him. Am I upset? I think I am. Of course I am.

The aunts shrug. "Eh. It's not so bad. It's only Dick."

Florrie recovers. "No, Dick's not dead."

The aunts look disappointed. I hope I don't.

Florrie clarifies. "It's worse than that. Dick's moved into town."

Now that I know that Dick is not dead, I think Florrie's right—the news that he's moved into town is worse.

"But why?" Rarely, if ever, do I whine. This moment is an exception.

Florrie feels personally responsible since she delivered the distressing news. "I don't know. He rented a flat over the hardware store. Three down from me."

"But why?" Whining louder.

Florrie shakes her head helplessly, looks as if she's about to sympathy cry for me. "I have no idea. He's always followed you and done whatever you did. Remember when you were pregnant, and Dick had nausea and mood swings and gained weight and bloated?"

The aunts cluck their tongues loudly in disapproval. They remember, too. Who could forget me making Dick dry toast every morning for nine months and driving out to pick up donuts and milkshakes for him in the middle of the night to assuage his psychosomatic cravings? Frigging hell that man was a ton of work.

"I do remember, unfortunately. Couvade syndrome, the doctor called it." I'm about to sympathy cry for my younger self.

Florrie shudders. "His ankles even swelled up, didn't they?"

She's killing me. "Florrie, you're making this so much worse."

She grimaces. "Sorry."

The aunts are uncharacteristically silent, but their judgmental thoughts are loud and clear. They exchange long side-eyes, reach into their apron pockets, and extract their well-worn tarot decks, then set about shuffling and dealing the cards on their folding TV tray table. They need answers pronto.

Florrie continues hypothesizing. "I'm just thinking that maybe Dick followed you up here because of his couvade syndrome. Like you got the urge to leave the city and move back home, and so he did, too."

"But this town was never Dick's home. He was up here hanging with pious Iris last month, but that fizzled out when he realized that she couldn't help him get to me. Unfortunately, he's still obsessed with me, and this is the next level of his stalking behavior."

Florrie, ever the optimist. "I thought of that, too, but I like the couvade syndrome theory better. It's way less scary."

"Couvade syndrome is just to do with pregnancy, Florrie. But either way, Dick is unstable, and that's always been concerning. He called me last night at three a.m."

"No way!" Florrie is as shocked by that news flash as I was by the call.

I drop my voice so the aunts can't overhear. "He told me some very bad men are trying to kill him, and he asked for my help."

Florrie whispers, too. "In killing him?"

"In saving him. And how would I do that?"

"Why would you do that?"

"Exactly. I hung up on him and told him not to call back."

Florrie, still hypothesizing. "Could that make you an accessory to murder if you refused to help him, and he actually winds up getting killed?"

The aunts are tsking and clucking louder now as they flip over Swords and Rods and all manner of doomsday cards in their psychic booth.

"Dick, he moved. The Tower card." Zia Angela proclaims the news.

Maybe not so psychic after all.

Zia Rosa looks extremely worried. "Also, danger and destruction."

They both gasp when they pull the Devil card next. "Big stuckness. Dick, he's obsessed to you. He can no let go of you, Gina. No good. No good."

Also, not so psychic.

"And he got the upside down Six Pentacles." Angela throws her arms up, the revelations are all just too much for her.

Zia Rosa fans her face with the skirt of her apron, she's getting that anxious. "Madonna. That's a big debt of money he owes that he's no paying."

"Tell me something I don't know. Dick still owes a million bucks in spousal support that I'm never going to see."

Zia Ange pulls the final card with a flourish of her hand and a kiss on the back of it as a prayer for good luck. "The last card is . . ." Dick can't catch a break. Both aunts cry out in anguish when Ange flips it over. "Three of Swords. He's the most negative card." So many Italian prayers being whispered.

"Sorrow!"

"Betrayal!"

And then the soothsayers lament in unison, "Death."

Both of Florrie's hands are pressed against her mouth, and she looks like she might faint.

Someone walks up behind us, and we all jump. It's just some random former student, years younger than Florrie and me. "Hey, this looks cool. Can I get my fortune told, too?"

The aunts recover instantly from the upset of Dick's reading when the young man pulls out a fifty-dollar bill.

"We no open yet. We open for the Halloween dance only. But sure, we do a special reading for you." The zias gather up Dick's deadly spread, reshuffle, and smile at the man. They shoo Florrie and me away.

"Sit, sit." The aunts make change for the fifty and make a fuss over their first customer of the weekend. Zia Rosa offers their new client a prosciutto sandwich with pesto and arugula—for five bucks. He's down.

Florrie and I walk out of the gymnasium in silence and immediately run into our old pal and the town librarian, Cordelia, in the hallway. She throws her arms around me. I love her, and I try hard to smile and look happy to see her, but I'm a crummy liar. She senses my fakery right off.

Cordelia displays uncharacteristic compassion. "I know. I heard. I'm sorry. Why would your loser ex move up here? We liked him when you were married, but he's not a local, so everybody hates him since your divorce. The whole town is on Team Gina."

Florrie corrects her. "Except Hugh's ex, Bible Babe. She thinks Dick's the greatest and that Gina's the worst."

Cordelia scoffs. "Iris McTavish isn't from here either, so she doesn't count. Also, she's a loose cannon."

All I can do is sigh in response. This town is actually that small. I was probably the only person who didn't know that my ex-husband had set up camp in Sunset Beach this morning.

Cordelia turns to Florrie, impressed. "The decorations in the classrooms look great, Florrie. You rocked them."

Florrie beams with pride. "Each room is a different theme based on the decade you graduated in. We've got fifties rock n' roll, sixties hippies, seventies disco, eighties Madonna's *Like A Virgin* bridal theme with crosses and—"

I interrupt her. "I'm sorry, Florrie. I'm not feeling well. I'm going to head back to mine."

Florrie looks immediately concerned. "I'll go with you."

"No, you've got loads of work to do here. I'm fine, really. I'm just burned out and need time to process this latest kick in the teeth."

"If Dick and the aunts are correct, you'll be needing your energy to arrange your ex-husband's funeral soon."

Cordelia's eyes widen in surprise. "What did I miss?"

I sigh in resignation. "The Devil and the Three of Swords."

Cordelia is intrigued now. "I want the deets. I'm coming with you girls."

Florrie feigns exhaustion. "I need a break, Gina. Let's do lunch."

Cordelia examines me closely. I'm obviously not passing her wellness test. "We all need a break. I'll bring the wine."

Florrie perks up. "Perfect. I'll swing by the bakery and grab us something yummy. See you at Gina's in twenty."

Both gals bustle out of the school and into the parking lot. There's no saying no to these boss babes. And to be honest, maybe some great gal company would do me good and save me from my harrowing thoughts that will likely torture me to death if I spend any more time alone today.

On the drive back from town, I freak out and calm down and freak out again. Then start all over. What does Dick think he's doing following me from Toronto to Sunset Beach? I will confront him about this. There's no way I'm letting him move into my hometown. He's going to have to make a life for himself elsewhere. It's been six years since our marriage ended. If the kids find out what Dick has pulled, they'll be livid.

Wherever Dick goes, trouble follows close behind, and I didn't need the aunts' tarot card reading to tell me that. I'm not going to let Dick dump his disasters on my doorstep, killers or no killers. He's never been one to pay his bills, so I'm sure there are dozens of people who would wish him dead. Add my name to the list after this latest news.

Chapter Seven

I arrive at the cottage before Florrie and Cordelia. I let a very happy Zoe out for a run and attempt to coolly answer the questions Hugh has for me about door styles, trying to focus on his detailed explanations, distracted once again by his bulging biceps and ropy forearms and also cringing with embarrassment and quite possibly regret from my earlier actions.

I threw every ounce of common sense out of my head when I threw myself bodily at this man. I followed my base instincts, and I gotta say, that rarely works out well for me. If I did that on the regular, I'd probably be doing a stint in the slammer—I mean, how many customer service representatives would I have assaulted by now?

Hugh's man, Ryan, works a few feet away from us, so there is no opportunity to address my earlier transgression. Or was it aggression? Whatever it was, it was out of character for me. The last time I threw myself at a man uninvited was never.

I choose a door and then deliberately turn my mind to wholesome and constructive thoughts. The bunkie is looking lovely. I can't wait until it's done and I can paint again. Making art centers me, and I am seriously off-center.

Minutes later, two cars pull up to park beside mine, an intervention I am in desperate need of. Saved by the gals. Hugh gets back to work; I cross to greet my friends.

Florrie gives Hugh a big wave while balancing stacks of pastry boxes and bags from her bakery. She has her little white fluffball of a dog, Snowflake, on a tight leash.

Cordelia unabashedly checks out Hugh, eyeing him up and down. He laughs at her forwardness. Despite the pseudonym, everyone knows that Cordelia writes erotica, and she's got the whole sexy librarian thing down to a science.

Florrie looks to the road, shields her eyes, squinting in the sunlight. "Hey, is that Vivi?"

Vivi is out for a walk. She smiles and waves. "Hey!"

Cordelia is ecstatic to see her old friend. "Hey, Vivi! My God, it's been years! You look amazing!"

Vivi looks uncomfortable, unsure whether she should stop to visit or keep on walking.

Cordelia barks at her. "Get your tight little ass over here, girl."

Vivi approaches, and Cordelia and Florrie embrace her with warm hugs.

One of Florrie's greatest passions is feeding people, and the more the merrier is her motto. "I've got loads of food here. Come for lunch, Vivi. Please."

"Yeah, you could use some meat on your bones. Come eat with us." Cordelia winks at Vivi. "And I brought loads of wine."

I'd welcome an extended diversion, especially one that includes smart women offering love and support. Wine and food are also good. "Join us, Vivi. It would be really nice for us to all catch up. I need all the shoulders I can get right now to cry on."

Vivi looks relieved that we're happy to see her and grateful for the offer of good company.

Hugh is still glancing over at us, smiling. It's hard not to look at Vivi with her shiny silver hair, softly lined face, and yoga-toned body. She's as attractive at fifty as most people twenty years younger. I make the introduction. "Hugh, this is my old school friend, Vivi."

He nods, and she waves.

Vivi follows us inside my cottage, as does Zoe, who is trailing behind Florrie's fragrant bags of food.

Cordelia turns back to a smiling Hugh. "You're welcome to join us, too,

49

Hugh."

She winks at him salaciously, and he laughs again. I think his cheeks may be a little flushed.

It's been noticeably quiet in the cottage since my four boisterous offspring departed two days earlier, and the pets are clearly happy to have visitors. Spook has come out from under the bed to rub against any and all available calves and greet his canine cousin, Snowflake. I'm also glad to have the place livened up and hope the high spirits of my gal pals might push out some of the lingering sadness of my babies leaving my home again.

Cordelia pops open a bottle of white and a bottle of red and carefully chooses long-stemmed glasses from my cupboard that will do justice to the fine vintages. Vivi puts the kettle on and peruses the blends in my extensive herbal tea collection. I choose a mellow Spotify playlist, turning my Beats Pill to just the right volume, and throw a couple of logs on the woodstove to warm up the cabin. The three pets curl up in front of the cozy fire.

"God, he's hot." Cordelia watches Hugh work through the kitchen window. "He's a Jeffrey Dean Morgan doppelgänger."

Vivi looks out over Cordelia's shoulder. "I agree. He mustn't have gone to our school. I definitely would have noticed him."

Florrie gets busy setting out appetizers of baked Camembert topped with fresh rosemary and dried cranberries to spread on a toasted twelve-grain baguette with a side bowl of marinated olives and feta. "Hugh didn't go to Sunset Beach High. He was living out in Walkerton, caring for a sick uncle."

Vivi is impressed. "Damn, hot and noble, too."

Florrie giggles. "Gina, you're strangely quiet on the subject of hot Hugh. Why is that?" Her teasing tone is obvious, and the girls whip around to get the lowdown.

Vivi is even more impressed now. "You and Hugh are a thing?"

I shake my head emphatically. "No, definitely not."

Florrie tsks. "Definitely, yes. At least they were until Gina pulled the plug and broke his heart."

Cordelia is dismayed. "Holy crap, what's wrong with you, girl? Give your head a shake."

I'm not sure why, maybe because I feel as if I'm basically in the center of an emotional support group, and it's my turn to give testimony, but the explanation pours out of me involuntarily, and I don't even pause to take breaths between sentences. "That's not exactly how it went down. We barely got started. I mean, kisses don't even count for anything these days, and all this wild stalking stuff happened with my ex, Dick, and with the ex of one of my readers, and with Hugh's stalker of an ex-wife, Bible Babe, Iris. So, I decided not to stay in town, and I was ready to move back to the city, and then my kids surprised me with a visit for my fiftieth birthday, so I stuck around, obviously. And now, I don't know what I'm doing or what I should be doing or what I want to be doing."

The three women stare at me slack-jawed. That was a lot.

Florrie clearly regrets setting me off. "I'm sorry, Gina. I shouldn't have said anything."

I'm embarrassed. "Oh my God. That was so much emotional junking. That's so toxic. I'm sorry."

The women recover from my surprise vent session quickly and switch into emergency girlfriend support mode.

Vivi is genuinely concerned for me. "No, no, it's good that you shared."

Florrie serves up her signature love and care by piling my plate high with hors d'oeuvres. "Yes, for sure. You must have really needed to unload, and we're all here for that."

I throw back my glass of wine. "No, it's trauma dumping. How to lose friends and repel people."

Vivi rubs my shoulder. "People find themselves doing that when they haven't actually processed their feelings."

"Guilty." I raise my hand. "No secret there. I prefer to eat them."

Vivi continues trying to assuage my trauma and my guilt. "My yogini discussed this in a yin class, and she said regular journaling, meditating, and breathing with intention are constructive ways to deal with trauma."

Cordelia has been noticeably silent until she can't stand anymore. "That might work for some people in some circumstances, but I'll tell you what you should have done, Gina. You should have let it go further than the kissing stage with Hugh. And I'll tell you what you should do now. You should let it go further than the kissing stage with Hugh. He's an amazing guy, and I think you're punishing yourself by not allowing a relationship to develop with him."

Vivi considers Cordelia's words thoughtfully and nods. "Actually, you may have something there. Sounds a little like self-sabotage."

"Oh my God, how am I this needy? And transparent?" I take a deep breath and try to calm myself down, but it's not happening. I remember the list that I recite to myself regularly of reasons why getting involved with Hugh is a bad idea and I blurt it out. "Aside from the freaky fact that Hugh and I both have unstable exes who happen to have formed an unhealthy alliance with each other, becoming involved with Hugh is not smart because he's working for me. And the truth is, becoming involved in a relationship with anyone is not smart because I've been out of the dating game too long, and I don't remember how to do anything that is remotely related to sex, romance, or partnering up period, in any way that would be considered normal. And because I've just started a whole new chapter in my life, and I need to do me right now, not focus everything, around a guy."

Florrie adds to my list. "And she needs to get her legs waxed."

The girls laugh.

Cordelia is our resident sex expert. "Sex and romance are like riding a bike. No matter how long a dry spell you've had, you just have to hop on lightly, take it slow, and let it come naturally. It's like a cellular-memory thing. Trust your body's intelligence."

And against my will, a true confession spills out at breakneck speed. "See, that's where I fail. My body must be way below average intelligence because I didn't hop on lightly and take it slow. My body literally blasted out of a cannon this afternoon, and out of the frigging blue, I jumped poor, unsuspecting Hugh's bones and laid a seven-minute-long wet one on his kisser. Then I got in my jeep and drove into town and listened to a pack of tarot cards tell me that my ex has moved into town and is probably going to die any day now, and apparently, it's on me to save him."

The three women are shocked into total silence. We stare at each other for a very long time. No one even blinks.

Chapter Eight

Weirdly, getting all that off my chest has me feeling better than I have in the past two days, but I'm nothing if not brutally honest with myself. "I'm not just rusty at the whole sex and romance thing. I'm cryogenically frozen in time. My sensuality is awakening the way prehistoric bacteria strains are waking up in the thawing permafrost in Siberia. We're both ticking time bombs and a danger to human life as we know it. Clearly, when it comes to dating, I don't know myself and can't trust myself."

Still silence. And then...

A burst of raucous, roaring, uncontrollable, tear and spit-spewing laughter from all four of us. And it goes on for a ridiculously long time.

We all clink wine glasses, chug that glassful, and then refill immediately. Finally, we quiet down to light chuckles.

Vivi is sincere. "I hope Hugh's still available when you're ready, Gina, because he seems like a great guy, and you deserve a great guy." Vivi pulls out her phone and is constantly taking photos and videos of us, the cottage, and what we're eating and drinking. She needs round-the-clock content for her two million followers.

I smile at my old friend. "We all deserve great partners, Vivi. Okay, girls, I feel a whole lot better for getting all that out. Can we not talk about me anymore tonight? Please? I exhaust myself."

Florrie jumps up from the table. "Okay, change of subject." Florrie presents the main course with a flourish. "Wait until you taste this baby! I put some nostalgic new dishes on the bakery menu for the reunion weekend. Nostalgic but evolved and reimagined."

Vivi videos Florrie's entrée.

Cordelia seems annoyed. "Vivi, do you film everything all day long?"

Vivi smiles serenely. "Pretty much. TikTok and Instagram have an insatiable appetite for reels. The first twoposts of you gals have already gotten over thirty thousand likes apiece."

"So exciting!" Florrie is stoked to know a celebrity and fills Cordelia in. "Vivi is a super-famous Insta influencer now. She's one of the most popular Silver Sisters on the 'Gram. Vivi's followers want to know what she's doing all the time." She turns to Vivi. "I love it when you post no-makeup and no-filter photos. They're so inspiring."

Cordelia is not quite as impressed. "I couldn't handle that. It's not my style. I'm more into anonymity. I like a mask, a costume, and a pseudonym like Mistress Delilah."

"And a whip." I wink at her.

"Chains are good, too." Cordelia nods.

We all laugh.

Vivi teases Cordelia. "Based on the amount of attention you gals are garnering on my Instagram page, I don't think you're going to be anonymous for much longer, Mistress Delilah."

Cordelia grimaces at Vivi, then turns to inhale the savory aroma of Florrie's entrée. "It looks like mac and cheese but smells way better than the stuff we ate in high school."

Florrie pops the Le Creuset casserole dish into the oven to warm. "Mac and cheese for grownups—winter greens mac and cheese. Macaroni with swiss chard, kale, garlic, olive oil, gruyère, and a topping of panko crumbs."

Cordelia swoons. "Sounds deliciously R-rated. Adults only." She tops up our wine glasses again.

It all looks amazing, but to be honest, as usual, I'm most interested in the dessert, and Florrie never disappoints. She's made giant salted caramel chocolate chip cookies and a gingerbread cake sprinkled with powdered sugar that will be perfect with tea later today.

Late lunch preparations complete at last, we're finally all seated around my kitchen table with wine and tea and food and loads of thoughts to share and conversations to catch up on. The last time we all sat together with no interruptions was probably twenty years ago when we planned a girls' weekend in the city, checking out Toronto's top eateries and having a blast in front-row seats at a No Doubt concert.

Cordelia never beats around the bush. She turns to Vivi; it's her turn to air dirty laundry now. "What happened with you and Sal?"

That question is always a complicated one but usually has a simple answer—things didn't work out. Even most long-term relationships have a best-before date, and we're not necessarily meant to stay in them forever, even though we do sometimes, despite the fact that they've soured. Life happens, and people evolve, and love ends. Mentally healthy humans remain flexible and open to change.

Vivi shrugs, is matter-of-fact. "Salvatore was married to his work. I didn't like being so low down on his list of priorities, but we had two young children, so I put up with a lot for years to keep the family together. I didn't want my kids spending every other weekend away from me and hanging around Sal and his motley crew. As long as I was in the picture, I could control what my children were exposed to. The day after they went off to university, I filed for divorce."

Florrie is genuinely concerned for Vivi. "Did you make out okay in the end? Are you all right financially?"

Vivi smiles. "I let him have the house. I really didn't want six thousand square feet of marble floors, arched entryways, fluted columns, and basement bowling lanes."

Cordelia shakes her head. "I always wondered how you handled the aesthetics in that house. You're such an amazing designer, and that place never seemed to jive with your taste."

Vivi laughs. "It definitely did not. The one thing I did want was my parents' cottage, and Sal agreed to that. I also got a small lump-sum settlement. The courts look at a person's income tax returns, and Sal's income was mostly off the books, so there wasn't much I could do about that. But I got my peace of mind, and that was worth everything to me." Vivi doesn't sound sad or sorry for herself. "And I started up my interior decorating career again after the divorce was finalized, and it's been going great, but I make most of my money from my influencing collabs. I'm good monetarily. You don't need to worry about me, Florrie. I'm a survivor. I think all us gals are."

Florrie looks relieved. "That's good to hear, Vivi."

Vivi shares a little more. "I didn't like the type of business Sal was in, either. I'm sure that doesn't come as a surprise to any of you."

There's an uncomfortable silence as we all struggle to figure out the appropriate response to Vivi's remark. Everyone in town knows Sal was connected, but no one says it out loud if they know what's good for them. He was tied in with the mafia in Hamilton, the exploits of which are constantly making headlines—blown-up cars and torched bars. Over the past few months, the organized crime war stories have escalated with three well-known mob families each having a son shot in the driveway of their home.

I've never seen Sal's name in the newspapers, so maybe he's not quite the kingpin he makes himself out to be. It's not my place to ask. If Vivi wants to enlighten us, she will, but maybe it's not even safe for her to divulge information about Sal's business dealings. Vivi has always known how to handle herself. She's no shrinking violet, but she knows when to keep her mouth shut.

Vivi shifts the conversation to lighten it, if you can call it that, although maybe it's just a safer topic for her to discuss. "Through the years, there's always been a parade of Brittanys and Ashleys. The latest one's a Tiffany. That's part of the life in Sal's line of work. It got to the point where his cheating didn't even hurt my feelings anymore. Still, constantly looking the other way was exhausting, and I was through putting up with that, too." It doesn't exactly cut the tension, but it's easier for Vivi to talk about Sal's personal affairs than his business affairs.

Cordelia's lips curl. "I hate to ask, and with a name like Tiffany, I can pretty much guess, but how old is this latest one?"

"Younger than my daughter. Twenty-three."

"Eeeeeeewwwww." All three of us grimace in disgust.

I pipe in with feigned enthusiasm. "And the good news is, we all get to meet young Tiffany this weekend. She and Sal have rented out the Steller estate, and they're going to be at the reunion."

Florrie is shocked. "That place goes for twenty thousand a week. He must be rolling in the dough. Is it counterfeit?"

Vivi laughs at Florrie but doesn't answer her question.

Cordelia is not impressed by men like Sal. And since Cordelia moonlights as a dominatrix, she knows a lot about men. Especially the freaky ones. "An old guy like Sal has got to spend a lot of moolah to keep a Tiffany happy."

"Apparently, Tiffany has her eye on my family cottage now. It's the next big bauble she's after in her quest to make Sal prove his affection for her. There are no waterfront cottages for sale around here, and I think nasty little Tiffany is looking to steal something else from me. She obviously doesn't know that I would have paid her to take Sal off my hands. He made me a lowball offer for the cottage, and I turned him down, but I know he'll be back."

We all gasp, horrified to hear this.

Florrie is appalled. "You don't have to sell your cottage to him. You said the court gave it to you in your divorce settlement."

"Sal's not one to take no for an answer." Vivi does look sad now. "It would break my heart to lose the old place. My plan was to start spending more time up here. I've had a number of requests to take on design projects from some of the well-heeled Toronto people retiring in this area. I'd keep my condo in the city but get the cottage up and running for year-round living and go back and forth between the two."

"That sounds like a fabulous plan." Florrie squeezes Vivi's hand. "It would be so great to have you here more often."

Vivi's voice cracks. "I don't want to lose my cottage. After my kids, it's probably the thing I care most about. All my good memories are stored there."

My blood boils instantly. "There's no way Sal's taking your family cottage away from you. We're not going to let that happen, so you don't need to worry."

Cordelia is the consummate ice queen when she wants to be. "No, he's not going to. We may have to team up to stop him, and if we do, Sal won't even know what hit him. Tiffany will last about thirty seconds in the ring with us."

We all chuckle because we all know it's true.

Cordelia exudes power, as the well-read librarian quotes a dead German poet. "We should forgive our enemies, but not before they are hanged."

Florrie pipes up excitedly, does her best Italian gangster impersonation—Marlon Brando with marbles in his mouth—and messes up the quote about revenge and serving it cold."

We laugh even harder and lift our wine glasses in a toast.

Florrie, "Happy reunion. To old friends and fresh starts."

Vivi, "To keeping our cottages and getting rid of trash exes."

Me, "To teaching all the young Tiffanys out there not to mess with us vintage broads."

Cordelia, "To resurrecting our dreams, rekindling friendships, and remembering how to romance all the hot Hughs out there without scaring the testosterone out of them."

We drink and eat and talk and laugh and heal for hours. Vivi records much of it on her phone. This evening, life is good. I should have known it wouldn't last.

Chapter Nine

W e've managed to kill the entire afternoon and evening along with three bottles of wine, and we've polished off most of Florrie's fabulous food. The four of us are full and drunk and feeling the late hour.

Vivi is a master of discretion. Her entire married life with Sal has revolved around secrecy and concealment. I didn't have to ask her not to mention anything about Team Outcast—I knew Vivi wouldn't bring it up unless I initiated the conversation. This weekend is supposed to be a fun one, and I hate to rain on everyone's parade, but Florrie and Cordelia need to know about the frightening letters and unsettling photos Team Outcast has sent on the off chance that this mystery person actually carries out any of their threats. The whole town needs to know. Hopefully, Floyd and Lloyd can make sense of it all whenever they can get around to looking into the matter.

I bite the bullet. Wet blanket time. "I have to fill you girls in on correspondence I've received from an anonymous old school chum who apparently still hates our guts thirty-three years later.

Vivi cringes but doesn't look surprised that I'm broaching the subject.

Cordelia rolls her eyes. "Let the high school theatrics begin."

Florrie looks completely shocked. "Somebody hates us? Is it Sissy Greensplat? I knew she didn't like you, Gina, but I never thought she hated the rest of us. That's not fair. We didn't try to steal her boyfriend."

"I didn't either ." Now I'm eye-rolling, struggling to keep this talk on track. Deep breath. "Yesterday, I received three emails from someone who apparently went to Sunset Beach High with us. I don't know who, don't even

60

know if they're male or female. They're coming to the reunion weekend, and they want to meet up with us but not exactly to reminisce."

Florrie is confused. "I don't get it. The only reason to go to a reunion is to reminisce about old times."

Cordelia is exasperated. "No, that's not why most people go to reunions, Florrie. Most people go to reunions to gloat, and many of them are hoping to find out that all their former chums from school did crappier in life than they did so they can feel better about their own crap lives."

"I don't agree with that idea at all." That outlook is not part of Florrie's reality.

Cordelia walks a fine line between realism and pessimism. "Wait until Saturday night when everyone's drunk at the dance and their true colors come out. You'll be singing a different tune then."

Florrie waves off Cordelia's negativity, turns back to me. "Who do we think this person is, and what do we think they want?"

"They signed their letters with the name Team Outcast. Does that mean anything to any of you?"

All three women shake their heads.

I continue, "They said we were stuck-up cheerleaders who never talked to them or included them, and they called us the Barbie Brigade."

Florrie is offended. "We weren't the Barbie Brigade. That was the popular girl crowd—Kelly Armprior and Wendy Stickle, and Sissy Greensplat. This person has their cliques confused."

Cordelia agrees with Florrie. "We weren't cheerleaders. Gina, you're the only one who ever tried out for the team, and you didn't make it because you sucked."

Cordelia remembers wrong, and I actually feel offended now, exactly the way seventeen-year-old me did when I was cut from the Whitecap Rah Rahs.

"I did not suck. Sissy Greensplat's boyfriend, Russ Carney, asked me to go to the movies with him, which was a death knell for my cheer career. I turned him down, but Sissy blamed me anyway and swayed the whole cheer squad against me, so I got thrown off the team.

"Ooooooh, that's right." Cordelia laughs loudly. "I forgot about those details.

So much drama!"

"It was a blessing in disguise. I wouldn't have been allowed to hang out with you uncool girls anymore. They had rules against fraternizing with nerds."

The women all nod, remembering full well the number-one popular girls' rule that you can only ever hang out with other popular girls.

Now I have to share the really bad news. "The worst part of Team Outcast's letter is that they also said one of us told them to do the world a favor and hurry up and die."

Florrie gasps. "None of us would ever do anything like that. We weren't mean girls."

Even Cordelia is horrified. "I never ever heard of anyone at our school doing something that terrible. Not even someone as nasty as Sissy Greensplat."

Vivi is realistic. "We weren't privy to very much of what the populars did. I'm sure loads of things went on that we never knew about, and lots of those things would have been very unkind."

Cordelia nods. "True."

I deliver more unfortunate details. "Team Outcast said they considered following that advice way back then, but then decided it would be better to get revenge on us now instead."

Florrie weighs the two options. "That's definitely better than the person killing themselves, but it's not so great for us. This person has clearly got the wrong girl gang. We just have to let them know that."

"I've been trying. They don't believe me. And they're bent on revenge."

"As in an eye for an eye?" Cordelia is suspect.

I don't hold back. "More like a dead person for a dead person, based on what they're writing in their emails."

"It's quite possible that ruining the reunion for us will be all the revenge this person needs." Vivi holds her baseline of calm. "I'm sure they're all bluster, but that doesn't mean we shouldn't take some extra safety precautions, just in case they bark and also bite."

The October air has turned a cutting cold, and a strong westward wind has whipped up off the lake, banging against the old wood-frame windows, making them rattle. The fire in the woodstove is dying down, so there's a slight chill inside the cabin. An aura of creepiness fills the space, and we shiver in unison.

"I'm going to pop outside to grab some more wood for the fire." I clap my hands to wake my fur baby for her bedtime potty break. "Let's go, Zoe." A sleepy Zoe stirs. "Does Snowflake need out again?"

Florrie perks up. "No, he's good, thanks."

Cordelia checks her Fitbit. "It's eleven o'clock. This was a nine-hour-long talk-a-thon."

"Just like high school." Vivi smiles groggily.

Florrie gets up from the table. "We'd better hit the road. We're expecting twelve hundred alumni to roll into town tomorrow, which means I've got twelve hundred name tags to write out before noon."

Cordelia scolds her. "Jesus, Florrie, why do you take on so much?"

Florrie shrugs. "Saying no isn't my forte."

Cordelia, "Can you clean my house for me?"

Florrie, "No."

Cordelia, "You're not that bad at it."

"You girls can't drive home now. We've all had too much to drink." I zip up my hoodie. "I've got two beds and a couch."

Vivi raises her arm. "I'm within walking distance."

I shake my head. "Extra precautions, remember? None of us should be out alone. Safety in numbers."

"I'm sure we don't have anything to worry about." Cordelia shrugs it off. "But better safe than sorry."

Florrie looks tempted by my offer. "I'd love to crash here, but I've got too much to do tomorrow."

"You can leave first thing in the morning." I take Florrie's keys out of her hand. "Go get washed up. Your toothbrush is in the medicine cabinet."

Vivi pulls her coat on, looks at Cordelia. "I've got extra beds at mine if you don't want to sleep on the couch here."

Cordelia nods and says, "That sounds good. I'll go to Vivi's, and then she doesn't have to walk home alone."

Hugs all around. Florrie lumbers off to the bathroom to get washed. Zoe and I follow Vivi and Cordelia outside.

"Wow, it is ridiculously dark out. And it's gotten so cold." Cordelia wraps her arm through Vivi's, and they clasp their coats tight around their necks.

Zoe trots off into the cedar forest at the edge of my property to do her business. Meanwhile, I cross to the woodpile to gather enough logs to keep the fire going for the rest of the night.

Cordelia turns around. "We'll wait until you're back inside before we go."

"No, absolutely not. I'm fine, and Zoe will be back in a flash. She's scared of the dark. You girls start walking, and text me when you get to Vivi's."

Vivi smiles. "Okay, thanks for a great night, Gina. No matter how the reunion goes, today will be the highlight of the weekend for me."

"Don't cast your vote too soon," Cordelia says with a chuckle. "Wait until you see what we've got planned for tomorrow night. We're going to take down a Tiffany."

The girls laugh, their voices trailing off on the gusts of the forceful wind, their bodies disappearing almost instantly on the pitch-black road.

I've piled up as much firewood as my arms can hold. Zoe startles me when she zips around the corner of the cottage as fast as a bullet and almost runs into me head-on. My big tough guard dog is afraid of the dark and hates being outside alone at night. Me, too.

"Inside, Zoe, time for bed." I take a few steps toward the porch when Zoe suddenly turns and takes off, bolting back into the woods. I yell after her, but she's not listening, and my calls don't carry far in the strong wind that competes to be heard above the loud crashing of the waves.

I dump my armload of wood on the porch steps and, frustrated and tired, head after the damn dog, hollering her name.

Florrie has followed Zoe's barking and my yelling, and she's rushed outside to check on us. I can barely hear her calling me now that I'm deep among the twisting trees, the blowing leaves flapping like flags, and bending branches scraping on creaking trunks. Nature's powerful sounds tonight are near deafening.

"Zoe! Zoe! Come!" I feel more and more frantic with each step I take into the black forest. Zoe rarely ever runs away like this, and never when it's dark out. Sometimes she chases a rabbit or raccoon, but she's always back in a minute or two. There's something wrong. Something very wrong.

I pick my way through the prickly cedar and pine branches, the sharp needles stinging my face and hands as they scratch and poke my skin. I try to protect my eyes. My ankles twist on the stones and uneven terrain. I can't see where I'm going at all, wish I hadn't left my phone behind on the kitchen table. I keep calling out to my dog. It's unlike her not to come to me after all this commotion and on such a fierce and wild night. So many terrible visions are running through my head. Maybe she's hurt. Or worse. There could have been a car on the road. Or a coyote pack hunting in the woods. Or a murderous former classmate skulking around in the shadows.

I turn to head in a different direction, away from the beach. There's no way Zoe would go to the water in the dark with a gale beating about. I try to retrace my steps back toward the road, but there's no straight line to take, the broad tree trunks turning me around and round. I'll have to get a flashlight from the cottage so I can see where I'm going and find Zoe if she's lying somewhere and can't get up. My biggest struggle right now is trying not to burst into tears.

I step into an opening between trees in the thicker forest, and boom—a hand drops down hard on my shoulder. I scream and try to leap away. The side of my head hits hard against the solid trunk of a tall cedar, and the stars I see in my mind are the only illumination.

"I'm sorry! Are you okay?" It's Florrie.

I rub my hand on my throbbing skull. I don't know whether the wetness I feel between my fingers is blood or tree sap, but my head hurts like heck.

I have to shout for Florrie to hear me over the howling wind and crashing waves. "Why did you sneak up on me like that? I almost had a heart attack."

"I didn't sneak up on you. I've been yelling for you since you left. You didn't hear me because you were yelling, too, and it's loud out here. I could barely see you. Where's Zoe?"

Now I am crying. "I can't find her. She ran away."

"Zoe never runs off in the dark. Oh no, what's happened to her?"

"I don't know. I'm scared that she's hurt. We need to get some flashlights to go look for her."

Florrie grabs my arm. "Okay, let's get back to the cottage. I ran outside without my phone. I didn't expect you to be so far from the house. We can call Vivi and Cordelia, too. They'll come back and help us look for Zoe." She steers me out of the woods and back toward the cottage.

Every third step, one of us is tripping on the uneven ground. A few minutes later, we're close to the road, and I hear something and freeze, yank on Florrie's arm to stop her walking.

"What is it?"

"I think I hear barking."

The two of us hold still and listen hard.

Between the wind and the water and my pounding heart, it's nearly impossible to pick up the sounds of anything else. Florrie shakes her head; she doesn't hear any barking.

We take a few more steps to head back toward the cottage, and as we near the edge of the road, I hear it again. Barking. It's Zoe. I know it. "That's her."

Florrie nods. She can discern it now, too. She points away from my place. "It's coming from down that way."

The road is more even than the forest floor, so we can run in the blackness and only twist and trip every five or six steps. We hold each other up to keep from flat-out falling and jog along, calling out for Zoe the whole way. Her faint barks grow louder as we get closer to her. I know it's Zoe, and I know she's alive, but I can barely breathe because I'm still scared for her in case she's badly hurt.

Three minutes later, we're nearing Vivi's cottage, and Zoe's barks are clear and piercing. And there she is. I can just make out the big inky shadow of my beautiful Giant Schnauzer on the side of the road. She's in the ditch and not coming to me, so I fight back more tears, realizing that she probably has been hit by a car and is injured. Finally, we're upon her, and my dog will not stop frantically barking and jumping around, so I know that she can't be badly hurt, but I don't understand what's wrong with her.

And then we see what she's barking at. What she's sounding the dire alarm over. What duty my loyal and clever canine companion is refusing to abandon in answer to her master's calls. There are two more shadows on the ground.

Lying in the ditch, not moving, are Vivi and Cordelia.

Chapter Ten

Florrie screams. I throw myself into the ditch, brush away the tangle of hair swept across my friends' faces so I can look into their eyes, but it doesn't help much. I can't see any details in the darkness. I call for Florrie to help me, and she pulls herself together, scrambles into the tall, dry grass next to me. As I cradle Vivi's head in my hands, Florrie does the same with Cordelia.

Now that the help she has been summoning has finally arrived, Zoe stops barking at last.

The women are breathing and groaning. They're not unconscious, but they're disoriented. A moment later, their eyes flutter open, and they focus. Thank. God.

We labor to help the dazed women sit upright.

Zoe nuzzles against my back, clearly as relieved as I am that we're together again. I twist around to kiss her big nose. I am so grateful for her and proud of my brave protectress.

Florrie squeals over the howling wind, her voice cracking and crying. "Holy mother of God, what happened to you two? Did you fall and knock noggins?"

The girls shake their dizzy heads, gingerly touch the backs of them.

Cordelia speaks as loudly as she can, but it's still not easy to catch everything she says. "We were walking to Vivi's. It was dark, so we had our phone flashlights turned on to help us see the road."

Vivi leans into my shoulder. "We had to yell to hear each other talk. I didn't know anyone was coming up behind us. But there was somebody there, obviously."

Cordelia tries to get her bearings. "I felt something smash down on the back of my head. It was so shocking, and it hurt like a mother. I went down on all fours and tumbled into the ditch."

"I heard Cordelia scream and saw her start to fall. I tried to grab her, but then I got hit from behind, too. I didn't see it coming, either."

Florrie's face is twisted with worry for the girls. "Do you think you were knocked out? You could have a concussion. We'd better get you to the hospital to have you checked."

Vivi shakes her head. "I don't think so. I was just lying there for a minute, dazed, trying to figure out what happened."

Cordelia is trying to stand up, but it's difficult to do on the slanted angle of the little gulley we're in. "I think we were more stunned than anything. I wasn't knocked out, and I'm not going to the hospital, so don't even talk to me about that."

Florrie and I look at each other, then look over our shoulders and up and down the unlit road. There's no one to be seen, but is there anyone who's unseen?

Could it be Team Outcast? Of course, it could be, and it likely is, and I can no longer pretend otherwise. This old schoolmate's threats are not empty, but I'll make sure they can't make good on them. I won't let them harm my friends or me. This revenger chose the wrong gal to goad.

The four of us need to get indoors ASAP. Once we're all safely locked inside, I'll let the police know what happened and call for medical care if the girls need it.

Florrie and I help a still-wobbly Vivi and Cordelia scrabble to their feet. Cordelia bends over to retrieve her purse that's in the ditch a few feet away. We find their two phones on the ground, screen down, the flashlights still on. Florrie and I hustle the disoriented girls toward Vivi's cottage as quickly as we can. Zoe stays right at my heels.

There are no lights on inside or outside at Vivi's place. The five of us form one tight, shivering clump at her front door. Vivi hands Florrie her phone to hold. She reaches into her pockets, feels around, searching for her keys.

Florrie sounds annoyed but is really more nervous than anything. "Vivi, why didn't you leave any lights on outside? It's not smart to come home in the dark."

Vivi actually is annoyed, it appears, with herself. "I always do leave lights on, but today I was just going out for a half-hour walk at noon until I ran into you girls and unexpectedly ended up spending nine hours visiting. I had no idea I'd be gone this long."

Cordelia voices the impatience and the fear that all of us are feeling. "We need to hurry up, Vivi. Whoever hit us could still be out here, and he could come back to finish the job."

Vivi is on the verge of tears. "I know that. I'm trying to hurry. I can't find my keys." Her hands slide inside every pocket of her jeans three times over.

"Didn't your family keep an extra key under that rock by the stump?" Every family on the beach has always known where every other family hides their spare key just in case the cottage owner isn't around and they need a neighbor to go into theirs to stop a leak, or close a forgotten window, or chase out a squatting squirrel.

Vivi's voice cracks. "We always did, but it wasn't here when I came up yesterday. I only had the one key, and I don't know where it is now. I must've dropped it."

I hate to think it. "Maybe your keys are in the ditch."

Even in the blackness, I can see how white Florrie's face has turned. She shudders. "That's not good."

The other three look to me for a plan. I can only think of one, and I don't like it much. "Okay, we've got two phones to use for light. Let's go back over to where you were knocked down and have a quick look for the keys. Maybe we'll get lucky." Obviously, after what's gone on tonight, none of us are buying that possibility, but nobody dares to say it out loud.

Safety in numbers, we link arms and walk back out to the roadside. We shine the phone lights over the ditch, but the fall switchgrass and bulrushes are tall and thick, and the gusts of wind are swirling it in all directions, making it impossible to find Vivi's keys in the matted vegetation.

I offer up the only plan B I can think of. I wish there were another way that

70

would have us indoors sooner. I have to yell to be heard. "This is pointless, and it's dangerous for us to stay out here. It will be a lot easier to find the keys in the daylight. We're going to have to walk back to my cottage for tonight."

Ten terror-stricken eyes flit back and forth, if you count Zoe's, and you have to count Zoe's because she is as frightened to stay out any longer on this dark and scary night as the rest of us.

No one speaks, or barks. We form a wall and walk down the middle of the road as fast as we can without breaking into a full-fledged panic sprint, because we probably couldn't keep that pace up the whole way back to my place, which could be very bad indeed if we do end up pursued from behind.

All of us, including the dog, incessantly check over our shoulders while we make our way down the desolate dirt road.

At last, the light from my porch glows welcomingly through the tree branches, and we cannot get there and get inside my cottage fast enough.

"What if the person who attacked us is Team Outcast, and they've come over to your place now, Gina?" Cordelia's voice is faint, but we all know exactly what she said because we were all thinking exactly the same thought. "What if he's right here right now?"

We stop dead in our tracks in the center of the road, fifty feet away from my property.

I turn to Florrie. "Did you lock my door when you came out to look for me?"

Florrie's eyes squeeze shut as she struggles to recall. "No. Yes. I think so. But I didn't take the keys with me."

"That's okay. I have mine. As long as you locked the door." I can feel the outline of the key in the pocket of my jeans.

Florrie's voice is trembling. "I hope I did."

Vivi squeezes my arm tighter. "What if he's right behind us and coming up close? We didn't see or hear him last time."

We all have the same thought at the same moment again and simultaneously make a break for it—a mad dash for the final stretch to the front porch. We're huffing and puffing, and some of us are squealing and squeaking as I

71

fumble to pull the keys out of my pocket. I finally grasp them and reach for the door lock.

Cordelia grabs my hand to stop me. "What if Team Outcast is inside your cottage?"

We freeze, consider the possibility. What should we do?

Zoe gives us our answer when she turns toward the thick cedar bush at the side of the cottage and starts growling menacingly at something the rest of us can't see.

"I'll take my chances inside." I struggle to unlock the damn door that sticks at all the worst times.

We're in full-on panic mode now.

Cordelia is trying to push me through the door that is not open yet. "Hurry up, Gina. You're gonna get us killed."

"That is not helping!" I see that Vivi has her phone out. "Vivi, stop videoing me!" I struggle a few moments more until, at last, the door flies open and four frenzied women and a freaked-out dog plow through the entrance sideways and all at once. After a rugby-worthy scrimmage, we are all inside the cottage; the door is slammed and locked behind us, and we stand in silent disbelief for a very long moment, trying to catch our collective breath.

Living always and forever in the moment, Zoe has already put the unpleasantness of the evening behind her as dogs do, and she immediately gobbles up her kibble, drains her water bowl, and is curled up in front of the woodstove next to a sleeping Snowflake and Spook the cat four minutes later.

I hand out Advil and tall glasses of water to Vivi and Cordelia to try to stave off the pounding headaches they are sure to develop from the blows they received. "Do you girls want ice packs to put on the backs of your heads?" They accept the pills, decline the compresses.

"What do you think Zoe was growling at?" Vivi is nearly inaudible.

I try to reassure her. "Could be the wind. It's making the trees sound strange tonight."

Florrie, making it worse, "Could be the killer."

I try again. "Let's stay as calm as we possibly can. We don't know that

72

we're dealing with a killer. I mean, the person who attacked you could have killed you, but they chose not to try. This is more like assault than attempted murder. Which is still really terrible, but preferable. Florrie, do you want to call the police and tell them that it's urgent now?"

Florrie nods, finds her phone.

Cordelia is preoccupied with going through the contents of her purse. "I don't think it was a robber. Doesn't look like they stole anything from my bag. Vivi didn't have her purse on her."

Florrie is dialing while pouring four jiggers of whiskey, and none of us object. "He may not be a killer or a thief, but this guy is dangerous. Floyd or Lloyd, or whoever's at the police station tonight, will want to be heading out looking for them ASAP." Florrie holds her phone to her ear. "It went to voicemail." She hangs up. "Probably only one cop on shift tonight to take calls. Should I dial 911?"

"It's not officially an emergency at the moment. Maybe just try again in a few minutes?" Cordelia puts her purse down, takes a seat at the kitchen table. "It's too bad we can't give any sort of description. Our ace detectives will have to figure out who it is without our intrepid assistance."

"There will be so many visitors in town by tomorrow. The Reunion Committee is not going to be pleased with the kind of bad press that a prowling mugger can bring." Florrie sets the liquid courage down on the table.

"Maybe they'll appreciate it." Cordelia attempts to look on the bright side. "A slasher lurking about town could add ambiance to the Halloween theme of the big dance."

We each take two fingers of the liquid medicine that Florrie hands out to soothe aching noggins and frayed nerves.

Vivi has another theory, and she sounds more nervous than she has all night. "Maybe it was Sal." Vivi is shivering. She takes a throw off the couch and wraps it tightly around her shoulders.

A long silence. The usual reaction whenever Sal's name is mentioned. Discussing a mobster with a family member, even a former family member, is an extremely delicate matter, and none of us really grasp the dos and don'ts of it, so we are always very careful.

"Why would Sal hit you and Cordelia and take off?"

Vivi shrugs. "Maybe he wants me to feel unsafe and frightened at my cottage, so I don't want to be here, and I sell it to him. Maybe all of this is him trying to scare me away to get what he wants."

Cordelia, not helping. "Maybe it was Tiffany."

Our eyes dart back and forth between each other. Awkwardness morphing into excruciating discomfort.

Cordelia expounds, "You said she's the one who's lusting after your cottage, not Sal. Maybe she's trying to rub you out to get it."

A verrrrry long, unsure hush.

Then Cordelia breaks the silence by laughing. Delirium? Maybe.

It's contagious. Moments later, we're all laughing, then howling, then stamping feet, crying, laughing. Yes, definitely delirium. And exhaustion. And stress decompression. And probably the whiskey too.

Florrie pours another round of shots. "Zoe was heroic. She caught wind of your attacker, or maybe she just knew you two were in trouble, but she wouldn't come to Gina for anything."

Vivi still shivering. "It's so cold in here."

I also feel the chill now. "I need to stoke the stove. I was going outside to get firewood when Zoe ran off."

Florrie picks up her phone to redial the police. "I'll try Floyd and Lloyd again." She gets through to a person this time and begins her explanation.

The others watch me closely as I open the door for a quick minute to snatch the logs I dropped earlier on the porch steps. Cordelia locks the door behind me as soon as I'm back inside.

I stoke the fire with lots of good dry pine, and the flames are leaping within minutes. "It won't take long for this little place to warm up and feel cozy again."

I pile the extra firewood into the copper box on the edge of the hearth, and then I see it.

Nailed onto one of the logs that I just carried inside is a large newspaper clipping. Not randomly stuck to the log. Not a faded piece of garbage that blew onto the woodpile outside and clung to wet bark. No, this is a carefully cut page from an old newspaper, purposefully fastened onto one of the logs. I know it wasn't there when I collected the wood before Zoe ran off. I definitely would have noticed it. Somebody has been on my porch in the last hour while I was pulling unconscious women out of ditches, and they left this for me to find.

I know I have to look at it, but I really, really don't want to. I can feel my breathing getting shallow. My heart is pounding, and my head feels as if it's starting to heat up. I haven't had a panic attack in years, but I think that's what's threatening. I'm still on my knees in front of the wood stove and don't want to stand up in case I pass out. I'm feeling so dizzy.

Florrie is still talking to the dispatcher at the police station, recounting all the details of what's gone on here tonight and arranging for them to come to my place so we can file a report. She notices that I'm struggling. "Gina, are you okay?" She hangs up her phone and drops down to the floor beside me. "What's wrong? Are you ill?"

Vivi and Cordelia cross to me, too. Instead of talking, I focus on trying to steady myself, on keeping my inhales slow and equal to my exhales, but my body is shaking uncontrollably. These past few days have all just been way too much, and clearly, my circuits are blown.

Cordelia sees the news clipping on the log and removes it from the nail, being careful not to tear the faded paper.

She looks at it, then holds it out for the rest of us to see. It's the front page of the *Sunset Beach Gazette* from October 1990 with a devastating headline that rocked the town for years after: "Sunset Beach High School Grad Killed in Tragic Train Accident."

Chapter Eleven

F lorrie helps me to my feet and I shakily cross to the couch and curl up on it.

Cordelia reads the harrowing headline and the heart-wrenching caption beneath the photo of a sweet young girl we used to know, then she holds it out for the three of us to look at. Of course we all remember Cassie Williams and the front-page news of what happened to her. No one in our town could ever forget that devastating incident and, especially, no one who went to school with timid Cassie. We are all struck silent with the sadness of her memory and the incomprehensible loss of a life cut short.

Cassie was in our year at school and was only nineteen when she was struck by a train while walking along the tracks one evening on the outskirts of town. She was wearing headphones, listening to a music CD, and it was thought that perhaps she never heard the train approaching her from behind.

The coroner was never able to determine whether her death was an accident or suicide, but the gossips in town perpetuated the suicide theory. I suppose that made for a more dramatic story, a juicier rumor. It was also crueler to her family.

Cassie did have a history of depression, as the newspaper article highlighted. From the little I knew about Cassie, it was clear that the troubled girl had many demons to battle and more than her share of hard knocks to deal with. The journalist never mentioned the fact that everyone knew Cassie had been the unfortunate victim of bullying for the majority of her school years. It was mostly two or three nasty boys who started harassing Cassie when she was a child and kept it going through high school, but it only takes one horrible person to crush a spirit.

It's a terrible truth that there are few things in this world more cruel than children, particularly if they weren't taught compassion in their homes. Compassion isn't something humans are born with; we have to learn it and practice it regularly for it and empathy to become a part of our nature. That was my number-one priority when I raised my own kids. I'm relieved to say that I succeeded on that front. My children are all unconditionally kind.

Cordelia sets the yellowed newspaper down on the counter and breaks the quiet with a hushed voice when she speaks to me. "Why would someone leave this here for you, for us, to find?"

Florrie brings me a glass of water. My breathing is beginning to normalize, the heat in my head cooling down. "I have no idea."

Cassie kept mostly to herself, but I remember her having a friend or two off and on who were also unpopular nerdy kids. Her mom had cancer for years, and Cassie had to hurry home after school most days to take care of her. The odd time our group of girls invited Cassie to join us on an outing or to a Saturday night bonfire party at the beach, she always turned us down.

I'm ashamed to say that we didn't ask Cassie to hang out with us because we really wanted to get to know her or because we were particularly interested in spending time with her. It was more out of guilt. We felt sorry for Cassie. The fact that was our motivation doesn't make our gestures all bad, but it doesn't make them all right, either.

Florrie's voice is laden with heartache. "The last thing I heard about Cassie was that her mother died from her cancer a few months after the accident, and her father and younger brother left town soon after. They moved back to the East Coast where the dad was from, Nova Scotia, I think."

Vivi sits down next to me on the couch. "Do you remember that time in the locker room after gym class when Cassie opened up out of the blue and told us that her dad was useless, and she had to do absolutely everything for her mom and her brother? She said she had to cook all the meals, bathe her mom, give her the medications."

"I remember. We were so surprised that she told us all that personal stuff." Cordelia warms up by the wood stove. "We were sympathetic, but I don't recall us offering her loads of comfort. We were probably in a hurry to go watch the boys' basketball game."

"I think her dad had a drinking problem. He was always down at the Safe Port Pub." Florrie puts the kettle on.

The panic attack has been averted; still, the episode has left me with a throbbing headache. The wine and whiskey haven't helped. "When I think back on that conversation now, it's obvious that it was a cry for help from a young girl who had no one else in her life to turn to. And we didn't do anything to help her."

Cordelia sits down at the table. "We can berate ourselves all we want, but we were just typical self-centered teenagers who didn't know any better at the time. None of us would ever ignore someone in need now."

"We were nice to Cassie." Florrie's voice is more hopeful than sure.

"She needed more than that." I can't let myself off the hook. Not even my teenage self.

"We really weren't capable of giving Cassie the support she required." Vivi doesn't sound as if she's making excuses, more like trying to come to terms with past mistakes and regrets.

"At least we could have steered her in the right direction, but we didn't even do that. We never told anybody what Cassie was going through." I wish so much that adolescent me had been years wiser.

"She asked us not to tell." Florrie reminds us of that fact but sounds heartbroken.

"It doesn't matter. We were so wrapped up in our own dramas, most of them manufactured and overblown, that we barely took any notice of Cassie's problems and couldn't be arsed to do anything about her veiled pleas for help." I don't like to hear the words spilling out of my mouth any more than the others do, but we all know it's the truth.

Florrie pours us each a large mug of chamomile tea. "If her parents couldn't be there for her, where were the teachers and guidance counselors? They must have known that something wasn't right. Why did no one do anything to help Cassie?" She passes out the hot drinks then sits down at the kitchen table.

Vivi squeezes my hand. "Kids like Cassie have always fallen through the cracks and disappeared. The blame lies at the door of the entire town for the bullying Cassie endured and the care she never received."

Cordelia is done with the guilt trip. "We can keep beating ourselves up, but two of us have already been beaten up tonight, and I don't think I can take much more. This isn't going to help Cassie or us right now."

Vivi tops up the teacups with hot water from the kettle. "You're right. We can't go back in time and make things better. All we can do is our best now."

I feel absolutely tortured, and I deserve to be. We failed a young girl, and we can never take it back. "The most pressing question is who would give us this newspaper. And why?" The puzzling in my brain is getting dangerously close to a breaking point.

No one has any answers.

Florrie checks the time on her phone. "Holy moly, it's almost two o'clock. No wonder we're all so exhausted. Either Floyd or Lloyd should be here soon. They said they're going to file an official report on Cordelia and Vivi being assaulted."

Cordelia rubs the swollen lump on the back of her head. "Do we think the person who hit us is the same one who left the newspaper about Cassie on your porch? It would be quite a coincidence to have two freaks out here on the same stretch of road on the same night."

I'm not so sure. "I don't know that we can jump to that conclusion. That would make sense on a normal weekend, but this isn't a normal weekend with the reunion going on. The town is packed with people who loved high school and are thrilled to be back but also some who hated those years and are only reminded of old hurts."

Cordelia is skeptical. "I can't imagine anyone seeking revenge for things that kids did to each other decades ago. That's a little extreme. But I guess the world is full of all types."

Florrie has her finger on the pulse of the reunion numbers. "There are an extra twelve hundred revelers in town already, and there will probably be a few hundred more who register for the reunion tomorrow, so Sunset Beach will definitely be bursting at the seams with all types."

"Most of them drinking too much alcohol, which makes the asshole ones extra brave." Cordelia holds out her glass. "How about another shot? I can be an asshole, and I could use some courage."

Vivi warms her hands on her mug of tea. "So maybe Team Outcast is the person who attacked us on the road tonight."

It seems like the obvious conclusion. "The most telling thing here is that we weren't cheerleaders. We were the cheerleader wannabes, the failed cheerleaders, so if this Team Outcast person doesn't know that, then they can't know us very well. Maybe they didn't even go to our school. We need to figure out who it is in case the police can't."

Cordelia stands up, begins pacing to assist her deductive abilities. "That's an important point. If they didn't know us well enough to know that none of us were cheerleaders, then that might narrow down the list of possible suspects."

Florrie offers up another possibility that's quite a likely one. "It's been thirty-three years. Maybe they did go to our school, but they've forgotten exactly, who was who, and what teams and friend groups everybody belonged to."

"Just our bad luck then that they targeted us, huh?" Vivi rubs her sore head. "I think we're forgetting there are people who wish us ill who didn't know us in high school. But they could be using this reunion weekend as a cover to harm us."

Florrie's eyebrows fly to her hairline as if she wouldn't have thought of that. "I guess you'd know about that sort of clandestine stuff from your years with Sal, but it seems like a stretch. Who are you thinking it could be?"

Vivi sounds pretty certain. "One of our exes."

Expressions of dread sweep across all our faces. We've all got exes, and they all elicit the same response. Ick.

Cordelia warns us. "Vivi could be right. High school reunions are like breeding grounds for exes. They come out of the woodwork when you least expect it."

My lips curl. "High school reunions are Petri dishes for exes. Colonies of rapidly replicating infectious bacteria that any thinking person would avoid like the plague."

"Eeeeewww." Florrie the foodie can't stomach that analogy.

"How about hunting grounds for exes." Vivi issues a dire warning based on her personal fears. "Sometimes they're armed and dangerous."

As chair of the reunion-planning committee, Florrie cannot allow this misinformation to spread any further. "The doomsayer dames. You three have got this all wrong because you've been wronged. I get it. Me, too. But reunions are happy times where we get to reconnect with old friends and enjoy surprise visits from people we used to know."

There is a knock at the door that startles all four of us.

Florrie catches her breath, then speaks in a singsong voice as she crosses to answer the door. "And this will be our third surprise visit of our reunion weekend. Vivi was number one, Team Outcast number two, and that will be Lloyd or Floyd, our friendly neighborhood police chief here to take our statement at last." Florrie throws the door wide open with great aplomb.

We all scream.

Loudly.

For a very long time.

Can't stop.

The two dogs go full Cujo and charge at the man standing in my darkened doorway.

Our surprise visitor is my ex-husband, Dick.

Chapter Twelve

We all jump up from the table. Finally, the screaming stops, although the barking doesn't let up. Three bodyguards spring into action. My defenders automatically glom on to me like chunks of scrap metal sucked up by an electromagnet. The women form an immediate, protective forcefield of flesh around me.

Florrie manages to scoop a frenzied Snowflake up into her arms. I reach around the wall of women to wrestle Zoe, pulling her back by the collar. She strains against my hold. She doesn't like Dick. Nobody in this cottage likes Dick.

It takes me a few moments to realize that Dick's face is even more terror-stricken than ours. He stands, shocked and stock-still at the open door. It surprises me that he looks older, but still so strong and fit—he's always adhered to his regimen of four gym visits a week. I bet he thinks Carly Simon's song is about him.

The dogs snap and snarl at Dick. I'm sure he didn't expect to be confronted with the sights and sounds of this mad matriarchy when he decided to darken my doorway in the middle of the night. He's stuttering out apologies that I can barely make sense of.

Like a sisterhood of spotted hyenas, my friends can sense Dick's fear, and they circle in to feed on his carcass, leaping all over him with admonitions, pointed fingers, and raised voices.

"We called the cops already. You're going down, buddy."

"What the hell do you think you're doing here?"

"What is your problem? It's the middle of the night. You scared the bejesus out of us."

"You're not allowed to come anywhere near Gina."

Florrie thinks to grab a frying pan off the counter, always her weapon of choice.

Dick raises his arms to protect his head in case Florrie opens a can of whoop-ass on him, which she looks as if she might do.

He offers an explanation that makes me laugh out loud. Dick is usually a much better liar than this. "I saw the lights on, so I figured you were still up, Gina . . . And I thought I'd stop by, you know, to talk. I called you the other night, remember?"

Florrie lifts the fry pan threateningly high. "No, you do not get to stop by or pop in or drop over at Gina's any time, ever. Or skulk around in the dark of night spying on Gina, which is super creepy but probably not the worst thing you've done tonight."

Dick holds his hands up in surrender. "I wasn't skulking or spying. I promise."

I find my own voice, emboldened now, since I'm feeling so well guarded by my scrappy pack of protectors. "Yes, I remember you calling me, also in the middle of the night. And I remember telling you not to call me again."

Dick is rubbing his gray, immaculately trimmed, three-day stubble-look beard. He's always done that when he is exceptionally nervous. "Yeah, I know. That's why I came over to see you in person instead."

I'm not scared anymore, but I'm angry and ready to go full Rambo. "You thought coming to visit me at two in the morning would be a good idea? You thought I would be receptive to that? You and I haven't had a face-to-face chat outside of a courtroom in six years, Dick. What is wrong with you?"

"I told you on the phone, Gina. I'm in trouble. I need you to help me." His pale gray eyes look a little watery, although that is sure to be some effect he's mastered. He's been known to turn on the waterworks in front of courtroom judges, but that was all performative. I've never seen Dick cry real tears. I don't think he's capable.

Cordelia leaps into the fray. "This behavior is called stalking, Dick. It's illegal, and you need to give it up. You've been harassing Gina since the day she packed you up and put you out for being a lying, cheating, narcissistic embezzler."

Dick is only slightly offended. "That's not true, Cordelia. I'm not a narcissist."

They never think they are.

Vivi is recording everything on her phone for her reels, as usual. I suppose this drama will make a great TikTok.

Vivi zooms in on Dick to get his reaction to the accusation she's about to lob at him. "The police are on their way here right now. And they're going to want to question you about a couple of women who were assaulted on the road out here tonight."

"The police?" Dick is clearly panicked now. "I never assaulted any women. I haven't even seen anyone tonight other than you girls now."

Vivi zooms in on Dick. "I've got you on video, and this reel could go viral. You want to tell your side of the story before the cops arrest your ass?"

Dick is tugging at his full head of silver hair with his hands. "I didn't do anything to anybody! I just came out here because I need to talk to Gina."

I let go of Zoe. "How long have you been creeping around outside my cottage tonight?"

Dick tenses as the big dog aggressively sniffs him up and down. "I just drove up two minutes ago."

Florrie sets her frypan weapon down. "Why are you even in Sunset Beach, Dick? You didn't go to our school, so we know you're not here for the reunion."

My voice is too loud, and the unnaturally high pitch is definitely hard on everyone's ears, including mine. "Is it true you moved into town? Why would you follow me up here? I know you met up and hung out with my contractor's ex-wife, Iris McTavish, a.k.a. Bible Babe, a.k.a. pious Iris, last month, and that is, next-level screwed up, but other than misguided connections that you're desperately trying to manufacture, you have no personal ties to this town. You don't belong here."

Dick smiles at me and cocks his head as if I'm a little soft in mine. I recognize that classic narcissistic trick where they try to make their victim think that they're remembering wrong, or worse, are losing their grasp on the facts.

Dick speaks to me calmly and slowly, the way one does to a young child who's failing to understand the situation at hand. "I do have ties here, Gina. I know a lot of people in this town. You and I came here every summer when the children were growing up. We had so many happy times up here at the cottage with the kids when we were a family. You remember all those good old days, right, Gina? We have countless beautiful memories here together." Straight out of the narcissist's playbook.

The girls leap in to stop the guilt trip wagon before it heads too far down memory lane, and I possibly hop on board. In truth, my survival instinct is too strong for me to let that happen.

"Don't listen to him, Gina. He was a terrible husband, and he's been a worse ex." Cordelia is tough as always.

Florrie moves to stand between Dick and me. "Dick, you need to leave. Now."

Dick tries to look hurt. He does a very good job. "And I always loved your girlfriends." He looks charmingly at the other three. "You girls look amazing, by the way. Have you had work done?" He openly and shamelessly displays his world-class schmoozer skills.

The girls are silent now, and I look at them, astonished. Are they falling for Dick's schtick? I sense a slight wavering. He actually is that good.

Dick carries on with his list of reasons why he has chosen to take up residence in my hometown. "And, of course, I love your zias, Gina. I'm sure they'd be glad to see me. They used to love feeding me, and I loved their cooking."

"My aunts do not want to see you. They don't like you, and they don't trust you, and you shouldn't trust them. If the aunts ever do offer you something to eat, I'd advise you to hire yourself a food taster to take a few bites of it first, then wait to see if they keel over dead before you indulge."

That old, familiar condescending smile stretches across Dick's lined but still handsome face, and without words, he says to me, *You're crazy, Gina. You don't know what you're talking about.* Dick could sell Botox to Tom Cruise.

Clearly, Dick has realized that his "woe is me" routine is not having the desired effect on me, so he goes into maximum overdrive. For Dick, his last-ditch effort, his last resort, is also the most difficult thing for him—to tell the truth. "I came up to Sunset Beach because I needed to get out of the city. I told you on the phone there's some not very nice guys after me. Their beef with me is a complete misunderstanding—I didn't do anything wrong." To clarify, Dick doesn't ever tell the whole truth and nothing but the truth. He tells a certain version of, or a fraction of, the truth, and it's always skewed in his favor.

Vivi has been recording everything. It's amazing how used to that you become after a while. At first, I found her filming us annoying, but now I hardly notice as she videos our every move and conversation as if we're all stars in a tacky reality show. Or maybe it's because it's not nearly as annoying as my loser of an ex-husband who's still trying to ruin my life six years later.

I have witnessed Dick attempting to dig himself out of a grave of his own making many times in the past two-and-a-half decades. It's an eye roll from me. "Not buying it."

Dick reasons he's going to have to let out a little more line to catch his fish. "Okay, so I owe these guys some money, and I'm going to pay them back. I just can't do it quite yet. I'm a little skint at the moment."

"Oh, I bet you are." The mother of all eye rolls from me. "But these money lenders aren't willing to wait until you're flush, right? You probably don't need all ten fingers and toes anyway, Dick. I hope they don't take your ears, though. I know how much you love wearing your Gucci sunglasses at night."

Vivi has been around this familiar cagey block more times than she would care to remember. She speaks from experience. "You been hanging out with Sal?" It's not really a question. Vivi knows the answer. "Cause it sure sounds like it, Dick, and that wouldn't be very good for your health."

"What? No." Dick feigns innocence. "Not that that would be a bad thing. How's Sal doing anyway?"

"I wouldn't know. We're divorced."

"Oh, sorry to hear that."

"No need to be." Vivi presses him further. "Maybe you've been spending time with some of Sal's business associates, then?"

Dick is rubbing his stubbly beard again. "Uh, these people might be acquaintances of Sal's. It's possible. I mean, I think they're in the same line of work. Car dealerships and electronic parts, isn't it?" Very, very nervous treading on this very, very thin ice.

Vivi puts her phone down now, so we know she's pissed. "I cannot believe you brought this garbage onto Gina's doorstep. She is the mother of your children, and you have willingly endangered her." Vivi turns to me. "Gina, you'd better get this conman out of here fast. This is not good. It's not safe for you or for him."

"Don't lend him any money, Gina. You'll never get it back." Florrie's tone says she's worried for me.

I reassure my cousin. "No worries there, Florrie. There's no danger of me opening my pocketbook for this guy. He still owes me a million big ones."

Dick ignores my comment, addresses Florrie's. "I'm not asking Gina to lend me money."

Cordelia quirks her mouth to the side, obviously curious and confused. "What are you asking her to do, then?"

"I just need a place to stay for a while. You know, to lay low. It's just temporary."

Cordelia throws her arms up. "You've got to be kidding."

I'm furious, and I pop off on Dick. "What you're telling me, Dick, is that you're going down, and you're willing to take me down with you. Nothing new there. You never think about anybody but yourself. You came to Sunset Beach to hide out. Of all the small, middle of nowhere places you could have disappeared to, you chose here because I'm here. But you're forgetting a key point. We're not married anymore, and we're certainly not friends. You shouldn't be coming to me for anything, ever. Certainly not because you're in trouble again, and you want me to bail you out. Or hide you out. I can't help you, and I don't want to see you. You really need to find a new town to hole up in. Stop endangering people who used to care about you." I point to the door. "Out!"

Dick knows he's shot his wad. He turns to leave at last. "Okay, okay, I get it. I won't ask you again, Gina. But if I wind up dead because you refused to help me, I want you to know that no matter what anybody says about you, no matter how many people blame you, it's not all your fault." A true narcissist to the end.

All four of us chime in unison, "Bye, Dick." And Dick is out the door, and it's slammed shut and locked up tight behind him.

Chapter Thirteen

It's three in the morning now. We're exhausted, we're stunned, we're freaked out. By the threatening letters and creepy photos from Team Outcast, by the physical violence of the attack on Vivi and Cordelia tonight, by the frightening and terrible reminder of the tragic death of Cassie Williams, and by the shock of my ex-husband turning up on my doorstep in the middle of the night claiming to have loan sharks circling him.

"Where the heck are the cops? I'll call them again." Florrie dials.

The rest of us fall onto the two couches like sacks of potatoes.

"Can your brain break? I think mine might be about to." My gray matter is stonkered, but I can't let it rest. "We still don't know how any of this absurdity ties together. We don't know who hit you girls, who Team Outcast is, or what any of it has to do with Cassie Williams. If I understood chaos theory, I could probably crack this."

Cordelia's eyes are shut. "You flunked eleventh-grade math, Gina. The only thing you're ever going to grasp about chaos theory is that you seem to be one of the fractals in the feedback loop. You're predictably unpredictable, and where Gina goes, chaos follows."

I protest weakly because all my strength is gone. "Hey, that's not fair. If I'm a fractal, it's because of my job, because I'm easily accessible online, so people reach out to me with their problems. And their grudges. And their threats. Okay, you're right. I am the chaos theory personified."

Vivi spells out her own theory. "We said that it seemed like whoever this was didn't know us very well in high school because they've got us pegged all wrong. We weren't the mean girls. We weren't cheerleaders, and we never bullied anyone. I'm betting all this is connected to our exes and their current squeezes. Dick, Iris, Tiffany, maybe some of Cordelia's former clients. It could even be Sal."

I'm too tired to be delicate with Vivi and the whole mob-connection thing. "I don't really see Sal as the knock-them-on-the-head-lightly kind of assailant. He's more of a cement-shoes, sleeping-with-the-fishes kind of guy. Anyway, Sal went to school with us."

Vivi extrapolates. "Yeah, but he was three years ahead, and he really never took any notice of us or what we were doing. He didn't know I existed until I was in my final year, and he came home for that summer to work at the garage after he got out of juvie."

Cordelia shortens the list. "It wouldn't be any of my clients who I've stopped servicing. They don't know my actual identity. I'm always masked during our sessions. And anyway, they're all submissives. They're not capable of asserting themselves in a dominant way, and even if they could, they'd never dare come after me or my friends." Cordelia makes a whip-cracking motion with her arm.

My head is hurting as if I got a smack upside the skull, too. "Team Outcast said they'll meet up with us at the costume dance on Saturday night and that they'll be easy to spot because they'll be dressed as the Grim Reaper."

"Obviously, none of us will be at the dance, then." Cordelia is a professional risk-taker, and even she doesn't want to take this one.

Florrie hangs up her phone. "What? We have to be there. That's the highlight of the reunion. We're giving out the awards that night. And I'm on name badge handout duty. And I've already got my costume. I'm not missing the dance. I've been working on this damn reunion for three years."

"And then they left this on my porch before I got home from Toronto yesterday." I take the photo with all our faces erased out of a drawer and set it down on the table. "Still want to go to the costume dance?"

Florrie stares at the photo in horror but then finds her resolve, or more likely, the famous familial stubborn streak takes over. "Yes, I will be in attendance at the Sunset Beach One-Hundred-and-Fiftieth Anniversary Reunion Halloween costume dance. This person is not going to scare me into missing these celebrations."

Cordelia looks at the photo closely. "I mean, I guess the guy wants to get caught. He told you he's going to be dressed as the Grim Reaper, so how hard will it be for the police to pick him up before he even gets inside the school?"

I struggle to open an eye. "Unless he's messing with us, trying to throw us off with the Grim Reaper clue. Or maybe he's just trying to scare us, and he has no intention of going to the dance."

"You think Team Outcast is a male?" Vivi is surprised.

Cordelia shrugs. "He's so threatening, I guess I'm just assuming it's a guy. If someone thinks we excluded them from our friend group, it could be a boy or a girl."

Vivi's tossing out possibilities. "Maybe it's a guy that one of us turned down for a date?"

"Still feeling rejected thirty-three years later?" One day not so long ago, that may have been hard to believe, but now the vermin are crawling out from under rocks at every turn. I suppose anything is possible.

Cordelia reminds us we weren't the most popular girls in town. "It's not like the four of us left a trail of broken hearts in our wake. We didn't exactly date a lot. We spent most of our Saturday nights together."

"I only dated Marty in high school. Until the bastard cheated on me with Rona Gillespi. He better not show up at the reunion, or I am finally going to tell him what a total piece of garbage he is." Florrie is still bitter after thirty-three years, so I guess it's true that anything is possible.

Cordelia isn't too tired to gloat. "So much for reunions being all about happy times where we get to reconnect with old friends and enjoy surprise visits from people we used to know."

Florrie sneers at her.

There's a knock at the door, and we all leap out of our skins. Florrie lets out a squeal. Zoe and Florrie's dog, Snowflake, wake instantly from their sound sleep and charge toward the door in a barking frenzy. Spook runs in the opposite direction, seeking his usual refuge beneath the bed.

Floyd calls through the door. "It's Floyd, your friendly neighborhood police chief."

I unlock the door and let Santa Clone inside. Floyd and his identical twin brother and co-police chief, Lloyd, are always jolly, sporting big white beards and bigger bellies.

"A girl's night in, eh?" Floyd ruffles Zoe's floppy ears and gives Snowflake a scratch, and they both calm down immediately and head right back to their beds, exactly where the rest of us should be. "Oh, hey, that you, Vivi? Haven't seen you in a few years. Where you been hiding?"

Vivi smiles at one of the many sweet people she grew up around. "It's been too long, Floyd. But I'm going to start spending more time up here. Going to get the old family cottage winterized and do some design work for clients in town."

"Oh, hey, that would be great. If you need a good contractor who's not too hard on the eyes, ask our Gina here. She found one." Floyd is teasing me, even at this late hour. It's how the personable old guy rolls. "But maybe you wouldn't want to share your Hugh, would ya, Gina?"

It is absolutely ridiculous that, at fifty, my body is still capable of blushing when I'm embarrassed, but I can't bend over to pick the dog dish up off the floor without my joints cracking audibly in four places. I shake my head, annoyed at Floyd, and he laughs a deep, bellowing guffaw. His pleasant presence is a comfort.

Florrie looks so tired. "Can I get you a tea, Floyd?"

"Oh no, I'm good, Florrie. I'm not planning on staying long. You Whitecap kids need your rest before all the festivities start up tomorrow. I hear there's a glow-in-the-dark tournament at the bowling alley and an Elvis look-a-like competition in the bandshell planned. I'm looking forward to the fishing derby and the butter tart bake-off myself. Old Mrs. Philpot gives me the loser tarts, and they're still way better than any store-bought. And that's just day one." Floyd sits down at the kitchen table and pulls a tiny black notebook and pencil out from his jacket pocket. "So what sorts of shenanigans have you young gals been up to? I heard you two got a whack on the noggin? What were you doing walking around alone at midnight on a dark and blustery night like tonight?"

Vivi and Cordelia look sheepish. A scolding from the elders in this town can still bring out the little girl in each of us. We heft our leaden bodies off the couch and take a seat at the table with Floyd.

Cordelia gives a quick explanation. "The four of us had been here for the afternoon, catching up, and then around eleven o'clock, Vivi and me walked back to her cottage to sleep there. It was dark, and the wind was loud, so neither of us saw or heard anything. We were walking and talking one minute, and the next thing we knew, Gina and Florrie were helping us climb out of the ditch, and our heads were hurting."

Floyd turns to me.

I shake my head. "We didn't see anyone when we were out there, either. Zoe ran off barking and wouldn't come back, so we went after her and found these two lying on the side of the road."

The other three look at me. I lay out printed copies of the three emails from Team Outcast along with the high school photo of us with our faces angrily scratched out with red pen, as well as the faded newspaper from 1990 with the headlines of Cassie Williams's train accident.

"I don't know if any of this is connected, but I received these anonymous emails and the photo yesterday. The newspaper was left on my porch while Florrie and I were out looking for Zoe but found these two. It all sounds somewhat threatening, so I thought you'd want to try and find this person in case they actually try to hurt somebody."

Florrie pipes up, "Or wreck the reunion weekend."

Floyd raises an eyebrow at Florrie. "Why would anyone want to go and do something like that?"

We're all silent because none of us know the answer. Shrugs.

Floyd takes his time looking at and reading everything. He flips the pages over and around, says nothing, nor do we.

Florrie opens her mouth to speak, but I kick her lightly under the table, and she bites her tongue.

All the jolly has disappeared from our Santa Clone. He's pure police business now. "Any ideas who this might be?"

We shake our heads.

"Anything else you girls might have forgotten to mention? Anything at all? Something you think is insignificant could be important."

The other three stare at me pointedly. I know what they're pressing me about. "My ex-husband, Dick, showed up here half an hour ago. He says he owes money to men who are threatening him. Apparently, he's moved into town, but I've asked him to leave, and I hope he's going to."

Floyd has perfected the poker face. He makes more notes in his little black book. "Anything else?"

Now Florrie spits out her question. "Do you think there's a connection between the emails and Vivi and Cordelia getting hit?"

Floyd, with his finely tuned small-town-cop skills, doesn't let on any of what he's thinking through his facial expression or his tone of voice. "Impossible to say for sure. It sounds likely, but then again, nothing is normal in town this weekend, and who knows what the reunion revelers will get up to once they start double-fisting tall boys. First thing they're going to find out is that their fifty-, forty-, or even thirty-year-old bodies can't handle a hangover like they could when they were back in high school. Should you two girls be going to hospital to have those goose eggs looked at? Might have a concussion."

Both women shake their heads.

Cordelia smiles. "Nightshift Nurse Nellie never does anything but send you home with an aspirin anyway. I'm surprised people haven't bled out in the hospital parking lot after being assessed by her."

Floyd belly laughs again. "Ain't that the truth. I think old Nellie's been running that little four-bed ER since I was a kid. She doesn't like to keep changing those sheets, so you've got to be in really bad shape for her to let you through the gates and mess up one of her rooms." Floyd gathers up all the photos and emails I gave him. "I'll have to take these with me."

I'm glad to see them go. "Please do."

Floyd turns serious again. "I don't want anyone out and about on these roads tonight. You four will have to bunk here unless you want me to give you a lift back to town. If so, you'll have to come along, too, Gina. I don't want you staying here alone. This is all bad timing, with the huge crowd flooding Sunset Beach over the next four days. It would be a lot easier locating this Team Outcast character on a normal weekend. Finding this guy now could be like looking for a black cat in a coal cellar. But don't you worry. We will find him. In the meantime, you're all to take extra safety precautions. No one goes anywhere on their own. And no one goes walking down deserted roads in the dark. Got it?"

We all nod obediently.

Floyd puts his little black notebook back in his pocket and crosses to the door. "Lock it up tight and call right away if anyone comes around. Or if you feel nervous. I'll have a car out here lickety-split to check things out." Floyd tips his hat and disappears into the black night.

I lock the door behind him. All four of us are cross-eyed with exhaustion.

Florrie checks the time. "It's four a.m. Let's hit the hay. Two to a bed. Just like the old days." Even with all the weirdness of the night, Florrie is still pumped for the weekend. "All the real excitement starts tomorrow when the celebrations go into full swing."

Vivi rubs her sore head. "I don't think I can take much more excitement."

We drag our weary bodies into the two bedrooms of my cottage and bunk down. We're sound asleep in seconds.

The same dream wakes me a few times during the night. Cassie Williams is standing on the tracks with a deafeningly loud train bearing down on her. She's screaming a warning at me, but I can't make out what she's saying. And then the locomotive barrels past, and Cassie is gone.

Chapter Fourteen

The whole lot of us are up four hours later, nobody looking like we've slept at all as we schlep into the kitchen, unshowered and still garbed in yesterday's outfits. But everything always looks brighter, less threatening in the light of day, so we all feel better than we did last night, even though we're knackered. The fear quotient has diminished, mainly because the survival instinct is so strong. Life keeps happening whether we're prepared to carry on or not, and we all have to keep up or risk being devoured by monsters, real or imagined.

When I'm short on sleep, I'm always ravenous with hunger. A body has to get the energy it needs from somewhere. I grab a couple of Florrie's leftover salted caramel chocolate chip cookies and wolf them down.

I let the dogs out for a morning potty session and gather an armful of logs to feed the woodstove. I pull a loaf of sourdough twelve grain out of the freezer and take butter, jam, and a large chunk of sharp cheddar from the fridge, and set it all on the counter for everyone to help themselves.

Vivi already has the coffee on. Florrie begins toasting the bread four slices at a time. Both scents smell divine.

I kneel down to stoke the fire, and it's roaring and throwing off much-needed heat within minutes. The smell of the burning logs mingles intoxicatingly with the percolating Arabica. Cabin life, the ultimate definition of cozy, is so rich for the senses, so healing for the soul. I need patching up on my soul, my heart, my head, my entire body—pretty much everything about me could use a lift, a tuck, or a transplant. Medic, we've got a woman down!

Vivi stands next to me at the woodstove, warming her hands, deeply inhaling the comforting morning aromas while recording our every task on her phone. Even running on next-to-no sleep following a wildly stressful night, this woman manages to look effortlessly lovely. Her silver hair gleams like pewter in the sunlight that streams in through the front window, and it's inspiring.

I wonder whether or when I'll ever be ready to embrace my own silver locks and let my natural grays grow in. I wonder whether or when I'll ever have enough confidence to stop hiding the real me beneath the layers of the toxic chemical concoction that is boxed hair color. To be honest, I've always enjoyed playing with different hair shades, and silver is just another color. It's also an admission to oneself that youth is gone, which can seem sad, but at the same time, it's an empowered statement to the world that your elder years are here, and you have decided to passionately seize this third life chapter and kick it's ass. Maybe I'll be able to talk myself into going gray sooner than I thought, but for the time being, I'm not there yet.

"I'm starving." Vivi finally turns her phone off, crosses to see what Florrie's fixing. "Florrie, you really don't have to go to all this trouble. It looks amazing, but plain toast is fine."

Florrie is upping the breakfast game, preparing food as if Gordon Ramsay is going to show up to taste test and tear a strip off her. "I cook when I'm nervous. It calms me down."

Cordelia slumps across the kitchen table, too exhausted to pitch in with breakfast prep. "Let's keep her stressed out, then. Florrie's cooking is the upside of vindictive exes and shadowy stalkers."

Florrie is furiously frying up eggs and sprinkling them with shavings of the sharp cheddar. She's slicing avocados and tomatoes and whipping up a quick glaze for drizzling over the *Bon Appétit*–magazine-worthy avo toast she's plating. She does all this faster than I could make toast and jam.

The bliss is busted minutes later when the power saws and electric drills start up at eight on the dot, and our communal headache is instantly catapulted into migraine territory.

"Bloody hell, is this what you wake up to every morning?" Cordelia, squinting in pain, looks especially accosted by the barrage of high-pitched grinding sounds that reverberate through my tiny cabin.

I pass around the bottle of Advil for anyone who needs it. Everybody does.

"Yup, every morning, and there's a long renovation road ahead." I pour myself a large mug of strong coffee, then hand the pot over for the others to imbibe.

Cordelia throws back her scalding java. "Hugh is hard on the ears, but at least he's easy on the eyes."

We all sit down to eat as Florrie sets out delicious plates of her inspired avocado toast topped with fried egg, sliced cherry tomatoes, and balsamic drizzle.

I take a ridiculously gargantuan bite, speak with my mouth full, inadvertently spitting toast crumbs across the table. These girls know me too well to notice or care. "It is absolutely delicious, Florrie."

The pleased chef beams as she always does when people enjoy her food. The other two nod and moan in appreciation as they chow down. Feeding people is Florrie's love language. Eating may be mine.

Vivi reminds me of today's itinerary. "We're still recording the podcast at our Madonna Madness party tonight for our graduating decade, right?"

"We're recording the podcast at a party? No, absolutely not. I never set that up."

Florrie raises her hand sheepishly. "I did. I thought you'd want to help out, Gina." Florrie sounds a little accusatory, as in, *You, haven't done anything for the reunion yet, Gina.*

And she's right. But I'm still not going to any of the reunion parties. "It's going to be pretty tough for me to host a podcast from this eighties party since I'm not going to be there."

Florrie switches from sheepish to miffed in a flash, and she preaches from the guilt trip pulpit. "It's a combination eighties and nineties party because we wanted to draw a bigger crowd from both decades' graduating classes. It will be more fun with more people there, and we'll raise more money for charity. And all the partygoers are expecting to watch the very famous Ex-Whisperer hosting the very famous Silver Sister from the Silver Lining live at the fundraiser they've bought tickets to attend in support of our local women's shelter." Florrie's indignant eyes bore holes right through my own sleep-deprived, crusty ones. She's wearing me down, but I'm not ready to cave quite yet.

Cordelia groans. "Oh gawd. That means half the people at the party will be ten years younger than us. I've been getting laser treatments on my crow's feet for the past five months leading up to this damn reunion. If I had known the nineties classes were going to crash our party, I would have gone for a full-blown browlift."

Vivi turns to Cordelia. "Well, it's good you didn't know, then. It's way cooler to age naturally. Step one, stop dying your hair."

Cordelia rolls her eyes. "Maybe once I give up my very lucrative sideline work—nobody wants a dominatrix who reminds them of their grandmother. Well, actually, some probably do, but none of the clients in my current stable."

Florrie knows enough to be nervous when she hurls the next curveball at me. "I kind of volunteered you for spicing up the eighties/nineties shindig, as in, Spice Girls spicing it up." Florrie is looking to make a quick exit now before I have a chance to wake up enough to properly react. She gathers plates at warp speed and dumps them in the sink. "You're Posh. Dress appropriately and be at the school by seven." She grabs her purse, pulls her car keys out, hurries to the door.

It's a hard no from me. "Absolutely no way am I dressing up as a Spice Girl to record a podcast or go to any party. Especially not Posh, or Baby, or any other pop princess who was in vogue thirty years ago."

Cordelia loves to push buttons and then sit back and watch the fireworks. "Gina's really more like Scary Spice, wouldn't you say?"

My rope is frayed, and I'm dangling from the end of it. "No, I'm definitely not Scary Spice." I think I'm offended.

Vivi leaps in. "Cordelia, you are Scary Spice. That's a given."

Cordelia acquiesces. "Yeah, I guess you're right. Florrie has to be Baby Spice."

"That's a no-brainer." Florrie understands the assignment.

Vivi shrugs. "I'm obviously Sporty. Gina, you can't be Ginger, so you have to be Posh. You've got a little black mini-dress. Just throw on a pair of high heels, and straighten your hair, and you'll be perfect. Oh, and look sulky. Posh never smiles."

"If I have to go anywhere dressed as Posh Spice, you can bet your ass I'll look sulky and will not be smiling."

Florrie bursts into song, belting out the Spice Girl power anthem "Wannabe" as she dances out the door with Snowflake in her arms.

I run to the door, calling after her. "It's going to be impossible to record with the background noises of the party. It's not doable."

Florrie yells back at me. "You and Vivi will wear headphones."

I am ticked off. "You should have asked me first, Florrie. Technically, we can't make that work. It's going to sound terrible."

Florrie waves me off. "We're going to record it in a little sound booth, and you'll do great, Posh. And hey, bring David Beckham along with you, will ya?" Florrie looks pointedly over at Hugh, who is working in the yard, and chuckling away at Florrie's loud singing.

I'm pleading now. I'm desperate. "And also, I don't want to do this!"

Florrie ignores me, continues singing over top of my begging. She's giggling as she closes her car door and zooms off.

I trudge back inside the cabin and am met at the door by Vivi and Cordelia, who are also making their exit and are also singing loudly together about *what they really really want and zigazig whatever.*

Annoying lyrics being sung by annoying women. My cranky mood has leveled up to totally pissed off.

Hugh is shaking his head, and I am shaking my fist. "Traitors."

Vivi calls over her shoulder with a big Sporty Spice smile as she girl-power walks down the road back to her cottage. "See you at the school at seven, Posh!"

Hugh stops chuckling long enough to grab me before I go back inside. "Hey there, Posh, could you please come here for a few minutes and spice up my life by going over the plumbing rough-in with me?"

I immaturely stomp toward Hugh and the bunkie. "Very funny." Cannot look him in the eye, also cannot think of a more clever retort. Everything about this moment is making me feel like an awkward thirteen-year-old, a stage I never wished to return to. Fervently hoping that he has no memory of me physically throwing myself at him yesterday.

Hugh is his regular cool-cucumber self, only further highlighting my own innate lack of composure. I step inside the bunkie with him, puffy eyes downcast, and Hugh goes over the layout for the sink and toilet with me. I struggle to focus—my new baseline.

When I thank him and turn to leave, he reaches out, gently taking my wrist to turn me around to face him. I pull my arm away, wait for him to speak because I sure as heck don't know what to say.

"Are you okay? I heard the police were here last night. I was glad to see Florrie and your girlfriends were with you when I pulled up this morning. You weren't hurt, were you?"

I'm flabbergasted. "How did you know the cops were here? It's only been six hours."

"News rides in on the waves in this town. Was it something to do with Dick or Iris? If my obsessed ex pulled some stalker shit again, I'll go talk to her right now." Hugh can't hide his irritation once his ex-wife, Iris, comes into the conversation.

"We both know there's no talking to your ex or mine, which is why you and I can't have a thing, or whatever it was we were attempting to have because, clearly, there will always be four people in this relationship, and that is two weirdos too many. But no, Iris wasn't involved as far as I know, but I don't know much. Dick popped by for a middle-of-the-night visit, asking for help because he's got some loan sharks circling around, so that was bizarre."

The cool cucumber is morphing into a red-hot chili pepper with each sentence I share.

"But Dick isn't the reason we called the police. Some anonymous former classmate dropped off creepy photos of me and the other girls and sent threatening emails to my blog."

Hugh looks as if his blood pressure is rising to dangerous levels.

"Even worse, somebody attacked Vivi and Cordelia on the road out here last night. They're not hurt badly, but they've each got a golf ball on the back of their heads."

"That's scary. Any idea who?"

I shake my head. "We don't even know if it's the same person or if we've got a couple of freaks on the loose. There are a ton of people in town for the reunion weekend, so it literally could be anyone who got their feelings hurt in high school and never got over it."

"That is literally everyone who ever went to high school, isn't it? Did anyone not get their feelings hurt?"

"High school was bad, but high school reunions are worse. Apparently, I have no choice but to dress up as Posh Spice and attend an eighties/nineties fundraising party tonight to record a podcast."

"Need a date?"

I figure he's joking. He must be joking. I mean, I'm basically a relationship dumpster fire, which Hugh has to have figured out by now. And he told me only yesterday that there's no way he would be attending any of the reunion festivities since he didn't go to our high school, and I don't know him well enough to be sure, but I'm thinking he might fundamentally dislike most people, or more likely he just distrusts them, which I totally get.

I laugh weirdly in response to his offer because I clearly suck at anything to do with dating, romance, or sex, and let's forget about love. How do I so deftly advise others in this challenging arena in which I'm completely developmentally stunted? That's easy—I ascribe to the philosophy that we teach best what we most need to learn. In which case, my qualifications as an utter failure in the world of relationships make me a bona fide dating and romance guru.

More embarrassingly bizarre chuckles escapes from my mouth. I am so cringeworthy that I spill my guilty guts all over this gorgeous man, who if he knows what's good for him, should definitely run for his life. "I want to apologize for the uninvited, unwarranted, bumbled booty call yesterday. I mean, it wasn't exactly a booty call, more like an ambush with like a snare and a net, and a trip line. I'm sorry. I don't know what happened. Please forgive but mostly forget if you can. Please forget so we can go on working together without the whole humiliation energy, on my end, permeating our days and annihilating what minuscule shreds of my dignity are still intact."

I am done. I am so done. Hugh looks at me for a long beat, and I cannot read his face and my level of discomfort is excruciating and I wish I could disappear into the cracks between the warped floorboards.

And then Hugh answers with the longest, deepest kiss of my life. And I sink into the perilous quicksand of relationships that should never be allowed to continue. And I think I want to stay here forever.

Chapter Fifteen

Following the torrid make-out session in the bunkie with my hot contractor, I'm feeling light and sort of silly, which, if I recall correctly, is a mental state called *infatuation* that children under the age of eighteen years old are often afflicted with. Damn, I hope I grow up quickly—like in the next couple of hours—before I make a complete and utter fool of myself. Once again.

Vivi texted earlier to say that, on her walk home this morning, she found the key to her cottage in the long grass of the ditch where she and Cordelia were attacked from behind. And also that the spare key, which went missing a day ago, after sixty years of being kept under the same rock on top of the same tree stump, had been replaced. So strange. And unsettling.

I message back that she should have the locks changed ASAP in case the person who "borrowed the key" had it copied, hoping that Vivi wouldn't notice it missing for a day. Vivi figures it was Sal. I hope it wasn't Team Outcast.

The aunts have been texting, asking me where I am and what I've been eating, and telling me how they could be dead by the time I ever get around to visiting them again. They went into detail about what I'm to do with their ashes since that's probably the shape they'll be in by the next time I see them, but they couldn't agree on the arrangements, so they launched into a lengthy text-fighting sesh. Zia Angela wants to be sprinkled in their veggie garden, but Zia Rosa wants her urn to sit on top of my mantel so she can keep an eye on me for all eternity. I don't need to tell them while they're still walking the earth, but they're both going to fertilize the zucchini patch. It's been less than twenty-four hours since I set up the aunts' tarot-card-reading booth for them at the high school, but still, I am a neglectful niece. I tell them I have to record a podcast at the school tonight, so I have some prep to do for that, but they coerce me into squeezing in lunch with them at Happily Napoli first.

Zoe comes for the drive into town with me. She hangs her big beautiful cement block of a head out the open window for the whole trip, even though the wind is frigid this morning. She loves a car ride and is happy to spend a couple of hours sleeping on the back seat while I do my thing.

Finding a parking spot on High Street in Sunset Beach this weekend proves to be tougher than finding one in downtown Toronto. The quaint little town wasn't designed to accommodate this many visitors. It's at burst capacity in the summer months when it's overrun with tourists, and it's the same this weekend, overrun with the returning prodigal sons and daughters who left their childhood homes for greener pastures and higher wages many years ago.

Reunion partyers, already filling up the pubs and restaurants, are spilling onto the sidewalks, beers, and wine glasses in hand. Zoe has lots to bark at, which will keep her entertained while I entertain my aunts. I magically manage to snag a parking space only a few stores down from the aunts' restaurant and hustle inside so my zias can feed me lunch and mete out a well-meaning tongue-lashing. Food and scolding are the aunts' love language.

Happily, Napoli is packed to the rafters, and extra waitstaff whisk back and forth through the swinging kitchen doors that look to be in perpetual motion. Usually, the aunts keep a small table open next to the kitchen for family and close friends who drop in to eat regularly, and also for themselves to sit when the pace slows enough that they can *mangiare* a little linguine and rest the swollen ankles they suffer from after being on their feet all day kneading pasta dough and stirring the closely guarded secret recipe for their homemade spaghetti sauce.

My usual table is taken, and I don't see any open ones. I don't see the aunts, either so I wait by the door, try to blend in with the red-and-white checkerboard linens and the plastic salamis hanging from the ceiling.

This is exactly what I didn't want. I didn't want to be standing out in the open, fully exposed to reunion revelers. I didn't want to risk throngs of people running up and throwing their arms around me, shrieking my name and me not knowing who in the heck they are, and worse, not caring. The reason we let relationships with old-school chums die a natural death after graduation is that we don't have anything in common with them other than growing up in the same geographic area.

I wait for the onslaught of long-lost schoolmates to rush me, telling me I haven't changed a bit and that they've missed me and that we must get together and stay in touch after the reunion. Waiting. Waiting. No stampede of old classmates desperate to reconnect. I'm not even noticed, never mind recognized. Maybe none of the customers here are from my graduating year. Maybe I have changed a lot in thirty-three years. I'm starting to feel insulted now. And pissed off with myself that I didn't treat myself like Cordelia and spring for the Groupon coupon for the facial laser treatment package that I deleted from my inbox twenty-five times.

I scan the faces of the diners, hoping I don't recognize anyone who hasn't recognized me. Everyone is chowing down on the overflowing baskets of fresh ciabatta and steaming bowls of baked penne and creamy carbonara, and none of them look familiar to me. What I do notice is that everybody looks so damn old. There are more gray hairs and paunches and marionette lines than you could shake a stick at. But there are also more smiles and more laughter and boisterous conversations than I normally see in any restaurant. Everyone here has been lucky enough to grow older and stay healthy enough to make the memory lane trip back to Sunset Beach. Actually, it's shocking how happy everyone looks, and my misplaced defenses fall away. All of us here do have more in common than geography. We have a shared history, even if it is an ancient one, and that's a lot.

"Gina, Gina, *sedere*." Sit down. The aunts appear from the kitchen, sweeping past me with huge plates of mushroom risotto and pesto ravioli and spicy sausage and anchovy pizzas held high over their heads. The delicious smells waft through the space, and I can feel my mouth beginning to water. After they set the dishes down in front of extremely appreciative customers, the aunts accost me and drag me toward the kitchen.

Zia Rosa always sounds angry with me, but I know she's not really. "You gonna eat in the kitchen. There's no space for you out here. You came too late. Why you late for lunch? You sick?" They're not interested in hearing answers to their questions.

Zia Angela pulls my ear to bring my head toward her and lower so she can whisper a secret to me. "Your exa Dick, he's living right across the road over Mr. Cuddy's Hardware Store."

I nod, also whisper. "I know, Zia. I asked him to move to another town. I hope he's going to, but I don't know."

She shrugs as if it's not all bad. "He orders the lasagne and the linguine alle vongole every night for the takeout."

I can't believe the nerve of Dick and the disloyalty of my aunts. "You let him buy food here?" So upsetting.

Zia Angela shrugs. "It's twenty dollars for the dinner. Who's gonna say no to twenty dollars? You *stupida*? We gotta pay for the electric bill, you know. We gotta keep the roof over *la testa*." She taps her own, then taps me upside the head and pushes me between tables toward the kitchen before I have a chance to respond.

"Gina? Is that you?" A small, round, blond woman leaps up from her table, chewing on a mouthful of rigatoni.

This is what I was worried about. I'm the worst with faces, and I don't have a clue who this woman is. I smile and wave and act excited to see her. I do fake so brutally. This person absolutely knows I don't recognize her.

"It's Sissy. Sissy Greensplat. Well, Carney now," she says with an inauthentic amount of pride. The evil little fae person bares her teeth.

Please, God, no. Not Sissy Greensplat. Sissy is the reason I got booted off the cheerleading team. Sissy is the girl who turned every popular kid, and everyone who had any hope or dream of ever becoming a popular kid, against me.

The aunts lumber over with a wooden chair from the kitchen and squeeze it into a too-small space at the end of Sissy's table. "Good, good. Gina, you eat here with your friends. There's no tables for you right now." Zia Rosa

motions gruffly for Sissy to scootch over. "You gotta make room. *Spostati.*"
Move over.

Panic, embarrassment, dread. I can't do this. I turn away from the table.
"No, Zia. I came here to see you and Zia Angela. I'm going to eat lunch in
the kitchen with you." I start toward the kitchen.

My aunt grabs my sweater, yanks me back to the chair she's pulled up for
me. "No, *sedere.* You eat with your friends." She's pressing me into the seat.

Sissy bares her teeth again. It might be a smile, but that's highly doubtful.
She doesn't say any of the things she should right now like, *Yes, please join us,*
or *We'd love to have you sit with us, Gina.* I am in agony.

There are three other people at her table, none of them smiling at me
either. Another couple who, big surprise, I don't recognize, and a man who
must be Sissy's partner and looks vaguely familiar. None of them are overly
welcoming. I am dying.

Moments later, the aunts shuffle back to us with a full place setting and a
minestrone soup for me along with more bread for the basket on the table.

Sissy points to the man next to her. "You remember my high school
sweetheart, Russ Carney. My husband now." She clutches onto his arm
possessively.

I wish I could tell her there is no need to send me a message about her
having a claim on Russ Carney. Not thirty-three years ago and not now. I'm
not interested, lady. Never was, never will be.

Russ Carney. The former captain of the wrestling team, who invited me to
the movies while he was dating Sissy and, even though I turned him down,
singlehandedly changed my popularity trajectory for the following four
years. He looks old and dull with a coolness factor of negative one thousand.
I stare into my bowl and slurp my soup without stopping, so I don't have to
speak to anyone.

Sissy introduces the other couple at the table. "And you must remember
the best flyer girl the Whitecaps Cheer Squad ever had, Wendy Stickle."

Wendy waves her arms over her head and squeaks loudly. "Give me a
W, give me an *H*, give me an *I*, give me a *T*, give me an *E!* Goooooooo,
Whitecaps!"

Cheers and clapping erupt throughout the whole restaurant.

I take back everything I said to myself minutes earlier. I don't have anything in common with anyone in here.

Sissy continues, "And this is her husband, Harry Smith. He didn't go to our school."

Wendy titters and leans into her husband's shoulder coyly, which she was a master at three decades ago, but she's not managing to pull off cute now. Harry Smith is unresponsive. He continues eating in silence like a walking dead man. "He's an inlander, but I married him anyway." An inlander is what people who live in towns along the shores of Lake Huron call all the poor sods who aren't lucky enough to live along the shores of Lake Huron.

I'm finally sitting at the popular girls' table, and I hate it.

The aunts bustle back with a piping-hot plate of pasta e fagioli and switch it out for my soup bowl. I don't get to order in Happily Napoli. My zias serve me whatever vegetarian dishes they have going. I've never complained. They don't know how to cook anything that's not spectacularly delicious. I shovel the pasta and bean dish into my gob as fast as I can, even though it scorches the back of my throat. I can't spend a minute longer with these former schoolmates than necessary.

The two women carry on a lively conversation about all the former classmates they've run into so far today and how every one of them looks old and has gained weight and has had too much Botox or not enough Botox. They compare notes on their mental scorecards for the competition of How Everyone's Life Has Turned Out—who's divorced; who did or didn't have children; what model of car people are driving; who's letting themselves go; who's trying too hard to cling to their youth. The women lower their voices to whispers when they discuss Sal being a "made man" and how Vivi was married to the mob. Their husbands are silent. Please shoot me.

I'm finished eating in record time and stand up to excuse myself. "Thanks for letting me crash your party. It's been a real trip down memory lane."

Sissy looks surprised. "You don't have to leave yet Gina. Stay, and fill us in on what's going on with you. You're divorced, right?"

Cannot get away from them fast enough. "I've gotta help my aunts out in the kitchen." I pick up my dishes from the table.

Sissy feigns disappointment. "See you at the party tonight then. I hear you're interviewing Vivi on your podcast. Make sure you ask her about her former mafia-wife life. I can't wait to hear all the juicy stuff about hit men and kneecapping."

The two women giggle like a couple of high school girls, and while the tittering sound used to tinkle when they were teenagers, it's now infused with the croakiness of vocal cords that are half a century old.

I dodge waitstaff zooming back and forth carrying precariously balanced bowls of fragrant Bolognese with mortadella meatballs and platters of roasted vegetable antipasto, and I time my entry through the swinging kitchen doors just right so as not to topple teetering trays.

The aunts are too busy cooking to chat with me. I kiss their red cheeks and thank them for the lunch.

Zia Angela leans over a ginormous vat of boiling water to kiss me back. "So sorry we can't sit with you. Too busy. Come back later for dinner, and we talk."

Zia Rosa is chopping peppers with the knife skills of a ninja warrior. "Angela, you *pazza*? Crazy? No, dinner is busier than lunch today. Gina, you go let Peppita and Peppeto outside to peepee. They're upstairs in the apartment."

Oh God, please no. Anything but that. I think I'd rather go back and spend the afternoon with Sissy Greensplat and Wendy Stickle than take care of the aunts' twin Chihuahuas for five minutes. Pet sitting Peppita and Peppeto is like trying to wrangle the demon duo of Damien from *The Omen* and Regan from *The Exorcist*.

"*Sbrigati!*" Hurry up. Zia Rosa points to the stairs that lead to their apartment above the restaurant.

I know there's no point in arguing. And obviously, the aunts could use some help. At least they don't put me to work washing dishes.

I let myself into the aunts' abode. It hasn't changed a bit since I was a kid. Every stick of furniture was purchased in the 1950s, including the wide-armed sofas, and is all still in pristine condition. That's mostly due to everything being draped in plastic so thick you could massacre an entire village in the aunts' apartment, and nothing would wind up bloodstained. There are more than ten thousand Catholic saints, and I think either a statue or a picture of each one of them is displayed throughout the aunts' home. Between the relics, the crosses, and the plethora of Mother Marys, there are decks of tarot cards, and crystal balls, and amulets to ward off the evil eye. The smell from a potent mixture of Lemon Pledge and frankincense incense permeates the apartment and clings to the clothes of anyone who enters.

The Hounds of Hades barrel out from a back bedroom at full speed, snapping and snarling and displaying their usual bad tempers. They leap all over me, scratching my legs wildly and getting in little nips when they can while I struggle to attach their matching leashes. In a tornado of fur and teeth and bulgy eyes, the twin Chihuahuas lead me down the stairs and out the back door to the aunts' garden.

The small yard backs onto a narrow laneway that the locals use when they want to avoid High Street, which is mostly just in the summer months when it's jammed with tourists. The yard is fully fenced in, so I can drop the leashes and let the little fiends run loose. I wander for a bit, inspecting the aunts' good-sized and perfectly maintained veggie patch. It's usually a vibrant riot of color, but it's been put to bed for the winter now, and it looks tired. I'd like to be put to bed for the winter right now, too. I sit down on the aunts' extremely uncomfortable wrought-iron outdoor furniture, also from the 50s, while the dogs chase dried leaves around my feet and scrap with each other over twigs.

There's an old shed at the back corner of their yard that the aunts use to store their lawn mower and gardening tools. There's a car parked in the lane behind it, which isn't unusual, but I think I've seen it before, and I wonder who it belongs to.

I hear a loud bang coming from the aunts' shed, and the dogs hear it, too, and race toward the suspect sound, yapping and growling. I follow after them but only manage to catch the back of a man in a heavy coat, hood pulled up over his head, who's moving quickly to jump inside his car. He was doing something in and around the aunts' storage shed, but I can't imagine what.

There's certainly nothing to steal in there. In a flash, he's in his car and racing off.

I didn't see his face, but from behind, the man looked a lot like my ex-husband Dick.

Chapter Sixteen

I t's strange for sure, but there are stranger things going on in this town right now than someone poking around the aunts' old shed filled with rakes and shovels, many of them broken. And I can't imagine any reason Dick would have to be hanging around the aunts' garden. Maybe it was a neighbor looking to borrow a tool. Maybe it was a killer looking to bury a body. I don't think I care. I just know I don't have the bandwidth to cogitate on this curiosity, along with all the other freakiness floating around right now.

Peppita and Peppeto have done their business, and I wrangle them back inside through the service entrance of the restaurant. They bark and yelp incessantly, calling out to their mammas. A minute later, both my frazzled aunts, who couldn't take any time out for me today, appear and scoop their fur babies up into their aprons to hand feed them penne drizzled with olive oil and coo Italian lullabies to the little monsters.

"Bambina."

"Bambino."

When I get back to my car and my sleeping giant Zoe, I appreciate my comparatively well-behaved and quiet canine.

The town is even busier now as more visitors pour in. The circus has geared up, and the reunion ride will last for another four days. I'm looking forward to getting back to my quiet cottage for the rest of the afternoon.

After Zoe and I enjoy a long, brisk walk along the deserted beach in front of my cottage, my energetic fur baby has finally reached a point of exhaustion and is out like a light, so she won't mind spending the evening at the cottage without me. Spook is drunk on the heat from the roaring woodstove and in classic feline style, is languishing full length on the warm stone hearth. I have showered and am waiting for my thick waves to dry so I can attempt to wrestle my hair into submission with my flat iron, à la Posh Spice.

I've packed up my podcast recording gear and have just made a lovely cup of cardamom and cinnamon tea and carried it and my laptop to my favorite chair to curl up next to the snoozing pets. I need to check my email and perhaps squeeze in a bit of actual work for a change.

It's getting dark outside already, and I hear Hugh and his man Ryan loading up their truck with their tools and pulling out for the day. Hugh will be back at 6:45 to pick me up for the podcast party. He insisted on accompanying me tonight, saying it wasn't safe for me to be going out alone. I'm not interested in playing the damsel in distress, and I don't need anybody to take care of me, but I don't mind the idea of a night out with Hugh.

I check my inbox.

And they're back.

> Dear Ex-Whisperer,
>
> You lied when you told me that you and your friends never bullied anyone in school, that your group was the nice girls. I left the proof on your doorstep. Did that newspaper headline jog your memory? Do you remember now? Do you remember being so cruel to me that I went for a walk and never came back? My life has been a train wreck. It's your turn now.
>
> Team Outcast

Bloody hell, this is making my skin crawl. I'm so confused. Is Team Outcast now writing as if they are long dead Cassie Williams? It sort of sounds like it, and that confirms what I already suspected, that they're completely out of their mind. At least now we know for sure that all these emails, and the photos, and the newspaper are connected. I'm not certain whether this is the same person who hit Vivi and Cordelia knocking them into the ditch, but I'd guess it's highly probable. Then again, there are a lot of weirdos in town this weekend as my lunch date with Sissy, and Wendy, and their zombie husbands proved. I forward Team Outcast's latest email to Lloyd at the police station then get up to double-check that my doors are locked. They are. I'm now feeling a little less brave and also extra pleased that Hugh is coming with me to the podcast recording tonight. Don't really feel like going out solo.

Dear Team Outcast,

I didn't lie to you. Neither my friends nor I were ever intentionally mean to anyone in high school, including Cassie Williams. You need to back the eff off and get yourself professional help for your mental issues before you wind up in jail or you hurt somebody or worse. The police are on to you, and so am I. You don't scare me. I don't believe in ghosts.

Affectionately Yours,
  The Ex-Whisperer

Delete.

Not sending. And not going to rewrite, either. I'm not email brawling with them. You can't argue a person back into their right mind. Obviously, what they most want is for me to engage with them, and although that is basically my job description, I am in the driver's seat when it comes to choosing who I interact with in my advice column. And if Team Outcast is actually the ghost of Cassie Williams, she's either going to show up at the foot of my bed, and I will die of fear on the spot, so she'll win in the revenge game, or she'll know the truth that it wasn't my friends or me who bullied her in school, and she'll go toward the light and give up the haunting hullabaloo.

The only thing truly haunting me right now is guilt. We didn't bully Cassie Williams, but we didn't stop the bullying, either. I'm not saying that, as young people, we were entirely innocent; no one in this town was, but we also weren't fully responsible for what happened to that poor young girl. I never witnessed anyone being cruel to her. I would never have allowed that at any age, but I knew that it went on. Three boys, in particular, orchestrated and perpetuated Cassie's pain and suffering through all her school years. Tom Lucknow, Jason Bragg, and Ethan Coleman. They were two years ahead of us and came from rough families. From what I knew of them, I think those boys passed on the abuse they learned and received in their own homes to younger, weaker kids who made easy targets and provided outlets for their pain and suffering. Bullying is a vicious cycle. At its worst, it can be a deadly one.

Three more to add to the list of people I hope I don't run into at the reunion—Cassie's three tormentors.

Enough. I put my laptop away for the night. Or maybe for the weekend. Or maybe for the year. I need a break, and I've arranged for one in a tall drink of water who's going to knock on my door to pick me up in an hour from now.

I pull up a 90s playlist on Spotify to distract me from the freaky effluvia and put me in the right mood for tonight. First up—Salt-N-Pepa, "Let's Talk About Sex." Oh God, pressure.

Can't help it. My body starts groovin'. Oh, screw it. I'll just go with it. An early girl-power anthem should be celebrated. I pour myself a Baileys on ice to forget my troubles and maybe prep to take on a few new ones if I level up my bravery and Hugh is game to join me.

I stand at the bathroom mirror to do my makeup. I recall a decent amount of useless details about the 90s, so I do know that Posh Spice was all about the smoky eye. I layer on the thick, smudgy eyeliner in charcoal gray, and I recreate her signature nude lip and top it with lots of Britney Spears gloss. Straightening my unruly hair proves to be a bigger challenge, but eventually, I wrestle my wavy locks into an acceptably slick and shiny Posh-like bob.

Janet Jackson's "Together Again" is up, and despite myself, I dance into the bedroom, drink in hand. I do own a couple of little black dresses, none of which I've worn in years, and I select the shortest one for my getup. I try on a pair of black velvet stilettos that I used to dance for hours in, but I'm pretty sure I wouldn't make it across the lawn to my car without going over on an ankle wearing them now. I have a pair of black over-the-knee boots with high heels, they're more supportive, so I elect to wear those. I figure they're sexy enough, definitely sexier than wiping out in a parking lot looking white-girl wasted, but in reality, just suffering from fifty-year-old ankles.

J.Lo's "If You Had My Love" spins, and two Baileys in, I am singing mangled lyrics and dancing along. This music isn't as bad as I remembered. I check myself out in my bedroom mirror. I'm looking as Posh as I possibly can, and I'm feeling kinda cute. I can't remember the last time I went full-out glam like this. Not too shabby and kind of fun, but I won't tell Florrie that. I'm still going to keep her on the hook to owe me big-time for my agreeing to this favor.

I have to let Zoe go for a potty break before I head out for the evening, but I think I'll wait until Hugh shows up. It's already dark outside, and despite my initial feisty response, I'm beginning to feel more creeped out from Team Outcast's last message. I sure hope they're not at the party tonight. Also hope they're not lurking about in my yard again. They're probably like most of the big talkers and threat makers on the Internet and are all online bluster and bravado when they're hiding behind a computer but aren't capable of showing up in the real world in any actionable way. Yeah, I'm going to hold that thought. It feels much better than the debilitating alternative.

Damn it. Not doing so great at holding that thought. The scary flipside is worming its way into my psyche. Team Outcast did drop off photos and an old newspaper on my porch, after all. And they may have hit Vivi and Cordelia on their heads, but fingers crossed, that's as far as their physical bravery goes. Unfortunately, my gut tells me that this troll isn't done with us yet.

There's a sharp knock at my door, and I almost leap out of my thigh-highs.

Zoe goes berserk. Spook makes a beeline for the bed, and I nearly trip over the frigging cat as he zooms past me.

I stumble to the door in my spicy boots, but I'm not about to throw it open without making sure it's someone that I'm not dreading seeing. "Who is it?"

A man's voice with a British accent calls through the closed door. "It's David. Who were you expecting?"

I freeze in my tracks. David? WTF? "Who?"

It's an East Ender London accent. I can pick this up because my daughter lives there. "It's David. We've got a date tonight, remember?"

I was thrown for a moment, but I recognize Hugh's voice now and open the door slowly.

Once I get over the initial shock, I laugh way too loudly. I'm normally hard to impress, but right now, I'm impressed so hard.

Hugh has arrived dressed up as David Beckham. He's wearing a Manchester United number 7 football jersey, and he spins around to show me that he's taped the name Beckham onto the back of the shirt. He's got soccer shorts, high socks, and cleats on. He's sporting a Beckham-style stubbly beard, and he's even coiffed his hair in the perfect Becks pomade comb-over.

I can't get over it—he's gone to so much trouble. He looks freaking hot and like such a royal goof at the same time, and it's ridiculously funny and I could really fall for a guy who looks and does like this guy.

Hugh/David seems a little too surprised when he takes me in from bob to boots. But then I realize that he has never seen me wearing anything other than jeans and a T-shirt except for the first time we met when I, too hungover to notice, answered the door in my underwear.

He wears a very deep look of appreciation. "Wow, wow, wow. You look absolutely stunning, Posh." Still with the accent.

Me, still laughing. "As do you, Becks."

Hugh leans in to kiss me, and it is as hot as he looks. I'll have to redo my perfect 90s nude lip, but it's worth it.

I pour one last shot of Baileys over ice for me and a generous three fingers of whisky for David. We toast, kiss, and throw the drinks back. Everything about tonight feels extremely reckless, and I'm surprised that I feel fine with that. Likely thanks to the Baileys Irish Cream. Whatever it takes.

Hugh lets Zoe outside for me and carries my podcast gear to load into his pickup. I leave all the lights on inside and out, tuck the pets in, and lock up my little cottage tight.

Hugh opens the passenger door for me, takes my hand as I climb up into the high truck. It's not necessary, but it feels good, so I don't object.

When he gets behind the wheel, he leans over to kiss me again before he backs out of the laneway. Again, it feels good, so I don't stop him.

Hugh shakes his head slightly, smiles as if he can't believe his good luck, repeats himself. "You look so gorgeous."

"Keep your eyes on the road, buddy."

"That's a tall order." He divides his focus between the road and me for most of the drive.

On our journey into town, I fill Hugh in on the latest from Team Outcast and how I finally got to sit at the popular girls' lunch table today after all these years and what a colossal letdown it was, and I tell him about a person who looked like Dick snooping around the aunts' garden shed.

Hugh is already accustomed to me being a lot and having a lot going on around me, and somehow, he takes it all in his stride, sort of how I imagine the Marlboro Man might. He may even be amused or intrigued by all the chaotic energy that constantly flits in and out of my life and engulfs me personally most of the time, but he doesn't let on. He doesn't need to. I know he's down with it all, or at least he's willing to put up with it all, and what more can you ask for?

We pull up in front of Sunset Beach High, and there are already quite a few vehicles in the lot. The school is on the main street, but a couple of blocks away from the shops, restaurants, and the beach—fewer distractions for the students. When extra parking is needed for special events like this one, the cars spill over into the funeral home and cemetery next door. The party doesn't start for another half hour, but the organizers are all here working hard at setting up. I see Florrie's and Vivi's cars parked nearby. Hugh carries my gear inside the school, and I manage to make it across the parking lot without wiping out in my high-heeled boots, so my night is off to a grand start so far.

Baby Spice rushes toward me, squealing loudly as soon as I step inside the decorated gymnasium.

"Oh my God, you look amazing! I knew you'd be a perfect Posh!" Then she takes in David Beckham and screams with delight. "Becks!" Florrie's strawberry-blond hair is in Baby Spice–style high pigtails. She's wearing a sequined shift dress straight out of 1996, white go-go boots, and a honking big crucifix necklace, probably borrowed from the aunts. She looks great.

Sporty Spice and Scary Spice dance across the floor toward us, and they look fantastic, too. None of us can stop laughing at the others. Vivi/Sporty Spice has a high ponytail, and she's wearing tight Adidas three-stripe track pants, a cropped sports bra, and platform running shoes. Cordelia/Scary Spice has her hair in tight curls, and her bust is bursting out of a leopard-print bustier complemented by latex pants, both of which she likely uses in the work she does when she is not fulfilling her duties as the town librarian, or writing triple X bodice rippers.

As if on cue, the four of us break into an awful a cappella rendition of "Spice up Your Life," complete with hip bumps.

Vivi is recording everything she possibly can to post to social media.

Hugh looks more than amused; he looks captivated. And the girls appreciate David Beckham right back and don't hold back on the compliments, lewd as some of them may be.

After we conclude our show, Baby Spice directs Hugh to the area up the stairs of the stage and off to the side, where there is a very tiny glassed-in sound booth. Vivi and I will record the podcast in there, and I follow him to start setting up the equipment.

A few minutes later, Florrie runs back up onto the stage, pulls me aside. She points to a table in a corner of the room draped in purple fabric with a tall vase of lilies and an arrangement of various framed photos lining the top. "Jenny Bumstead made a celebration-of-life table. It's a memorial to everyone from the school who's passed away."

I look over at the tribute table. It looks sort of like a cross between a science fair project and a funeral service display. It's kind of nice but also kind of morbid. Jenny Bumstead was our resident Debbie Downer, so it makes sense this would be her contribution to the celebrations. "I think maybe Jenny Bumstead has left a few dead people off the roster. I mean, the school is a hundred and fifty years old. There's gotta be a whole lot of former Sunset Beach High students who have kicked the bucket by now."

Florrie looks more than solemn. She looks a little scared. "It's only a memorial for dead people from our two graduating decades, the eighties and the nineties."

"Oh, so there can't be that many then, can there?"

Florrie shakes her head. "No, there's only six. But I looked at the photos, and there's something really freaky about them." Florrie pauses either for dramatic effect or because she doesn't want to tell me about this freaky thing but knows she must.

I'm afraid it's the latter. My stomach turns. I know I'm going to hear something that I really do not want to hear. "Go on."

"So one of them is Cassie Williams, of course. Two of the deceased passed away from cancer, but they went to school ten years after us, so we didn't know them, but we know the families, the Browns, and the Macintoshes."

"Okay...what's the bad news?" Spit it out.

"Well...the other three former high school students who died are Tom Lucknow, Jason Bragg, and Ethan Coleman."

The three boys who bullied Cassie Williams to death.

121

Chapter Seventeen

I instantly feel cold and shiver involuntarily. My aunts would say that someone just walked over my grave. "How did the three boys die?"

Florrie looks over both her shoulders before she whispers. "They all moved out of town thirty-five years ago as soon as they finished school, and I don't think any of them ever came back. It makes sense that none of them wanted to stay in touch with their families—they didn't come from good homes. I heard Tom was killed in a boating accident. Jason moved to Calgary and worked on the oil rigs. I think he overdosed up there. I don't know what happened to Ethan, but I'll ask around tonight. It's a pretty weird coincidence, though."

"It's more than a weird coincidence." I can't help it, another shudder. "It's a pattern."

I tap Florrie's arm when I hear someone approaching, and we halt our conversation. She quickly goes back to work overseeing the table seating arrangements.

Vivi climbs up the stairs onto the stage to join me, and as she does, I appreciate for the first time that we'll be in this sound booth and not in the audience where Team Outcast could sneak up from behind and gut me with a shiv. I watch helplessly as my imagination runs away at a full gallop.

"Any instructions before we get started?" Vivi's ready to do this.

Hugh finds a beer, steps off into the opposite wing of the stage, and takes a seat on a wooden gearbox to watch our recording and keep to himself. He's not interested in rubbing elbows with any of the revelers. He's not exactly a social butterfly, and these aren't really his people. All the same, I'm glad he's here with me.

It's showtime, so I put on my game face, explain a few technical details to Vivi. "The guests will be able to hear us talking if they tune in to the speaker system, which won't be easy for them to do with all the chatting and other background sounds going on. Probably no one will actually be listening to us, and the show will be edited later for the actual podcast, so there's really no pressure. We're going to keep it loose and just have a nice, relaxed conversation. We'll see where it goes. I'm going to ask you about your influencer work and collaborations. I think people will be interested in that. Anything you want to focus on?"

Vivi nods enthusiastically. "I'd really like to talk about the importance of repping older women in media and give the Silver Sisters a shout-out. It's an untapped goldmine for marketers, and elder gals like us want to see themselves in books and films and also be seen and heard generally. Representation is always an issue for women of color, so it's especially crucial for them."

"Got it. That's great. Any topics you want me to stay away from?"

"My marriage. I realize you're the Ex-Whisperer, so that's where your listeners expect you to go, but I can't discuss Sal. You know that."

"Sure, no problem. We'll figure a way around it. Florrie's tried to arrange a way that the audience can ask us questions at the end of the show, so people might ask about your personal life, but we'll steer them away from Sal. And like I said, we'll edit out anything we don't want to keep in there."

Vivi looks relieved. "Great, thanks, Gina."

Early birds are beginning to arrive, and I see Florrie shooting back to the door to start collecting admission tickets and ticking names off registered guest lists.

Vivi and I put our headphones on, and I count down, "Four, three, two, one, and we are live."

I play the intro to my *Ex-Whisperer Files* podcast, then introduce Vivi, and we begin our banter. We cover a lot of the topics Vivi wanted to, and then we devolve into mostly focusing on the reunion, and what high school reunions mean in general, and juicy stories we've heard about other reunions and old flames and crushes and hookups and the fireworks that can ensue in relationships when old meets new. The talk is flowing great. We're having lots of laughs and are managing not to offend anybody directly. Thankfully, the sound doesn't seem too terrible. I'm not hearing any of the background noise, which is dialing up by the minute as more and more partyers arrive and choose their seats at the forty tables for eight that line the perimeter of the gymnasium.

Current high school students dressed smartly in white and black walk around serving trays of cheeses and crackers and mini quiches. There's a cash beer and wine bar, which is already crowded, naturally.

I lose my train of thought for a moment when I see a non-alcoholic punch bar being operated by Hugh's ex, Bible Babe. Vivi has my back, and she carries the convo while I recover from that curveball. Iris didn't attend our high school. She didn't even move into town until years after our group had graduated, but she insinuates herself into everything Sunset Beach for the sole purpose of attempting to recruit unsuspecting passersby to join her church. And also, so she can spy on/make trouble for Hugh and me whenever possible. I catch Hugh's eye in the opposite stage wing and motion toward Iris. Hugh leans around the curtain to see what I'm indicating, and he throws back his head in exasperation when he sees his apron clad ex, looking like Ma from *Little House on The Prairie*, pushing fruity-colored 7 Up in tiny plastic cups. She doesn't have many takers.

I quickly realize that this is only the start of the parade of the exes. Next up, Vivi is thrown for a loop, and I take over with the talk-show chatter while she tries not to throw up when Sal makes a grand entrance Tony Soprano–style with his twenty-three-year-old goomah on his arm and an entourage of six wise guys who look like gorillas in too-tight, too-shiny suits. They sure don't fit in with the low-key crepe paper streamers and blue-and-white balloon arrangements, although the disco balls are right up their alley.

Sal chooses a table in a far corner so he can sit with his back to the wall to make sure he can see everyone who walks into the joint and know that nobody can jump him from behind.

Tiffany may be dressed up as a 90s-style Britney Spears à la "...Baby One More Time" in keeping with the party theme, or she may just be so young that she actually regularly wears a schoolgirl uniform of plaid miniskirt, knee socks, and a white oxford shirt with her hair in braids, except she's made it sexy with her shirt tied in a midriff-baring knot and high heels. Either way, much to our disappointment, Tiffany does manage to pull off the look brilliantly.

The next time I look out from the sound booth, the place is packed, and the party is in full swing. There is definitely nobody listening to me and Vivi prattle on, and I'm more relieved than insulted. So many people are mingling and table hopping. The booze is flowing, and I marvel at the amount of hugging going on.

There's a crowd of curious rubberneckers gathered around Sal's table. He's the man of the hour. I can see Sissy Greensplat leaning into Sal for selfies that she'll be posting right after she applies her FaceApp filter to them. Tiffany seems to be relishing the attention, looks like she's ready to start signing autographs.

Florrie scurries up the stage steps and approaches our booth. I'm sure there would have been a better way to communicate the partygoers' questions to us, but Florrie tapes papers onto the plexiglass facing us so we can read the handwritten notes. They partially block our view of the fete, which is frustrating, because I'd been hoping to have a panoramic perspective in case I'm somehow able to spot Team Outcast among the crowd of paunches, bald heads, and jiggly jowls. Vivi continues speaking, and I try to focus, choose some questions to read out loud that are on point with the topics she wanted to hit on. I ignore the nosy ones clearly asked by Sissy, Wendy, and the rest of the cheer squad that focus on Vivi's personal life, particularly her marriage to a mobster. Vivi can read the notes stuck to the sound booth walls, too, and from her slow headshake, I can tell they make her feel crummy. Can't wait for the two of us to be done recording so we can grab a drink, or four.

It doesn't seem as if Sissy and her girl gang got the memo that they're not in high school anymore and that they're three-and-a-half decades older than they were in their glory cheer days. Not to be nasty, but yeah, actually, I will be nasty—it doesn't look as if any of them could do a deep knee bend never mind fly through the air in the splits, but it also doesn't look as if they're aware of that fact.

I mute my mic, talk to Vivi privately. "Oh my God, the old squad is lining up in formation to do one of their victory routines. This is way too painful to watch."

Sissy, Wendy, and six or seven other tumbler queens are standing in the center of the gym, spilling their red plastic cups full of Bud Light all over the floor.

It's way too difficult to focus on this interview anymore. "Let's sign off. This one can be a shorter podcast. No one cares that we're yapping away up here anyway. Florrie thought we'd be a big deal, the resident celebs, but she didn't count on Sal stealing the show."

Vivi speaks from experience. "Stealing is one of his many talents."

We remove our headphones, and I turn the sound mixer and computer off. Hugh sees and comes over to help pack up the recording gear.

The cheerleaders kick off their chunky heeled shoes, start sliding around in their stocking feet.

Vivi laughs so hard she chokes. "The Whitecap Sneerleaders."

I laugh so hard I snort. Unfortunately, I do so at the exact time that Hugh opens the sound booth door. So attractive.

Hugh carries the equipment off the stage to put it out in his truck. Vivi and I follow him down the stage steps, with me doing my best not to topple over in my teetering Spice Girl boots. The DJ is blasting the old classic "Barbie Girl," and the crowd loves it.

I notice that Sal is staring hard at Vivi and doesn't take his eyes off her as we cross the gym. Tiffany notices, too, and does her best to distract Sal by adjusting her bosom exaggeratedly. Vivi purposely doesn't even glance in Sal's direction as she cuts through the crowd; she concentrates on videoing the festivities.

Florrie and Cordelia book it through the crowded space to meet up with us.

Cordelia looks freaked out, and it's not just because Sissy Greensplat has thrown her back out attempting a pike jump and is now lying in the middle of the painted basketball key. Someone is helping out by getting her another beer.

Scary Spice looks scared. "Did you see the dead people's table?"

Sporty Spice laughs. "Would that be the stoner table or the goths?"

We look around, and Vivi's right—it's a return to cliqueville. It's as if everybody's seventeen years old again, and they've found their old groups, the brainiacs, the artsy kids, the jocks, the cool kids, and have regressed right back to where they were thirty and forty years ago.

No one has told Vivi about the three dead boys yet.

Cordelia does. "Jenny Bumstead set up a memorial table for classmates that might have come to this eighties and nineties party but couldn't make it because they're six feet under."

Vivi rolls her eyes. "Of course, our Debbie Downer did that. Kind of nice, kind of creepy."

Cordelia continues, "Agreed. We've lost six former students, but the really weird thing is that three of the deceased are Tom Lucknow, Jason Bragg, and Ethan Coleman."

Vivi makes the connection instantly, as we all did. "The three boys who bullied Cassie Williams."

We all slowly nod in unison.

"Wow. That is freaky." Then Vivi screams loud enough to make the closest fifty people near her turn to look, and she jumps in response to the hard smack in the ass she receives. She spins around to see Sal standing behind her, Tiffany behind him. Seven goodfellas behind the VIP couple.

Sal smiles his crooked, barfight smile at his ex-wife and looks her up and down admiringly. "How come you never dressed up as a Spice Girl when we were together? Might've saved our marriage."

Vivi looks down on her ex-husband because he is a lowlife and because he is two inches shorter than her, especially with her platform sneakers on. "Sal, the entire New York City Fire Department couldn't have saved our marriage. It was a towering inferno that eventually collapsed, and you're the one who lit the funeral pyre."

Sal looks extremely annoyed with his ex-wife already. "Always with the big words, trying to show off how smart you are, huh Vivi? That you're smarter than me." He turns to one of his soldiers. "Hey, Big Benny, you know that word?"

Big Benny looks dumber than a stump. Also, looks like he could rip one out of the ground with his bare hands. "What word, boss?"

"*Pyre*. You heard that word *pyre* before?"

Benny shakes his head. There may be the sound of something rattling inside it. "Pie or what? Pie or cake? I like cake better, myself. Cannoli are my favorite."

"Cannoli aren't a cake, Big Benny. They're a pastry."

Big Benny shrugs. "Oh, sorry, boss. I don't know so much about dessert."

Sal hasn't taken his steely eyes off of Vivi the whole time he's been speaking to Big Benny. "See what I mean, Vivi? You use these big words that nobody else knows because you like making people feel stupid. Makes you feel better than everyone else, right?"

Vivi's arms are crossed over her chest tightly, self-protection in body language. "*Pyre* is a big word? It's a four-letter word, Sal. Like *jerk*."

Tiffany pipes in. "Four letter word like *cun*—"

With one sharp look, Sal shuts Tiffany up before she can spit out the last consonant of the insulting word.

Vivi turns her back to Sal, looks to the three of us. "Let's go find some classy people to mingle with, shall we, girls?"

Now Sal looks angry. Tiffany is rubbing his shoulders from behind, desperately trying to get his attention and get back in his good books. Florrie looks petrified for Vivi. Cordelia is ready to lay into Sal or at least tighten the loose schoolgirl tie that's dangling around Tiffany's skinny neck to silence her vocal cords for a while. I squeeze Cordelia's hand to warn her not to do anything. Just before we step away from the repugnant little group, Hugh joins us, and I can see he's trying to read the tense situation but doesn't know who any of the players are. Still, he wades into the fray with a rescue attempt. "Everything okay here, Vivi?"

Sal is clearly furious at handsome Hugh stepping on his toes by swooping in to defend what he still regards as one of his women. Sal looks ready to attack, but he visibly works to get a hold of himself and changes his course from wrath to ridicule. He laughs disparagingly at Hugh. "Hey, Vivi, this mortadella pretty boy with you?"

I see Hugh's fists clenching and unclenching. I move over to squeeze his hand now, warning him not to do or say anything else that might set Sal off.

Vivi knows to step in and redirect Sal's attention. "No, Sal, he's not. Is Britney Spears here with you?" She effectively diffuses the situation, at least for now.

Sal laughs a little more good-naturedly now, remembering he brought along the arm candy for a reason. He slides his hand possessively around Tiffany/Britney's tiny, bare waist. The power display makes him feel better. But he's not done yet. He always has to get in the last word. That's the rule. "Hey, David Beckham, your wife Posh wears the high-fashion pants in the family and makes all the money now, huh? And you're just a washed-up footballer."

Sal snickers at what he thinks is a zinger, then looks over at his men. All Sal's henchmen know enough to laugh along with their boss when he signals them to. Their guffaws are a little over the top.

"We'll see you Spice Girls and Spice Boy on the dance floor." Rick James's "Super Freak" is blasting, and Sal is digging it. His head bops as he steers Tiffany around the room, just in case any of his former classmates haven't yet seen him to know how well he's made out in life. He barks at his men to get drinks from the bar for him and Tiffany.

Hugh is confounded. "That guy does know I'm not actually David Beckham, doesn't he?"

We four girls chuckle quietly at that, but mostly just feel worried for Vivi, and frankly, sorry for her. She's put up with so much from Sal over the years, and it doesn't look as if it will ever get any better for her. Sal is never going to go quietly into the night.

Vivi isn't thinking about herself. She's used to this treatment from her ex. "I'm sorry you had to endure Sal's ill temper, Hugh. He truly is an asshole."

Cordelia sees that and raises her. "A dim-witted asshole."

Hugh shrugs it off.

Florrie giggles. "That's for sure. Maybe not quite as dim-witted as Big Benny, though. I might come up with a new dessert for the bakery, call it pyre cake."

Vivi laughs, too, but looks around warily and hushes us. "Careful what you say."

"Let's go check out the memorial table." The five of us weave through the mass of dancing, drunken bodies who are feeling and acting like teenagers and for which they will surely pay a steep price come morning. Initially, I keep an eye out for anyone acting strangely, but that turns out to be basically everyone, so instead, I watch for anyone who seems to be watching me. I can't shake the feeling that Team Outcast is nearby.

Sissy and the rest of the cheer squad have broken formation and are now just dancing like a bunch of Beckys and singing along loudly about super freaks and kinky girls that you don't take home to mother. They obviously think they look a lot sexier than they actually do. If drunkards can slur their dance moves, that's what's going on.

On the way to the dead kids' tribute table, I yell into Hugh's ear to fill him in about Cassie's tormentors having all died prematurely. His Jeffery Dean Morgan bushy brows rise in surprise. Damn, he looks good.

The five of us gather around the shrine-like display and solemnly take in the gold-framed photos of the dearly departed resting upon the fabric-draped table. All of them look far too young to die, even if we know for sure that some were truly horrible people.

The former students of Sunset Beach High are memorialized on large sheets of Bristol board with magic marker sad faces drawn all around their names, and decals of doves, and crosses, and angel wings, and praying hands stickered everywhere. Jenny Bumstead is more of a scrapbooker than an artist, and it shows.

I lower my voice out of respect for the dead. "Does it say anywhere here how Ethan Coleman died?"

We all read the mass cards and newspaper clippings tacked up on the backing of the display.

After a few minutes, Cordelia finds what we're looking for. "Ethan Coleman fell to his death off a tenth-story balcony."

We all exchange astonished and fearful looks. There is a very long silence while we process this information about the three men and their untimely and coincidental deaths.

Florrie speaks up first. "So all three of the boys died in accidents."

Vivi offers an alternative. "Or all three were suicides."

And I voice what we're all thinking, but none of us want to say out loud. "Or all three were murdered."

Chapter Eighteen

"So you're thinking that this Team Outcast character killed the three boys who bullied Cassie Williams?" Hugh doesn't sound convinced. "Like he's some sort of vigilante?"

It doesn't sound so far-fetched to me. "It certainly seems like a possibility. He said in his emails to me that he wants revenge for Cassie being bullied. Those boys are the ones who bullied her, and now they're dead."

Florrie is frightened. "But Team Outcast isn't stopping there. They want revenge on everyone who they think bullied Cassie, and they think that includes us even though we didn't do it. We could all be in mortal danger too."

Hugh's jaw clenches at Florrie's words, and his hands curl into tight fists.

Cordelia is trying to make sense of it. "Who would take up her cause so strongly? A family member? Or maybe a best friend?"

Florrie fills Hugh in. "Her mom died of cancer right after Cassie's accident, and her father and brother moved out East after that. Cassie never really had any friends."

Vivi has a good point. "Why would Team Outcast wait thirty years to avenge Cassie's bullying?"

I text the information about the three dead boys to Floyd and Lloyd at the cop shop to keep them abreast of the situation, not that they're returning the favor. They're either not sharing information with me, or else they're not working on the case at all.

I look up from my phone to state my theory. "Maybe because they just moved back to the area from out East?"

132

I'm about to ask the group whether they've noticed anyone acting suspiciously when an inebriated Sissy Greensplat moonwalks over to us, unfortunately. We all cringe, including Hugh, and he doesn't even know her.

"Sad about the dead kids." But Sissy doesn't look sad. She continues dancing on the spot, despite no one joining in.

None of us respond to her comment.

Sissy glances at the memorial display. "The only one in our year who didn't make it was Cassie Williams. But I mean, is anybody surprised? That girl was seriously depressed. I used to tell her to find a fricking smile and quit pulling everybody down with her." Sissy is still jerking her body off beat with the music.

Another mystery about to be solved, I'm sure of it. "Is that why you put that letter in Cassie's locker telling her she should kill herself?" It only takes a moment before Sissy confirms my conjecture as fact.

She sneers at me with even more disdain than I remember her having back in high school. "People should learn to take a joke. Teenagers are mean. It's part of the job description."

A hot bile of hatred bubbles up into my throat. "And you were the Queen of Mean. Sounds like you still are."

Sissy points a finger straight into my face. "Still judgy after thirty-three years." She oozes bitterness and envy. "But that's what you do for a living, right? You judge people and call it advice."

The five of us are stunned into silence by Sissy's obvious admission of guilt, but more shaken by her clear lack of remorse. She flips her hair in a feigned motion of triumph, then performs the worst old-school robot moves the 80s ever witnessed on her way back onto the dancefloor.

Before we're able to recover from our shock another ex-perience decides to pop off. I'm surveying the space nonstop, but even I don't notice right away in the darkened room with all the noise from the crowd and the flashing, colored disco lights. Out of the corner of my eye, I catch sight of a body standing very close behind Hugh, almost touching him but not quite, breathing into the back of his head, like a shadow, or a mugger. Then I realize that it's Hugh's ex, Iris. Flipping Bible Babe. She has her eyes closed and looks as if she's deeply, longingly inhaling his scent, or else trying to suck the lifeforce out of him. It's super creepy, and I'm sort of stunned into silence, but before I can say anything, she does.

Iris whispers loudly into Hugh's ear from behind him, "I wish I knew when I was going to die."

Hugh, startled, reels around to face the freaky ear whisperer, staggers backward, bumping into the memorial table knocking down half of the framed photos of the dead folk. He looks alarmed and enraged at the same time. "What the…"

Iris smiles at her ex-husband endearingly, as if he's just told her he loves her. She repeats herself patiently in a sickeningly sweet voice that is at odds with her words. "I said I wish I knew when I was going to die."

Florrie can't help herself. "Eeeeeeeewwww."

Vivi is frowning, obviously trying to figure out the identity of this strange person she's never met before. Iris has stripped off her prairie pinafore dress and gone full throttle with the 80s theme of the party. She's fully decked out in neon workout gear, a fluorescent-pink leotard, lime-green tights, highlighter-yellow leg warmers, and a bright-purple headband. She looks like a middle-aged Olivia Newton-John from *Xanadu* after a roller-skating smash-up.

I cringe and inch behind the girls to use them as a human shield between me and Bible Babe. I may or may not be cowering.

Hugh rubs roughly at his ear, probably trying to get the cooties out of it. He looks mostly recovered from the shock of having weird Iris whispering freaky words to him and is transitioning into vexation, his usual mood when his ex is in the vicinity. "What the hell is wrong with you, Iris?"

Iris purses her lips and scolds. "Please don't curse around me, Hugh. You know I don't appreciate it."

Hugh rolls his eyes. "Please don't come around me, Iris."

Cordelia doesn't mince words. "You wish you knew when you were going to die? That's a really effed-up thing to say, Iris."

Iris clarifies in her usual, preachy way, "If I knew when the good Lord was planning on calling me home, I would go to the people who have wronged me and grant them forgiveness." Iris stares pointedly at me. "And the people who've wronged me would have the opportunity to make amends, to make things right." Iris stares pointedly at Hugh. "People would realize what's really important and who they really love before it's too late."

Hugh shakes his head in exasperation. "You're off your rocker, Iris. You always have been. Let's go get a drink, girls." He can't get away from his ex-wife fast enough.

We four Spice Girls are still in shock from the information about the three dead boys and from Pious Iris, who's an expert at getting under the skin of unsuspecting people. I'm certain the sight and sound of her alone can cause people to break out in hives. My arms are itchy.

Iris won't be deterred. She ignores Hugh's less-than-kind comments and pushes past Cordelia, squeezing in next to Hugh to pay her respects to the departed souls on the tribute table, none of whom she knew. She makes quite a show of her rehearsed prayer in honor of them. We all watch her dramatic performance in stunned awe.

Pious Iris lifts her arms widely, heavenward. "Father, we pray to you for our brothers and sisters whom we love but see no longer. Let perpetual light shine upon them." She reads the names off the bristol board. "Rest in peace, Tom, Jason, and Ethan, Cassie, Bob, and Phyllis." Iris proceeds to rectify the toppled framed photographs, standing them back upright on the display while exuding an air of superiority and somehow one of accomplishment as well.

Hugh takes me by the arm to lead me away, and the other three girls follow us as we make a beeline for the bar.

Iris calls out to Hugh, "We're still married in the eyes of the Lord, Hugh. We always will be." She holds her left hand up and points to the old wedding ring she refuses to remove from her finger. "I don't believe in divorce!"

Hugh closes his eyes for a long moment, then takes our drink order and lines up at the bar. We wait nearby to help carry the refreshments once he gets them, which could take a while based on the crowd in the queue.

"So, have any of you noticed anyone suspicious lurking around tonight?" I keep my voice down due to the nature of my question, but none of the girls can hear me over the speakers blaring, "Life Is a Highway," so I end up yelling, "Has anyone seen Team Outcast here tonight?"

The three girls jump at my words, and six eyes, wide with terror, begin darting around the room.

"Where is he?" Florrie grabs my arm.

I yell louder. "I don't know if they're here. I'm just asking if you've seen anyone strange looking."

"Everyone here looks strange." Cordelia is sardonic as usual.

Vivi shakes her head. "No one's stuck out as a potential murderer to me. Except for Sal, maybe."

I shudder involuntarily, just can't shake the feeling that I'm being watched.

"There are definitely some weirdos and weirdness creeping around tonight, but we're safe here. Let's try to have a good time. We could all use some fun." Cordelia reaches for my hand.

She's right. I squeeze her hand in reply and try to shake off the eerie feeling that relentlessly slithers up my spine. I pat Florrie on the back. "The party's a roaring success, Florrie. You did an amazing job."

Florrie beams. "I didn't do it all myself, but so far, so good. I'm super pleased with the turnout."

Cordelia is impressed with Florrie but not with many of the partygoers. "You must have done a good job with the icebreakers. Everyone is already extremely comfortable with each other." She points to a couple a few feet away from us.

Florrie is shocked. "Oh my God, isn't that Judy Kennedy making out on the dance floor with Steve Kane? I remember that's how they spent the entire prom night."

Cordelia remembers, too. "Yeah, and they didn't go to prom together. Not much has changed. They both came here tonight with their spouses, but it looks like they've each managed to ditch the old ball and chain for the evening."

Judy Kennedy comes up for air—lipstick smeared from nose to chin—and gives me an exaggerated wink, then holds up a too high, high-five for me to return. I. Just. Can't.

"Why is Judy signaling you?" Florrie's voice is a mixture of confusion and wariness.

The girls all turn to me to hear my explanation.

"I think I know who wrote the Ex-Whisperer a letter about reunion plans to reignite a long- extinguished flame with her long-in-the-tooth beau." I'm aware my lips are curling in disgust. "She signed it, Still Crazy After All These Years."

"Fitting pseudonym." Cordelia's words drip disgust.

"And then there's that lot." Vivi nods in the direction of the packed dance floor.

Sissy Greensplat and all her old cheer teammates are propping each other up. Some of them are on all fours, and the others are attempting to climb up onto the backs of their comrades in an extremely unwise attempt to form a drunken human pyramid. Just like the old days.

"Hope you've got paramedics standing by, Florrie." Vivi is legitimately concerned.

And there it is. Screams, and shrieks, and laughter—only because they're too wasted to feel pain at the moment—emanate from the pile of bodies in the collapsed pyramid in the middle of the dance floor.

Hugh shows up, displaying seeming superhuman powers by balancing five very full plastic cups in his large hands. We take our drinks from him and grab an empty table.

We lift our red goblets in a toast. "Thank God we're not them."

"Cheers."

We marvel at all the different cliques lumped about the gymnasium.

"The jocks didn't age very well."

"Why are they all still wearing Maple Leafs shorts and crushing beer cans?"

"They peaked in high school and then failed to launch."

The first thing anyone would notice if they looked around this room is how much everyone has changed in three decades. Half the heads are gray, the other half are dyed. There's no one without lines. Even the ones who have their faces filled and tucked can't do much to hide their crepey necks or age-spotted hands. And the truth is, all of that is so perfectly fine. What's disappointing is what you realize as soon as you talk to many of these same people. Too many of them haven't changed at all on the inside since high school, and that is not okay. We're supposed to have evolved with age. We're supposed to have grown up and grown kinder, gotten better and wiser. The people who have done that are my people. The rest I can't be bothered with.

We humans have such innate curiosity that we want to know how things turn out. We want to know the ending to every story we hear. Our old high school classmates, were woven into the fabric of our history whether we liked them or not. Those teenage years were short-lived in the big picture of our lives, but they were also magical, and one of the most intense periods we would ever know in both good and bad ways. The triumphs were monumental, and the defeats soul crushing, but both the positive and the negative experiences helped to shape who we would become.

Cordelia picks a familiar face out of the crowd of drunken dad dancers. "Hey, look. It's Dave Rimlick. He was the biggest stoner in school. Remember when he got kicked out of science class for lighting up a doobie with a Bunsen burner? He was voted most likely to fail at life."

Vivi has the lowdown on Dave Rimlick. "Apparently, he's an accountant now married to a physician, and they've got three brilliant kids and a beautiful home. The happy couple do annual family ski trips to the French Alps and keep a sailboat in the Caribbean."

Cordelia sounds a little bummed. "Wow, good for him. He basically ended up doing better than all of us combined."

A good-looking, well-dressed man approaches our table smiling shyly. "Gina Malone, do you remember me?" He's tall and slim with long, curly silver hair and a stylish gray beard. It would be tough for anybody to pick him out in a high school yearbook.

I suck so hard at this game. "Ugh, I'm terrible at this. I can't remember faces I met thirty minutes ago, never mind thirty years ago. Give me a clue?"

Craig takes the empty seat next to me. "I sat beside you in twelfth-grade history and geography."

Worst clue ever. Now I seem like a horrible person who didn't notice the existence of boys that I didn't have a crush on. I kick Florrie under the table in a plea for help.

Florrie understands the assignment. "Craig Berger!"

I leap in, trying to make it sound as if I knew his name before Florrie called it. "Craig Berger! Of course, I remember you." Awkward smile from me. I really don't.

Craig's too smart to buy my charade. "You don't remember me. It's okay. I didn't expect you to. You were the prettiest girl in the school."

Embarrassing and not true. The other girls give me long side-eyes.

Hugh looks at Craig a little more closely now, then reaches out his hand to shake Craig's. "Hugh McTavish."

Craig offers his hand to Hugh. "I don't remember you."

Hugh shakes his head. "I'm from here but went away to school."

"I object. I don't think Gina was the prettiest girl in school." Cordelia's offended.

"I agree. She was cute but also extremely annoying." Vivi jumps on the teasing bandwagon.

Craig chuckles. "You four were all pretty and were also the nicest girls in the school. I never worked up the nerve to speak to any of you, but I always wished I had. I was the number one nerd of Sunset Beach High. The yearbook committee voted me *Most likely to Discover a New Chemical Element*."

Florrie is impressed. "And did you?"

Craig laughs. "Something like that."

I lift my glass to touch Craig's. "That seems to be the secret to success. All the high school kids who flew under the radar crushed the whole best-life contest."

"Revenge of the nerds." Craig raises his drink cup.

"Looks like the nerds grew up, got handsome, got rich, and got the girl." Cordelia looks at Craig appreciatively. "What do you do?"

Dropping his voice, Craig downplays his noble position. "I run an NGO that helps support women and children in impoverished nations. Mostly in the Middle East and Africa."

Cordelia looks at us, eyes wide. "Like I said, the nerds win."

By the way her focus zeroes in on him, I know that Vivi is intrigued. "Did you come to the reunion on your own, Craig?"

Craig nods. "My wife passed away a few years ago. Breast cancer."

We all make sad faces.

Florrie's shoulders slump in sympathy. "Oh, I'm so sorry to hear that. Did the two of you have children?"

Craig smiles. "Two beautiful girls. One's in law school. One's doing her medical residency."

Vivi's eyes go dreamy as she visually begins to melt. "You must be so proud."

"I am. They're my whole world."

Hugh changes the subject to lighten the conversation. "So, Florrie, what's on the reunion schedule for tomorrow?"

Florrie answers excitedly. "It's the butter tart bake-off in the day. I better be taking home that first-place ribbon or pastry is going to roll. There's also a vintage car show on High Street. And your ex, Pious Iris, has organized a seven deadly sins scavenger hunt for the churchgoing folk."

"She'll do anything for attention." Hugh closes his eyes in exasperation, throws his drink back.

Craig laughs. "That's your ex-wife? The woman from the *Xanadu* movie? She started doing jumping jacks and singing "Physical" when I walked past her non-alcoholic punch table, and she invited me to a New Testament Bible Trivia night tomorrow at the Silver Star Café. I told her I wouldn't be very good at that since I'm Jewish. She didn't speak to me again."

"Good to know. Maybe if I convert to Judaism, Iris will leave me alone. I'll go get another round for everyone." Hugh heads to the bar. He needs another drink, pronto.

Florrie continues with the itinerary. "And in the evening, there's a choice between a bonfire party on the beach or glow-in-the-dark bowling at Shake Rattle and Bowl."

Vivi shakes her head. "Not a tough choice for me. Kingpin Sal will definitely be at the glow-in-the-dark bowling party, so I will definitely be at the beach bonfire."

Cordelia gives Vivi a heads-up warning. "Speaking of Kingpin Sal . . ."

Chapter Nineteen

Sal appears at our table, stands next to Vivi, taking in the new guy sitting next to her. He doesn't look happy. Tiffany and Big Benny take up the flank.

"Sorry to interrupt your little tête-à-tête." He looks imperiously at Vivi. "That's French, by the way, but I'm just wondering if you've had an opportunity to reconsider my purchase offer for your parents' old cottage. It needs a lot of work, Vivi. It's a money pit, and my offer is more than generous. I'd be doing you a favor, taking it off your hands."

Vivi exhales in exasperation. "I already told you, Sal, my cottage is not for sale at any price. I got it in the divorce settlement. You got everything else. Please stop asking me about it."

Tiffany busts in, sounding indignant and clueless. "Well, the only thing I wanted in your divorce settlement was that cottage."

Vivi stares the mouthy space cadet down. "If you marry Sal and divorce him, you can ask the judge for whatever you want. In the meantime, stay the hell out of my divorce and my cottage."

Tiffany sneers at Vivi. "I wouldn't take a dump in that nasty shack. It's a teardown, but there's no waterfront available anywhere that Sal and me can build a nice big summerhouse on. And I want to be on the lake, right Sally?" Tiffany whines but somehow manages to make it sound cute, if a little disturbing. "What Tiffany wants, Tiffany gets. Right, sugar daddy?" She walks her fingers across Sal's chest.

Sal isn't listening to Tiffany. His eyes are laser beams drilling through Craig's skull, and Craig is acutely aware of this. He shifts around uncomfortably in his chair.

Craig's not going to stick around for a family business discussion of a family he doesn't even know. He picks up his drink, stands to leave. "Nice seeing you all again. We'll probably bump into each other at the costume dance. I'm going as Moses. I'll be the one smashing the stone tablets." He smiles and steps away.

Vivi runs interception. She stands up, too, grabs Craig's arm. "Do you want to dance, Craig? This old song is one of my faves." Madonna is singing "Holiday."

Craig looks way beyond shocked. In truth, I think we all do. Vivi is usually so retiring, but it's refreshing to see her going for it. And she needs an escape route from Sal.

Craig smiles broadly, can't believe his luck. He sets his drink back down. "Wow! Sure, you don't have to ask me twice." He's pure enthusiasm as he takes Vivi's hand, and they dance out onto the middle of the gym floor.

Sal is not pleased. Not at all. He stomps back to his table, and Tiffany and Big Benny trail after him. Sal is relentless. And dangerous.

"What a creep." Cordelia's lips curl.

Florrie is always nervous when Sal's around. Most people are. "A scary creep. I hope he doesn't force Vivi to sell him her cottage. It's such a beautiful old place, and those two want to tear it down. Imagine the monstrosity they'd build there."

My blood is boiling. "That's not going to happen. I don't know who's creepier, Sal or Tiffany."

Cordelia is disgusted. "That preschooler seems to be the one pushing for the cottage."

Hugh returns with a round of drinks for all. He sits down next to me and discreetly strokes my thigh beneath the tablecloth. I return the favor.

Cordelia stands to leave. "Well, kids, I'm going to peace out."

"Really? It's still early. Don't leave." Florrie is disappointed.

"I have to be at the library to open it up bright and early. And I've got a date with a client in the afternoon, so I need to catch some sleep tonight. You guys have fun. I'll see you at the beach bonfire tomorrow night." Cordelia leans over and gives the three of us kisses on our cheeks.

Hugh waits until she's gone, then asks, "Is she okay?"

Florrie reassures him. "She is. Cordelia dates for work, not for fun, so she's not much of a party girl."

Another amiable-looking male with a quasi-familiar face that I'll never be able to place approaches our table.

Florrie's mouth drops wide open—this guy is definitely not a stranger to her. "Marty O'Hare?"

Marty drops down onto one knee and, takes Florrie's hand in his, kisses the top of it. He's all chivalry and fakery. Always has been. I recognize his old mug now, and I'm not happy to see it. I know it's not good for Florrie to, either. Marty was a theater geek and the star of every play Sunset Beach High ever put on. He was also a star in Florrie's eyes until he cheated on her with Rona Gillespi and smashed Florrie's young heart into smithereens.

Marty tries to turn his charm on me. "Well, hello there, Gina Malone, or should I say Victoria Beckham? You are looking lovely as always. Haven't changed one iota since 1989." Marty reaches for my hand, obviously looking to do a second take on the hand-kiss scene. I pull my hands away and place them around Hugh's neck. Marty improvs and reaches for Hugh's hand to shake it instead. "And who is the lucky man? Ah, David Beckham, I see, suave."

Hugh looks at Marty a little skeptically, not really his type of guy. "Hugh McTavish every other night."

Florrie is acting more ridiculously coquettish than she has in thirty years, and I stare hard at her trying to remind her not to get caught up in Marty's act, but she doesn't notice my eyes boring into her. She can't take her own eyes off of her old love.

Marty slides into the chair next to Florrie and scooches it over as close to Florrie as he can get it. "I've been meaning to pop into your charming bakery since I rolled into town yesterday. I remember what a great cook you were." He winks at her. "I missed that. Among other things."

Florrie is florid.

I'm pretty sure my eye roll is so big it makes a loud clunk. Florrie hears it

144

psychically and kicks me under the table warning me to behave myself.

I think Florrie actually coos like a pigeon. "What are you up to now, Marty?"

His normal voice is braggadocio and loud, as if he's speaking to the back row from stage left. "Still a theater professor at University of Ottawa, but I'm chair of the department now."

Florrie's eyelashes flutter. "That doesn't surprise me. You were always so talented."

I just can't. "How's your wife, Marty? Did she come to the reunion with you?"

Marty knows exactly what I'm doing, but he's unfazed. The consummate professional, he can snap back smoothly when an actor goes off script. "Unfortunately, Moira and I separated quite some time ago."

Bull. "Let me guess. You're still living in the same house, though, right?"

Marty's face twitches with annoyance, but he recovers instantly. "Practicalities dictate that I currently reside in the basement of my matrimonial home, yes. My heart, however, moved out years ago."

Florrie kicks at me again, but connects with Hugh's shin. He grunts, takes the knock as a cue to intervene.

"They're playing my song. Let's dance." Hugh takes my arm, but I don't budge. He pulls a little more insistently, and Florrie cocks her head, clearly telling me to vamoose, so I huff in protest, reluctantly follow Hugh onto the floor.

I am pissed and stand there without moving. Hugh shuffles his feet around, but who in the world can dance to this song anyway? "Def Leppard's 'Pour Some Sugar on Me' is 'your song'? It's not even danceable."

"No, it's not. I hate this song. But clearly, you and this Marty dude aren't overly fond of each other, and Florrie didn't want you interfering."

"Interfering in what? The guy cheated on her the night before senior prom, and he's probably looking to cheat on his wife now. I'm protecting Florrie. She's got too big a heart, and this musical theater dork would love to jazz hands all over it."

"He was a little boy thirty-three years ago, and Florrie's a big girl now. She can handle herself."

Vivi and Craig boogie over to us.

Vivi looks happier than I've seen her all weekend. "What's going on? Who's that with Florrie?"

"Marty O'Hare." I spit out his name.

"No!" Vivi is scandalized.

I look at Hugh smugly. "See what I mean?"

There is a massive smash a few feet away from us that startles the entire crowd in the gymnasium. For a fraction of a second, I think I've been shot by Team Outcast. I nearly jump out of my LBD and bang hard against Hugh's chest. Everyone stops dancing and spins around to see a hammered Sissy Greensplat who has full-body crashed face-first into a table of twelve. The table has broken in two, and food, drink, and dishes have flown everywhere and all over everybody within fifteen feet of the calamity.

I am done here. "Time to go. I'm starving. You guys want to come back to my place and order pizza?"

Vivi's game. Her dance partner looks as if he just won the lottery. Vivi slips her arm through Craig's, and we head back to our table to collect Florrie. I notice Sal staring very hard at Vivi and especially hard at an unsuspecting Craig.

I make the announcement to Florrie. "Let's go, gal. We're going to head back to my place."

Florrie looks disappointed at my suggestion. "Why don't we all go to the bakery, it's closer and I can whip us up something delicious. How does grilled veggie panini with herbed feta and avocado sound?"

Everyone's nodding enthusiastically.

My mouth starts watering instantly, but I don't want Marty to join us. This snake needs to be cut off at the head. "No—"

Florrie cuts me off at the head first. "Come on, Marty, join us. I'll give you a tour of The Bakehouse."

He's on his feet in a flash and has a possessive arm around Florrie's shoulder already. I really don't like him.

Craig looks at Vivi hopefully. "Do you want to drive with me, Vivi?"

Vivi smiles at him. "I've got my car here. Let's all just take our own vehicles and meet at Florrie's bakery."

"Sounds good!" Florrie's in a hurry to get out of there before I say something to stop Marty from joining us. Not that anybody could.

Marty breaks into song, loudly, as all theater geeks are wont to do, about seeing Florrie in all the old familiar places.

I can't be sure, but I think Florrie is swooning. I'm throwing up a little bit in my mouth.

Our group departs to meet up at The Bakehouse, and I, for one, am relieved to get the heck out of Dodge. The strain of peering over my shoulder all night long watching out for Team Outcast has left me with a kink in my neck that has me feeling like a contortionist auditioning for *AGT*.

Florrie unlocks the bakery door, and I move up close behind her before anyone else gets inside, follow at her heels while she switches on the lights.

I whisper, "I thought you said if Marty showed up at the reunion, you were finally going to tell him what an asshole he was."

"I did. He apologized."

"Florrie, you know Marty hasn't changed. He can't be trusted, and he's going to break your heart again. He's not good for you. And one more detail, he's married."

"Separated."

"Not divorced equals still married."

Florrie looks at me patiently. "Gina, you don't have to worry about me. He can't break my heart again because he doesn't have it to break. I'm only enjoying a good time with old acquaintances. We're just going to eat a panini, okay?"

"Promise?"

"Yes."

"Okay." I relax, subdue my mother-hen clucking.

Florrie speaks quietly, so only I can hear her. "Oh, and after the sandwich, I might munch on Marty for a little dessert."

I gasp. Florrie laughs loudly as she darts behind the counter to fire up the panini press and escape my judgy face.

The others are piling inside now.

Hugh carries in a forty-ouncer of whiskey and two bottles of wine. "I made a liquor store run this afternoon and, luckily, still had the goods in my truck."

Vivi and Marty pull up seats near the counter where Florrie is already grilling peppers and chopping fragrant onions at breakneck speed. I slice ciabatta and pull down six plates from the wooden shelves. Hugh pours the drinks.

The food smells delicious, and we chat while we wait on it. Marty is too loud and super irritating, of course.

Twenty minutes later, I turn to Vivi. "Is Craig coming, or did he bow out?"

"He said he was. But maybe he changed his mind." Vivi sounds slightly concerned and possibly worried and probably disappointed.

Florrie scoffs. "Not the way he's been looking at you for the past hour."

"I'd have to agree there, Vivi." Marty the predator puts in his two cents. "That man isn't going to give up the chase this easily."

Hugh is pragmatic, as always. "Maybe he had car trouble. Want me to drive back to the school and check?"

Vivi shakes her head. "No, it's okay. I don't know what he drives, and we didn't exchange cell numbers or anything. If he doesn't show up, I shall take that as an 'I'm just not that into you.' And no big deal. We had fun dancing and chatting for an hour. It's all good." All grown up and emotionally repressed.

"Craig's pretty cute." Florrie has her hopes up for Vivi.

Vivi sounds wistful. "Yeah, he seems pretty great."

A vehicle pulls up, and headlights glare in through the bakery window.

Florrie is excited. "There's our man. Just in time for a midnight snack."

Craig climbs out of his car very slowly. We all turn to watch as he lumbers unsteadily toward the door of the bakery, stopping momentarily to lean against the hood of his four-by-four. All of us are alarmed.

"Is he okay?"

Hugh leaps up, strides swiftly to the bakery door to open it. Craig meets him and falls against Hugh's shoulder. Hugh wrestles him inside the shop, and Marty jumps up to assist as well. We three girls can't help but scream.

Craig is bloody and bruised and maybe even broken. He's had the living daylights knocked out of him.

Chapter Twenty

With help from the two guys, Craig stumbles to a chair and collapses into it.

"Oh my God, were you in a car accident?" Vivi rushes to him. "Gina, call an ambulance."

I grab my purse to find my phone.

Craig shakes his head; he doesn't want to be touched. "No, I wasn't in an accident, and I don't need an ambulance. I just need to sit for a bit. I could use a drink, please."

Florrie pours him a glass of water and brings it over. "We have to get you to the hospital. You need stitches for sure."

Vivi fills a pot with warm water and grabs a clean cloth to wash the blood off Craig's face. "What happened to you?"

"I got hit from behind in the parking lot, and then the guy went to town on me when I was on the ground. He had a baseball bat."

"Did you recognize him?" Hugh looks up and down the street through the large store window, then locks the bakery door.

Craig winces when he tries to move his head. "It was dark, and he had something black pulled over his face. He was a really big dude, though. Strong."

The rest of us look at each other, all thinking the same thing.

Vivi rubs her eyes with her hands. She is beside herself. "How big? Like Big Benny big?"

Craig looks up at her, confused. "You mean the guy who was with your ex-husband tonight?"

Vivi nods nervously.

Craig nods, too. "Yeah, about that size."

Vivi smashes her fists on the table in frustration. "Damn him. Sal is a freaking menace. He's on a mission to make my entire life miserable. I am so sorry, Craig. This is all my fault. If I hadn't asked you to dance tonight, Sal never would have sent his goon after you."

Hugh and Marty draw the blinds on the bakery windows.

I pick up my cell phone to dial. "I'll call the cops. Sal is going to have to answer for this."

Vivi's fury is palpable. "Don't bother, Gina. It won't do any good. There are never any consequences to Sal's actions. That's the nature of his business—he gets away with murder. You'll only make it worse for Craig if the police get involved."

Craig wants to appease Vivi. "I don't need to report it if Vivi doesn't want me to. Maybe it would make things worse for Vivi, too. And what would I tell the cops anyway? I didn't get a look at the guy."

"The best thing any of you can do is stay as far away from me as possible." Vivi gathers up her belongings. "I'm going to go to the cottage and pack up, head back to the city. And, Craig, I hate to say this, but maybe it would be safer if you skipped the rest of the reunion weekend, too."

Craig looks sad now on top of being in ridiculous amounts of pain.

Florrie turns to Vivi. "Do you think it was one of Sal's guys who attacked you and Cordelia on the road last night, then?"

"You were attacked last night?" Craig is alarmed.

Vivi falls into Florrie's arms, starts to cry. "I don't know. Anything's possible when Sal's involved."

Hugh weighs in. "I think if Sal sent someone to harm you girls last night, you and Cordelia wouldn't have walked away with only lumps on your noggins."

I'm not so sure myself. I turn to face Vivi. "Vivi, yesterday you wondered if you and Cordelia being hit could have been Sal trying to scare you into selling the cottage. After Tiffany's whine-fest tonight, it crossed my mind that maybe you're right about that. Maybe that's why your key to the cottage

151

went missing, too, so you don't feel safe staying there."

"Are we thinking that Sal is Team Outcast, then?" Florrie is trembling, clearly terrified.

Craig is really confused now.

Marty, too. "Who is Team Outcast?"

Hugh looks at the other men. "Long story, but I'll fill you both in after we open that bottle of whiskey. You're gonna need it."

I shake my head. "No, I don't think Sal is Team Outcast. I think Sal is here for Vivi alone. Team Outcast is here for our whole group. The reunion has brought hundreds of people together and reunited old friends, reignited old passions." I'm looking at Florrie and Marty. "And reopened old wounds too. It's the perfect storm—a collision of the good, the bad, and the ugly. And we're witnessing it first-hand."

Vivi cries harder now. She's so worn down by her horrible ex-husband's relentless harassment. "Sal doesn't care about giving Tiffany the cottage. He just wants to take it away from me because it makes me happy. He is actually that spiteful. And in the end, Sal always gets what he wants, so it will probably happen one way or another. I don't know why I'm even bothering to fight it."

I wrap my arms around my friend. "It's not going to happen, Vivi. We're not going to let it happen. And you're not going anywhere. Not without us anyway."

Florrie throws the question out to everyone. "Should I still make the food?"

Everyone is starving. Even Craig manages to nod his throbbing head in affirmation.

Marty looks more closely at the cuts on Craig's face. "I don't think they'd be able to stitch those up, but you should probably get looked at anyway. I'm sure they'll want to X-ray you. You likely have a concussion at the very least."

Craig grimaces when he attempts a shrug. "They'll just tell me to rest. I think I may have a broken rib or two, but they don't do anything for that, either. I'm mostly bruised."

"This is broken rib medicine." Hugh pours a whiskey for Craig and passes it to him. "I think the guy knew exactly how to beat you up to make it hurt like hell and scare the shit out of you but not be bad enough to put you in hospital and get the cops after him."

Craig gingerly takes the drink. "I think you're right. I guess this counts as my first barroom brawl." He shoots the whiskey and winces. "I may have to turn in my Whitecaps nerd club card."

Hugh pours him another one, along with one for Marty and himself. "You girls want a shot?"

We all decline for now.

"The Spice Girls need food first." Florrie is back behind the counter, pressing melting gruyere between toasted panini.

I assist her in plating the gourmet sandwiches, and Vivi helps Craig clean up his wounds.

It's three in the morning by the time we've finished eating and talking, and we're all beyond exhausted.

Craig and Marty are both staying at the same motel up the road, so they leave their cars parked in front of The Bakehouse and amble back to their rooms together. Vivi spends the night with Florrie, so she doesn't have to go home alone. I need to get back to my place to rescue my poor dog.

Hugh drives me home and stays with me while we let Zoe outside, then he checks all around my cottage inside and out and kisses me long and longingly at my door, but tonight is not the night for anything more than that. I lock up, and he drives off. In four hours, he'll be driving back up my laneway to carry on working on my bunkie.

I toss and turn all night thinking about bullies—three of them dead and a few more wandering around town carrying baseball bats and old high school photos with the faces scratched out. I'm guessing we're all having bad dreams tonight.

As usual, morning is announced by the screeching of Hugh's power tools, and it comes way too early for him and for me.

I stumble out of bed and feel my way to the coffee pot. I intend to spend a couple of hours wrapped around the warm carafe. The pets are happy to have me home, and I'm happy to be here and have grand plans to do absolutely nothing. The way things are going of late, I fully expect fate to have other ideas, but I'll enjoy my solitude while it lasts.

Once I'm sufficiently caffeinated, I respond to the multitude of messages from my fabulous, amazing, incredible children. We all hop on a five-way FaceTime call and spend over an hour catching up. Nothing is ever more healing for me than sharing time with my babies, even if it's through the ether as circumstances and distance dictate presently. We discuss our next in-person visit and decide that I should go to them since they were just in Canada. So, for Christmas this year, we'll all meet up in London and have a week there, followed by a week in Iceland for the holidays, cause why not? I'm a sucker for the Northern Lights and also for the brilliant Icelandic custom of Jolabokaflod, which entails spending Christmas Eve reading the book that each person receives that night while consuming large amounts of chocolate. Sounds like the perfect celebration to me.

I shower and change into my uniform of faded Levi's and a white tee and pull a fleece hoodie over top. I put away my sexy Spice Girl gear, and I'm surprised that I kind of miss being Victoria Beckham. That was one memorable night, equal parts fun and terror. Seems to be the trajectory that my life is on.

Time to take Zoe out for a walk, and my pup is thrilled at the prospect, jumping all over me and nearly knocking me down. When I open the door, there's a sharp autumn chill in the air, so I throw on a coat and a cute toque, grab the leash, and off we go. I wave to a tired-looking Hugh and hardworking Ryan as a very happy Zoe, and I carry on down the road.

We walk for a good hour, passing by Vivi's cottage on our way back. Her car is parked in front, and she runs outside when she sees us and calls me over. She looks panicked.

"Everything okay?"

Vivi looks around before ushering Zoe and me inside and locking the door behind us.

"Looks like you were right about a copy of my house key being made by whoever borrowed it for the day. I just got home twenty minutes ago from town, and somebody had been inside here while I was out."

"How do you know?"

Vivi picks a business card up from her sideboard. "This was left here." She hands it to me to read.

I'm confused, but not for long. "Portsmouth and Sons Architects? Why would...?" And then it dawns on me. "Sal and Tiffany?"

"Just Tiffany. I called the architect and pretended to be the sneaky little wench, and he fell for it. He said he's looking forward to meeting Sal sometime after I surprise him with the news of the plans we discussed. He said he liked my idea of tearing the old cottage down and building a big Greek Revival with two-story columns and lots of marble statues of goddesses. Can you imagine that blight on the beach in our little maritime village? The architect probably threw his business card down on the table as a matter of course, and Tiffany didn't even notice. He thinks Tiffany is the owner."

"This is next-level entitlement that's borderline psychotic."

"She's that confident that Sal will get this cottage for her. They're both used to getting whatever they want, and that's what scares me."

"This is really terrible, Vivi, but I've got to say I'm relieved it was Tiffany and not Team Outcast who had your key and entered your cottage."

"That's only because you don't know Sal and Tiffany."

God, I really hope she doesn't have a point there.

There's a knock at the door that makes us jump, and Zoe go wild. Vivi crosses to answer it. "I called a locksmith to rekey the door."

Vivi greets the man, and he gets to work changing the locks.

"You want a cup of tea?"

"Sure, I'll stay with you until the locksmith finishes up."

Vivi makes us a jasmine green, and we sit at her antique kitchen table that looks out over the expansive lake.

I've been dying to ask. "Have you heard from Craig?"

Vivi looks sad when I bring him up. "That balloon definitely got shot down before it got off the ground. I called him to see how he was doing. He's got a shiner, a blinding headache, and a tender ribcage, but he's up and about. He and Marty went to Florrie's bakery for breakfast this morning. He didn't ask me to join them, and I think he's smart enough to keep his distance from me."

Like many of us by the time we get to fifty, I think Vivi is used to disappointment. Unfortunately, though, it never seems to feel any less soul-crushing.

I smile at my friend. "Being alone is absolutely fine for loads of people, but I don't think you're one of them. I just know it. You're going to have a life partner when the timing's right."

"That timing can't roll around until Sal is pushing-up-daisies, so I guess once he's dead and buried, I'll start keeping my eye out for Mr. Right. Unfortunately, that tough bugger will probably outlive us all." Vivi tops up our mugs with hot water. "I bet Florrie was happy to have Marty stop in for breakfast."

"There are so many things to worry about right now, not the least of which is Marty moving on Florrie and slaughtering her heart once again."

Vivi smiles at me. "I think Marty has changed a wee bit since our old high school days, Gina. We all have. Life has been an iron fist in a velvet glove, and those of us who are still here have figured out how to roll with the punches."

"And sometimes Life has taken that velvet glove off. That's when it really smarts."

"That's true. I just think you should give the guy a chance. He doesn't seem so bad. Florrie's not the naive teenage girl she once was. The worst that can happen is Marty makes her feel good for a while, and then he turns out to be the jerk she's thought he was for the last thirty years, and they both go back to their old lives."

I sigh far too loudly, but I am exhaling so very much emotion. "Okay, I guess you're right. I'll back off and let Florrie have some fun. And I suspect some bumps and bruises, too, but she'll survive. We all do. Speaking of bumps and bruises, Craig, on the other hand, seems like a super nice guy.

CHAPTER TWENTY

Hot, too. Who knew high school nerds could grow up into men like Craig?"

Vivi warms her hands in the steam from her tea. "Not me. He is so sweet. Too good, I think. Feeling worthy is something I'm working on, but I'm a long way off from believing that I deserve a guy as great as Craig seems to be."

"You're dead wrong there. We need to figure out if Craig is a good enough guy to deserve you. You're the whole package, Vivi."

"The whole package with Italian designer baggage. Sal Fortuna couture. It's expensive—could cost you your life."

We both laugh at Vivi's joke but also are both aware that there's a scary bushel of truth to what she said.

The locksmith is finished. He hands Vivi the new keys, and she pays him cash.

"I'm going to have to find a new hiding spot for the spare key."

We step outside with the dog and choose a new secret rock after the locksmith drives off.

"Want to go grab lunch at Happily Napoli? It's been twenty-four hours since I've seen the aunts. They'll be sending out search parties any minute now."

Vivi brightens. "Sure. I was going to try to get in there today. I haven't seen your zias yet since I got to town, and I know I have to, or they'll be putting the evil eye on me."

"You got that right. I'm starving. Pick me up in ten."

"Will do."

I jog the rest of the way home with Zoe.

There are four cars parked in front of my place and at least eight people standing on the roadside taking photos of my cottage. Zoe barks madly at them, and when they hear her and see me, they all hurry to jump back inside their vehicles. Three of them drive off before I can get close enough to stop them, but I manage to reach the last one before the driver can back up. A woman I don't know smiles and waves to me through her driver's window. I motion for her to roll it down. She opens it, one inch only.

"Can I help you?" I sound accusatory on purpose.

157

The woman's eyes widen as if she's nervous, possibly even afraid of me, and definitely afraid of Zoe. "No, we're fine, thank you. We'll be on our way now."

Something's up, and I feel angry before I even know what it is. "What are you doing on my property, and why are you photographing my home?"

The woman looks petrified now. She rolls her window back up and speaks through it, keeping it closed. "We're just following the instructions."

"What are you talking about?"

"For the seven deadly sins scavenger hunt. When we figure out the answers to the clues, we have to take photos of the places to prove we were there. We're trying to win the game. It's a fundraiser for the church."

Okay, I am verging on furious. "Why are you at my house?"

The woman appears extremely uncomfortable as she grimaces through the glass. "You're *lust*." She shrugs.

I almost fall over. The woman reverses and quickly speeds away. I see two more cars coming down the road and slowing in front of my cottage. I flip them the bird and let Zoe snarl and snap in their direction. They don't stop, but their phones are up, snatching pics as they roll past.

Exasperated, I turn around to see Hugh on the roof of the bunkie. He calls out from there, "That's the tenth car in the last hour. We're part of Iris's scavenger hunt for Jesus."

"Yeah, I figured that. Frigging Pious Iris the Bible Babe strikes again." I stomp into the house, feed the pets, stoke the woodstove, and am back out on my front porch just as Vivi drives in to pick me up.

We head into town, and the streets are even more packed than yesterday. There's a huge crowd at the marina for the fishing derby. We can't even get close, not that I'd want to. It takes a good ten minutes to find a parking spot near Happily Napoli, and if we didn't know the owners, there'd be no chance of getting a table.

We walk along the sidewalk toward the aunts' restaurant, and just as we're about to step inside it, a hysterical woman bursts out through the door and crashes headlong into the pair of us. Vivi and I stumble backward, try to keep the sobbing woman from face-planting on the pavement. It's Sissy

Greensplat. I wonder whether she's weeping because this is how bad her hangover from last night is.

When Sissy sees that it's me, she cries even harder, if that's possible, and buries her snot-flinging face into my shoulder, which is sopping wet in three seconds flat.

Vivi stares at her incredulously. "Sissy, what's happened?"

"It's Russ." Sissy's wailing is verging on screaming.

Passersby stop to stare.

I hate to ask, but what else can it be? "Did he die?"

Sissy's face turns thundercloud black. "No, but I wish he did." She looks almost demonic.

Vivi steps away from her. "Whoa."

"Russ cheated on me."

I'm not surprised, but I do my best to act as if I am. "Oh, I'm so sorry to hear that. Did it just happen? Last night at the dance?"

Vivi asks her question carefully, sensitively. "Did you catch Russ with another woman?"

"No. I just had a tarot card reading with Gina's aunts, and they told me. I didn't have a clue." Sissy pulls herself together in an instant. "I'm going to kill him." She storms off across the street to hunt down her husband.

Vivi and I can only stare at each other in disbelief. The frickin' aunts.

Chapter Twenty-One

Moments later, two more women walk out of the restaurant crying.

I stop them on the sidewalk. I can't let the aunts go around upsetting people like this, even if one of them is Sissy Greensplat. "Are you crying because you got upsetting news in a tarot card reading from those two old Italian women, because I've got to tell you...."

One woman blows her nose into a tissue. "No, they're booked up for the rest of the weekend. We can't get in for a reading." The women are crushed with disappointment. They sniffle as they walk off without knowing what their futures hold.

I call after them, "You're better off, believe me." I turn to Vivi. "I just can't go in there and face the aunts right now. I won't be able to hold back, and I know I'll regret what I say to them."

Vivi shrugs. "Lunch at The Bakehouse?"

"Much better idea." The two of us cross the street to Florrie's.

Just as we arrive, we see Cordelia coming up the sidewalk. She calls out to us. "Wait up. I'll join you. I've got to be back at the library in an hour." When she catches up with us, Cordelia gives me a gentle jab with her elbow. "Don't forget you're doing the reading from your new book on Sunday."

"It's in my calendar, but do we have to? I hate doing readings, and I mean, who's going to show up? People can barely move today because they're so hungover, and there's still two nights of parties to get through."

Cordelia ignores me, if she even heard me, because the bakery is just as packed as Happily Napoli was, and people are streaming in and pouring out, jostling through the narrow doorway. We elbow our way inside and are hit with a wall of the most delectable smells.

Florrie is behind the counter with a staff of eight, and they are all working like machines. People are lined up the whole length of the shop, and employees run back and forth to stock shelves with loaves of bread and tarts and pies, which are all scooped up by customers as fast as they're laid out. We squeeze into a spot on the end of the counter and lean in, to wave hello to Florrie.

She looks as if she's in a temper, which is unusual for Florrie. I wonder if Marty has already dashed her dreams and stomped on her heart.

Two minutes later, a young girl hurries over with three cappuccinos and a huge focaccia with goat cheese, olives, and sundried tomatoes sent by Florrie to keep us going until she can get around to taking our lunch order.

The moment Florrie has a quick break, she darts down to our end of the counter.

Cordelia is impressed. "Looks like you've got a license to print money here today."

"Business is booming partly because of the reunion and partly thanks to Bible Babe. Apparently, The Bakehouse is one of the stops on her seven deadly sins scavenger hunt. Loads of good Christians are coming in to take photos of the place, but they're leaving with bellies and bags full of baked goods. My place is on Iris's map as *gluttony*, and it seems the faithful are giving in to temptation and pigging out on my food."

Cordelia laughs, spitting her focaccia across the counter.

I'm chuckling about it now, too. "My place is *lust*. I hope Iris put her own home on the scavenger hunt map for *envy*."

Vivi is filming the entire scene in the bakery for TikTok, but she puts her phone down when she takes in Florrie's face. "You look angry about something, Florrie."

Florrie's face is flushed from the speed she's working at but also from something more. "I'm furious. The damn butter tart bake-off was rigged. I should have walked away with first place, and instead, I got disqualified! The judges said I displayed unsporting behavior. I had a bit of a meltdown because Karen Higgs was trying to sabotage my tart tin just like she did in home ec class in eleventh grade."

Cordelia is perplexed. "Unsporting? Is baking a sport now?"

Vivi shrugs. "I guess it should be if bowling is."

The most pressing question for me, "How do you sabotage a tart tin?"

Florrie looks at me exasperatedly, flicks her tea towel in my direction. "We've got vegan Irish stew with white beans and Guinness, comes with rosemary and sea salt rolls. Sound good?" Florrie darts to the other end of the counter to rescue a young server who's having trouble with the till.

We yell after her, "Sounds great!"

Our food appears minutes later. It is delicious. Florrie is too busy to chat with us again.

We don't stay any longer than the time it takes to wolf down our lunch so that we can make room for the line-up of famished diners who now spill out of the bakery and along the sidewalk.

It takes some gentle shoving to make it out the door through the crowd and onto the street.

Cordelia asks me, "Have you heard from Team Outcast again since the email they sent you last night?"

I shake my head. "Nothing, thank God. But I also haven't heard anything from the police. I guess they're not too bothered by the letters or the old photos and newspaper. Those things sure as heck are disturbing me, though"

Between the library and her clients, Cordelia knows everything that goes on in town. "I don't think that's it. I'm feeling sorry for Floyd and Lloyd right now. They're overwhelmed with the crowds and extra security needed for all the reunion goings on."

Vivi's in agreement. "I heard there's been record-breaking numbers of DUIs and disorderly conduct. Floyd and Lloyd aren't set up to deal with all this chaos. They don't have the resources."

I hear them. "Well, I suppose in the meantime, all the detective duties lie with us, then."

"Also, the protection duties. We need to watch out for each other." Cordelia gives us both a hug. "I've got to get back to the library."

"Are you coming to the bonfire party on the beach tonight? That's really going to feel like old times." Vivi wants to nail Cordelia down. "It'll be fun. Promise you'll come. Who knows when we'll all be together again next after this weekend?"

Cordelia gives a thumbs-up. "I've got a client at seven, but I promise I'll be there once I've got him whipped into shape."

"Yikes." I flinch. "Don't be too hard on him."

Cordelia winks. "If I'm not hard on him, he'll want his money back."

Cordelia spins around to hurry off, but she stops in her tracks. We all do. We all see him at the same time, and we stop and stare across the road.

At my ex-husband, Dick.

Dick is jogging down the alleyway next to the aunts' restaurant heading toward the street. He keeps checking back over his shoulder and in all other directions. He looks almost frantic and totally sketchy. He sprints across the road in front of traffic, and one car—obviously an out-of-towner because a local would never—honks his horn at Dick. Dick doesn't stop or even slow down. He keeps running until he reaches a door three down from Florrie's. His keys are out of his pocket in a flash, and he unlocks it quickly. Dick glances our way and locks eyes with me for a moment before he disappears inside. He looks absolutely terrified.

Cordelia and Vivi turn to me. We're all speechless.

Cordelia's mouth drops in shock. "So, he actually does live above the hardware store here?"

I nod. "Apparently so."

"What was he running from?" Vivi glances up and down the street, her tone sounds suspicious. "He looked scared to death."

"Maybe really bad men actually are after him to pay up. You never know the truth with Dick, but yeah, he did look very scared."

And then we spot an imposing figure lumbering out of the same alley that Dick just ran out from. The man looks up and down High Street but clearly doesn't see what or whom he's searching for.

It's Big Benny.

Vivi sounds grave. "Looks like Dick is telling the truth this time."

Before Hugh finishes working at my place for the day, he asks whether I'd like company at the beach bonfire party tonight. I tell him I'm going with Vivi, but he can join us if he wants to. He does want to. He offers to pick the two of us up at eight. It's a date. Or maybe not quite.

It's warmer than usual. There's no rain in the forecast, and the winds are light. It's going to be a gorgeous night on the beach, but a dark one—the sun sets completely by six o'clock at this time of year. It's super casual, jeans and sweaters and Docs and BYOB. This is the only reunion activity I'm not dreading.

Hugh is right on time. He wraps his long arms around me as soon as he steps inside my cottage, and he kisses me deeply. Dammmmmnnn, he's good at that.

He lets Zoe outside for me while I reapply my lipstick.

He's brought Baileys and wine and whiskey, as usual, and nice little thermal cups to keep our drinks cold. Vivi is already on her porch when we pull up at her cottage, and Hugh hops out to open the door to the back seat of the pickup for her. He's the perfect gentleman. And smoking hot.

We drive past Shake Rattle and Bowl as we head through town to the main beach. The bowling alley parking lot is packed, and crowds of people are milling about, drinks in hand. Almost all of them are wearing neon-colored clothes, fluorescent green, pink, yellow, and orange. Is it 1985 or glow-in-the-dark bowling? It's hard to tell.

Vivi scans the lot. "There's Sal's car, of course. He'll be rocking superstar status tonight with his bowling bravado. I just hope nobody is stupid enough to score higher than him. They could wind up with ten pins up their keister."

I'm relieved. One less weirdo to deal with tonight. "I'm so glad the glow-in-the-dark bowling is on the same night as the bonfire so Sal can't crash our party."

Hugh is serious. "I'm glad they're scheduled on the same night, too. I wouldn't want to dress up like a neon Teletubby to do glow-in-the-dark anything."

The beach parking is jammed, too. Hugh lets us off with the folding chairs and the bags of booze and leaves to find a spot on the road.

When I pull out my phone, I pick up a text from Florrie, who lets me know where she's set up on the beach. Also, that Marty is with her. Ugh.

"Do you think Craig will be here tonight?" I try to gauge where Vivi's at.

Vivi looks genuinely worried. "I really hope not. I mean, I'd love to get to know him better, but not while Sal is in the picture. I meant it when I told him it would be safer for him to skip the rest of the reunion weekend. I hope he took me seriously. I would already have headed to the city myself if I wasn't so worried about leaving my cottage unoccupied and coming back to find Tiffany squatting in it."

Hugh trots up behind us. We all grab some gear and make our way to the edge of the lake, where the most amazing fire is sending sparks twelve feet high. It's a great turnout. I think there are as many people here as there are at the bowling alley, a few hundred for sure. There are all ages, and the music is from all decades, which is nice.

Florrie texts me again, and I follow her directions around a couple of grassy dunes until I come across Marty and her sharing a marshmallow roasting stick. We set up camp next to them.

"Florrie, you must be exhausted from your day in the bakery. That was crazy."

"I am wiped. We broke sales records and ran out of absolutely everything. But it was great, thanks to Bible Babe and the troops of closet gluttons she sent my way."

Hugh rolls his eyes. "Oh no, don't tell me. Your bakery was *gluttony* on her scavenger hunt?"

Florrie beams. "Sure was. And I rode that sucker all the way to the bank."

Marty offers up his roasting skills. "Anyone for s'mores? I brought all the fixin's." He has a picnic basket with graham crackers, chocolate, and a jumbo bag of marshmallows.

Vivi raises her hand, and Marty leaps up to be of service. I've got my eye on Marty. He actually doesn't seem all that bad, which makes me think that he actually is all that bad because he is an actor, after all. Fooling people into believing things and pretending to be someone he's not is what Marty does for a living. I'm still more than a little worried for Florrie's tender heart, but

I'm trying my best to keep my mouth shut on the matter.

The rhythmic sound of the gently rolling waves is incredibly relaxing. The fire throws dancing shadows across the bodies milling about on the sand, making it very difficult to see people well. I don't recognize that many here, not that I remember faces anyway. I do, however, spot Sissy Greensplat and her seemingly estranged husband, Russ Carney. I'm relieved to see that she didn't carry through on her threat to kill him following the aunts' Molotov cocktail of a tarot card reading. It does seem as if she's making him suffer, though. They're at opposite ends of the beach, Russ alone on a rock, nursing a beer and perhaps drowning his sorrows, and Sissy chatting up an old beau complete with batting eyelashes and flirty lip licking.

A tall, lanky guy in a classy cardigan appears and moves close to Vivi. I remember this one.

Vivi looks shocked when she sees Craig smiling down at her. Then she looks happy. Then she looks nervous. "Craig, I told you to leave town. I wasn't exaggerating. It's not safe for you to be anywhere near me. Next time will be worse. It always is."

Craig looks very calm. "I hear you, and I believe you, Vivi. But I don't want to leave the reunion. Or you. Not yet." He puts his arm around Vivi's shoulder, and it looks as if she decompresses for the first time today.

I impart a word to the wise. "Just as long as you're not tempted to go glow-in-the-dark bowling."

"I'm more the triathlon type." Craig smiles at me.

"Now there's a sport." Vivi raises her glass.

"Don't go next door, either." Florrie points down the beach.

The largest summer home on the beach is next to the flagpole on High Street and only a stone's throw away from tonight's bonfire site. It's the rock-walled estate that Sal and his entourage have rented for the weekend, and we can see it clearly from where we sit. Not many lights on right now, but there are a number of black SUVs with heavily tinted windows parked in front. Some of Sal's soldiers would have stayed behind to keep guard on the place.

A minute later, Cordelia texts, and she finds our group after a bit of a search through the crowd.

"Wow." Cordelia takes in the gorgeous scene. "Now, this brings back good memories."

Hugh hands Cordelia a tumbler of wine, for which she looks extremely grateful.

"How'd work go today, Cordelia?" Florrie is always dying to hear the deets.

Cordelia plays dumb. "Great, thank you. Lots of kids borrowing lots of books."

"Not that work, your other work."

Cordelia smiles devilishly, lifts her thermal wine goblet. "It went well for me. The other party is feeling a little like Craig did last night, but that's the whole point, isn't it? No pain for him, no gain for me."

An awkward-looking dude wearing a hoodie pulled up over his head sits down on a large rock close to our group. He's alone and not drinking. No one else seems to notice his presence. I wait for a bit in case friends join him, but no one does. After a while, I whisper to Hugh. "Any idea who that guy is?"

Hugh glances over at the man on the rock. "It's hard to see." He shakes his head. "I don't think I recognize him, but I barely know anyone here." Hugh is clearly unconcerned.

I can't get a good look at the guy either, but the flashes of his face I do glimpse look very familiar. I can't place him, but know I've seen him somewhere before.

When I catch the eyes of the three girls, I nod toward the dude, and they each check him out and shrug, also untroubled. They carry on drinking and chatting and making and eating s'mores. A large cluster of people has started dancing in the sand, and it's getting wilder as the liquor flows.

A while later, when I look back towards the rock, the mysterious man is gone. A shiver runs down my spine. Something's not right. Or maybe everything is fine, and I'm just being paranoid. Feels a whole lot better to run with that theory. I throw back my wine, and Hugh pours me another. I close my eyes, inhale the stirring scent of the roaring bonfire, and tune into the cheerful sounds of old friends laughing. My tense muscles begin to relax at last.

Sometime afterward, the crowd parts, and I see the man in the hoodie again, standing still, and staring at me. The dancing bodies shift, and the man vanishes once more. The next time I see him, he's moved closer, and I get a better look at his face. I remember where I'd seen him before. He was the man who turned up early when I was setting up the aunt's tarot reading booth in the school gymnasium and paid to have his fortune told. He's quickly engulfed by the sea of people, but I can feel his eyes on me.

After a while, I look over my shoulder, and he's back sitting on the rock near our group. My hackles are up. I know this guy will approach us. It's not long before he's on his feet and walking toward me. I grab for Hugh's arm and draw his attention to the man entering our little circle. Hugh takes a few steps forward to stand between me and the stranger in the hoodie.

"How's it going?" Hugh speaks first.

The dude sort of smiles and grunts a response in Hugh's direction. But he looks directly at me. "Hey, you're Gina Malone, aren't you? The Ex-Whisperer?"

I try to sound friendly, but he's giving me the creeps for no viable reason, which, if it weren't for Team Outcast breathing down my neck, would make my feelings mostly unkind, and I hate that. The little voice inside me is sounding alarm bells, but I don't completely trust my instincts right now. I'm on edge, but so far all this guy did was build up his courage to come and talk to the Ex-Whisperer at a reunion party. No crime there. Obviously, none of the others are picking up weird vibes from this person. I force myself to converse with him. "That's me, but I'm off duty this weekend."

The guy shuffles his feet, seems unsure of how to proceed. "Oh, too bad. I had a question for you."

The others overhear and turn to look at him now.

Florrie studies him. "You look familiar. Did you have an older brother in our class?"

This guy is probably five years younger than us.

"I don't have an older brother, but I used to see you girls around town when I worked at the gas station."

Florrie is trying to place him. "Do you still live here?"

He shakes his head. "Moved away a long time ago."

I pipe up. "Don't you remember him, Florrie? We met him at the school the other day. He showed up early and asked the aunts to predict his future."

Florrie nods and smiles. "Oh, that's right. You had your tarot cards read, and you got one of the aunts' famous sandwiches out of the deal too."

The man twitches anxiously, shifts from foot to foot, as if he's ready to run away.

Hugh reaches out to shake his hand. "Hugh McTavish."

The guy seems reluctant to shake, but he does. "Sean."

I'm curious now but try to keep it sounding light. "What did you want to ask the Ex-Whisperer, Sean? I'll try to get a message to her for you."

Sean stutters nervously. "Yeah, uh, I wanted to get some advice on bullying."

Hackles up for everybody. Okay, so the little voice inside me turns out to be right again, as per usual. The others all move in closer to listen to our conversation.

My blood runs cold. "That's not really the Ex-Whisperer's area of expertise. But are you being bullied? Because I can share some resources with you where you can find help. Bullying is a very serious problem."

"I was bullied as a kid." Sean stares at me unflinchingly. "And I know people who were bullied."

I stand up now. My gut tells me that I may need to take flight, even though my forebrain knows that's silly. I could never outrun this guy. Better to use my mind to defend myself than my muscles. Also, Hugh, Craig, and Marty have all moved in close to me—I've got surplus muscles everywhere. "Oftentimes, when people are bullied as children, it affects them for their whole lives."

"And sometimes it ends their lives." Sean's eyes are quivering with the anger we can hear rising in his voice.

I'm pretty sure I know who I'm dealing with now. What I don't know is what this person is capable of. "That's true, too. And very tragic. Did that

169

happen to anyone close to you?"

"Why? Do you care?"

"Of course, I care. We all have scars that we carry from our childhoods, and lots of times, we don't get around to dealing with them until we're adults. But it's important to get the support now that we couldn't get as kids. Like I said, I can give you some resources for people who can help you."

Sean looks at the three men gathered around me and seems to tense up even more. He's still only speaking to me. "Did you ever bully anyone?"

I stay calm and make sure that my voice sounds firm and strong. "No, I never did. I wasn't bullied either, luckily. And none of my friends ever bullied anyone."

Sean looks at Vivi, Cordelia, and Florrie.

Cordelia speaks up. "It's true. We'd never hurt anyone on purpose."

"Lots of times, people who were bullied as children grow up to be bullies themselves. Is that what happened to you, Sean? Do you bully people now?" It's a question I already know the answer to.

Sean spits into the sand, then looks pointedly at all four of us women. "Some people deserve to get a taste of their own medicine."

Florrie is trying to confirm what we all suspect. "What's your last name, Sean?"

Sean's face is covered in shadows, even with the light from the fire flickering across it. I don't remember ever seeing him before this week. "Williams."

Sean turns away, and three broad strides later, he disappears into the dancing crowd.

We all stare at each other in disbelief.

I state the obvious. "That's Cassie Williams's brother."

Chapter Twenty-Two

To be honest, Cassie Williams's brother looked far more confused and hurt than dangerous. I know you can never know for sure what a person will do when they feel so broken and empty that they have nothing left to lose, but I hope Sean Williams just needed to hear us say that we weren't bullies, that we weren't the cause of his sister's torment or death. He also needed to bully someone just like his sister Cassie was bullied, and probably the way he was, too. He wanted us to know what it feels like to be on the receiving end, and I hope the things he did to scare us got that out of his system. Fingers crossed, he's going to leave us alone now. Side note: my biggest downfall is being optimistic to a fault.

The three guys are ready to chase after Sean Williams, and I suppose, bring him to justice.

I stop them. There's no point. "There's no reason to grab him. We know who he is now. It's not going to be difficult for the police to pick him up." I pull out my phone and send a message to Floyd and Lloyd with the latest information on the identity of Team Outcast, not that they have time to care about it much at the moment.

Cordelia shudders. "Yeah, we know who he is, and he's creepy as hell."

"Knowing who he is, doesn't make me feel any better." Florrie is distraught. "We told him we never bullied anyone, but we didn't get a chance to tell him that we liked his sister, that we would never have done anything to hurt his Cassie."

Vivi is creeped out, too. "It didn't look like he believed us anyway. He's definitely holding us at least partially accountable for Cassie's death. We

171

could still be on his hit list."

"Oh my God." Florrie buries her face in Marty's shoulder.

Hugh tops up everyone's drinks, and we all move a little closer to the fire to warm up and a little closer to each other on the off chance that there actually is safety in numbers.

Even hard-hearted Cordelia is beginning to soften with empathy for Cassie's tortured brother. "No excuses. This Sean is out of control, and he obviously has some major problems, but the poor guy has clearly never gotten over his sister's death. We know Cassie was the one who raised him and took care of him, so it had to be a totally devastating loss." She fills the three guys in on the details they probably haven't heard. "A few weeks after Cassie died, his mom passed away from cancer. Then right in the middle of his high school years, his abusive alcoholic father took him out to the East Coast to live."

Marty, Craig, and Hugh all shake their heads in sympathy for the anguished man.

"Some families get hit so hard." Craig has been through some of these life trials himself, including being bullied as a young person and losing his own wife to cancer.

"Like you." Vivi gives Craig a hug.

Marty seems especially sad for the man. "None of what he did to you girls is normal or acceptable, but he's likely suffering from mental illness of some kind and may not be receiving any treatment for it."

I try to work through the conversation that I'll have with the police. "What are the cops going to charge him with? Sending letters to a public blog that sound like vague threats that were never followed through on? I get menacing messages from online trolls every day. Can they charge him with dropping off an old newspaper on my porch and old photos with some of the faces scratched out? It's not even considered trespassing if you're delivering something to a residence or workplace." I know all about this. Every time Dick came creeping around my house, he'd have something dumb to drop off just in case he got caught. "Hopefully he doesn't escalate, but so far, none of the things that Sean Williams has done are illegal."

Hugh begs to differ. "It's illegal to hit people in the back of the head while they're walking down a road."

I'm not holding out hope on that one. "I'm sure that incident is already a cold case as far as the cops are concerned."

"We don't know that it was Cassie's brother who attacked us." Vivi's convinced she knows who her assailant was. "I really do think it was Sal. He wasn't trying to kill us, or we'd be dead. He was just trying to scare me away from staying at my cottage."

Cordelia doesn't have much faith that the mystery will be solved. "Floyd already said there's no proof to pin the assault on anybody, so there's nothing he can do about it. Vivi and I didn't even go to the hospital, so Sunset Beach's ace detectives aren't going to pull overtime hours to crack this case."

"But there is that other thing." The thing that kept me awake most of last night. "The three dead boys who we do know bullied Cassie Williams. They would have been on Sean's revenge list for sure. Maybe he didn't set out to murder them. Maybe he was trying to give them a taste of their own medicine, and things went too far."

Hugh counters for the sake of sorting through the facts that we know. "All three of those deaths were ruled accidents according to those newspaper clippings we read at the school last night."

"Does that not seem like too big a coincidence to everyone?" Cordelia's voice is steeped in suspicion.

Craig weighs in. "It does sound like a big coincidence. But there is such a thing as a big coincidence."

Florrie is sheepish. "Your aunts would say that maybe Karma paid those three boys back for what they did to Cassie."

"That's why we're not asking my aunts for their opinion on this."

Marty has an opinion, too. His is a little more grounded. "From what I know of detectives, they never like to reopen a case they consider solved. Especially when there's no evidence to indicate foul play."

I realize I sound petulant now and possibly ridiculous. "Well, maybe we have to gather some evidence ourselves, then. The letters and photos he sent to us weren't illegal in and of themselves, but surely they constitute circumstantial evidence since three other people who did bully Sean Williams's sister wound up dead."

Vivi is pragmatic, and I know she's trying to calm me down. "So we give the experts the information we have, and we let them handle it, Gina. It's impossible for us to run around the country trying to gather evidence regarding three accidental deaths of people we don't know and have no rights to access information for. No one is going to help us."

Cordelia takes me by the shoulders to talk some sense into me. "And why would we want to do this? To what end? It's not going to help Cassie or her brother, and it's sure not going to help any of us. It sounds like an impossible feat to boot."

I don't even know what I'm feeling anymore. I don't think anyone should get away with murder if Sean Williams did kill those three bullies, but I feel sorry for him at the same time. I feel even more sorry for Cassie, and there's a good dose of guilt in that mix, too. Fear and anger have coiled through my brain, creating some chemical concoction that has left me completely off balance. "I know you're all right, of course. I think maybe I'm losing it."

Florrie wraps her arm around my shoulder. "You've been under a lot of strain. We all have. We need to lighten things up and enjoy this bonfire."

I nod. I get it. I try to come back into my body and feel the sand under my feet. "You're right. I'll just pass along what we know and what we suspect to the police, and they can handle it, which will probably mean that they'll do absolutely nothing."

Vivi sits back down. "As long as Sean Williams leaves us alone, we don't have to take any of this on."

Craig stands behind Vivi and rubs her shoulders. "It's already been dealt with through the system, and we all know the system is broken, but I'm not sure that any of us are in a position to fix it. The important thing here is that you four women are safe."

This is the part where I get stuck and can't just go back to having fun at the beach party. "But that's the wild card. Is Sean Williams going to go back to where he came from and leave us alone now? Did he believe us when we told him we never bullied anyone?"

Cordelia throws her arms up. "Until we know the answer to that, all we can do is keep each other safe."

Hugh takes my hand in his. "I'm certain the cops will pick Sean Williams up as soon as they read the information you sent them, and then you'll know where he is and what's going on. He's not going to be able to make any threats in secret anymore as Team Outcast. He'll know everyone, including the police, have got his number, at which point he'll probably be too scared to stick around here. Floyd and Lloyd are going to take this matter a lot more seriously than the disorderly conduct of a bunch of drunk fifty-year-olds who have forgotten what year it is and are flirting with their old exes." He looks straight at Florrie and Marty.

Their mouths drop at the insinuation, and then we all break into much-needed laughter.

"To disorderly conduct!" Marty lifts his cup. "I say we all get drunk as fast as we can."

Florrie chimes in. "And get flirting!"

"Hear, hear." We're all in agreement and lift our glasses in a toast.

The seven of us join the very large crowd of dancers kicking up sand when Beyoncé and Jay-Z sing "Crazy in Love." And I must say, it is really fun and therapeutic. It's so cute to see Craig making an obviously monumental effort to move his sorely battered body to the beat, and he refuses to take the rest breaks that Vivi suggests.

Once in a while, I find myself checking around the perimeter of the party, looking for sightings of Sean Williams, but I don't see him anywhere at all, and I'm starting to think maybe he did get what he came for and has moved on now.

Perhaps it's wishful thinking, but it's probably more of a personal survival mechanism. My circuits are blown from this chronic stress, and I need to find a way to get back to my center. For now, imagining that Team Outcast has dipped and grooving to some Mary J. Blige is doing the trick brilliantly.

After a very long, very fun set of dance tunes that span a good forty years, we head back to our camp chairs and flop into them to indulge in a little more wine.

Even though it's getting late and the temperature is cooling off, the crowd hasn't lessened, nor has the party shown any signs of slowing down.

I notice Vivi watching something intensely at the far end of the beach. She looks concerned, and I follow her gaze. I immediately see what's holding her attention.

Three black SUVs are pulling into the swanky cottage that Sal has rented for the weekend. Lights on the grand estate are turning on to flood the grounds. The glow-in-the-dark bowling must have wrapped. I know Vivi is worried that Sal will come down to the beach to check out our bonfire party, and I am, too. It's probably time for us to head out.

I tell Hugh and the others, and they have no problem with our making a quick exit. Craig is especially anxious to bail, and who could blame him? We fold up our camp chairs, gather our bottles and bags, and hurry along the shore in the direction of the parking lot. We almost make it.

Sal cuts us off on the beach with Tiffany and four other burly sidekicks trailing behind him. We halt in front of them, exchange tense looks with each other. Sal is still dressed *Big Lebowski* style in an oversized black bowling shirt with yellow and orange cartoon flames licking up the front. "Hey, hey, hey, you guys missed a great night at the bowling tourney. You woulda loved it, Vivi. Yours truly took home the first-place trophy, of course. Scored two sixty-nine." Sal waits for the kudos and applause from our group.

There are none. But there is a very long, very awkward silence.

Vivi is clearly unimpressed, and Sal knows it. "Good night, Sal."

Sal's face darkens. "Where are you kiddos scrambling off to?"

Vivi squeaks out a reply. "None of your business."

Sal holds his arms up in front of Vivi to block her way. "Hold up. Stay for another drink. Let's have a catch-up chat. I got that special merlot you always liked." Sal snaps his fingers at one of his goons carrying a large cooler, and the man opens it, pulls out a bottle of red, and hands it to Sal, who presents it to Vivi with a flourish so she can read the wine label.

Vivi's not interested in the showy bottle and is more annoyed than nervous now. "No thanks, Sal. I don't want your wine, and I don't want to catch up with you. It's late. We're going home."

Sal tries not to sound ticked off, but it's not working. "What do you want, Vivi?"

"I want you to leave me and my friends alone." She looks over at a visibly bruised Craig. "And I want you to stop bugging me about the cottage. I'm not selling it, and I'm not discussing it with you any further."

Tiffany leans over Sal's shoulder. "We'll see about that. It's not safe for a woman alone way out there, you know."

Sal shoots Tiffany a reproachful look that shuts her up.

Hugh takes my arm. "Let's go, guys. It's late."

We all step to the side to move around Sal's group when Sal leans down and smashes the bottom of the wine bottle against a rock. All four of us women scream involuntarily, except Tiffany, who giggles. The red liquid gurgles on the sand like a pooling bloodstain. Sal holds the bottle up, the lethal, jagged end pointing straight at Craig.

Sal is fresh out of niceties. His voice is forceful and sinister now. "I think we are going to talk, Vivi. We're going to talk whenever I want to about anything I want to. Including the cottage."

Vivi has had years of practice perfecting the steely coldness she presents now. "Okay, Sal, you and I will sit and talk. But my friends are leaving." She cocks her head toward the parking lot, motioning for the rest of us to go.

I take Vivi's arm. "We're not going anywhere without you, Vivi. All of us are leaving together."

Sal laughs, finds my defiance amusing. "I don't think so, Gina."

His goons take a few long strides toward us. Tiffany drops back to a safe distance. The gloves are off. Hugh and Marty drop the gear they're holding, bracing themselves for whatever's next. Florrie screams.

Chapter Twenty-Three

Vivi yells, "Don't you dare, Sal!"

A few people around the bonfire have noticed the commotion and stopped dancing to stare. No one is coming over to intervene in the brewing fisticuffs. Everyone knows who Sal is, and everyone knows better. We're on our own.

Sal moves swiftly toward Craig with the broken wine bottle raised at face level. The other goons move in on Hugh and Marty, who are no slouches, but with two massive men against each of them, it will be quick work for Sal and his gang.

There's a sudden burst of prolonged, high-pitched yelping, and I'm not sure whether it's coming from Craig or Marty. It's so tough to see in the shadowy light of the bonfire.

Florrie screams; Vivi yells; Cordelia screeches, and I run into the fray in a desperate effort to stop whatever horribly painful thwacking is happening to at least one of our men.

The frantic, high-pitched squealing carries on, and my eyes make out the shape of two large rats, or as I quickly realize, two rabid Chihuahuas, from which the sound is emanating. It's the aunts out for their nightly prebedtime dog walk with Peppita and Peppeto.

The aunts are as frenzied as their dogs.

"Che succede?" What's happening? Zia Rosa bellows fiercely at the burly men who have Hugh, Marty, and Craig by the scruffs of their necks.

"E' tutto a posto?" Is everything all right? Zia Angela shouts out in concern.

Sal stops dead in his tracks, broken bottle poised against Craig's face. He signals his soldiers to stand down.

Sal turns toward the aunts, tucks the jagged glass weapon behind his back, smiles charmingly. *"Non succede niente."* Nothing is happening. *"Va tutto bene."* Everything is fine. *"Come stai?"* How are you, "Signoras Angela e Rosa?"

"Salvatore Fortuna." The aunts drag out the vowels in Sal's name in a reprimand that really doesn't require that anything more be said, but it's the aunts, so they're not about to leave it at that.

Their voices are filled with accusation, and they point at Sal as the guilty party in the group.

"Ti stai mettendo di nuovo nei guai." You're getting into trouble again. Zia Rosa shakes her fist at Sal as if she's ready to rain holy hellfire upon on his head.

"Non preoccuparti." Don't worry yourself. But Sal looks worried, even he's afraid of the aunts. *"E tutto a posto."* Everything is all right.

"Give me this." Rosa waddles across the sand to grab the jagged wine bottle out of Sal's hand. "Madonna." She tsk tsks.

"I phoning your mother." Zia Angela looks skyward, raises her arms to the angels. "Your grandmother will be crying at the gates of Heaven for you. You're breaking her heart." Zia Angela crosses herself, kisses the crucifix around her neck. "Shame, shame, shame. You go home now, Salvatore."

If the aunts had a wooden spoon, they'd be whooping Sal's Italian ass with it.

Sal, Tiffany, and the four mobbed-up men hightail it back to their fancy digs.

Now the aunts turn their tempers in our direction. The seven of us stand in silence before them like a bunch of kids who know we're about to get grounded.

Surprising us all, Zia Rosa shrugs nonchalantly as if to say, whaddaya gonna do? "Who's hungry?" For Zia Rosa, the answer to every problem is food. Makes sense to me.

"You want some spaghett?" Zia Angela, too.

We all burst into laughter, relieved on so many levels and also happy to be invited for a midnight meal. Who in their right mind would say no?

"Gina, bring your friends to the restaurant. We got a nice manicotti in the oven." The aunts shuffle off with their yapping dogs to finish up their nightly walk.

The rest of us look at each other, faces flushed and bodies still shaking with adrenaline. We don't waste any time hustling over to our vehicles and putting some distance between us and Sal's place.

The aunts arrive back at Happily Napoli about the same time as we are all parked and out of our cars. They unlock the door to the restaurant, and we follow my twin zias and their matching dogs inside. It smells delicious as always, and they have the guys push two tables together to make a long one for the nine of us.

Hugh has brought a couple of bottles of wine in with him. I pour water for everyone, and Florrie lights candles along the length of the red-and-white checkered tablecloths.

"*Sedere. Sedere.*" The aunts insist that the seven of us sit down at the long dining table, and they begin the midnight buffet brigade.

The restaurant is comfy and cozy. Everyone's mouth is watering in deep appreciation of the appetizing smells and kitchen sounds filling up the space, and we're all overflowing with gratitude. None of us expected this end to the evening. Half an hour ago, we all thought we'd be spending the rest of the night in the ER. The two miniature evil hounds are underneath the table, biting at everyone's shoes, but I even feel grateful for those little ghouls right now.

The pasta parade starts with spaghetti, as promised, featuring the aunts' otherworldly tomato sauce and meatballs made with fresh ricotta, chopped Italian bacon, and garlic, onion, and basil from the aunts' garden. For me, they bring out a special vegetarian bucatini with lemon and parmesan. Baskets of grainy bread to dip in olive oil and balsamic vinegar are endlessly replenished.

It is a sight to behold, and Vivi is busy videoing and taking photos of absolutely everything and everyone. "My TikTok is going to blow up with this."

The aunts love posing for pictures with their culinary creations, and Vivi can't get enough.

I don't think any of us realized how famished we were. By the time we finish our pasta, we can barely breathe, but the aunts present a second course of the perfect late-night snack, and it would be criminal not to make room for it, so we do. We may all end up in the ER tonight after all.

Mozzarella en carrozza is the Italian version of a grilled cheese sandwich. Thick bread slices are bread-crumb crusted and pan-fried with a volcano of gooey mozzarella between them and marinara dipping sauce on the side. They make a round of espressos for all, even though it's one in the morning, and set out a plate of chocolate and almond biscotti for dunking. I'm convinced that the aunts are right—good food is the answer to almost every ill. Possibly because when a person is as stuffed as I am right now, all bodily resources must be concentrated on digestion so the brain can no longer expend energy ruminating.

None of us want to leave, and that may be because we're all so full that none of us feel capable of moving but move we must.

Florrie reluctantly initiates our exodus. "Guys, we've got the Halloween costume dance later today, and I know the bakery will be a zoo again. I need to get to bed. Can someone roll my body home?"

We clear all the dishes from the table and carry them into the kitchen, but the aunts won't hear of us washing up. They assure us they'll have staff showing up in a few hours' time who will tend to the cleanup. Everyone kisses everyone else's cheeks, and we all thank the aunts profusely for the amazing food and also for saving our skins from the wrath of Sal and his goombahs.

Craig and Marty leave their cars and walk Florrie across the street to her apartment and Cordelia around the corner to her home, where they will then double back to their motel two minutes further up High Street. Hugh drives Vivi and me to my place. She's staying with me tonight, so neither of us are on our own.

Zoe and Spook are happy to see me, but I'm way too exhausted to give them much attention, plus, my stomach is so full that it hurts to bend over to pet them. They both wind up sleeping on my bed with me, which is usually against the rules, but guilt.

I'm not falling asleep. Could be the midnight espresso, or it could be the fact that I feel like a python that's just swallowed a goat whole. Pretty sure I look like one, too, and like a python, I don't need to ingest food for the next two months. Thank God Hugh and I didn't choose tonight to take our relationship to the next level. I imagine what that would have looked like in my current bloated state, and it's nothing short of horrific. A song we danced to at our beach blanket bingo party earlier tonight keeps replaying in my head, mocking me, "Da Ya Think I'm Sexy." We both know I'm not—screw off, Rod Stewart.

I don't remember falling asleep. I slip into a food coma and stay there until morning. I'm quite certain the rest of our gluttonous little gang would've done the same.

Vivi has the coffee on before I get up, and I follow the glorious smell into my little kitchen. Neither of us are interested in eating breakfast—for weeks. I let Zoe outside, then feed and water the pets.

Vivi and I sit at the window with our steaming mugs of life sustenance and stare at the beautiful lake, the cat on her lap, the dog on my feet. Vivi looks a million miles away.

I bring her back to earth. "Happy Halloween."

She smiles. "Oh right, that's today. Happy Halloween."

"That was pretty intense last night."

Vivi nods. "That's for damn sure."

"I meant the midnight supper." I elbow Vivi.

Vivi laughs. "That, too. The whole Sal thing was super scary, though. I think we all dodged a bullet. Literally."

I refill our coffee cups. "We might have a few more yet to dodge. The skirmish didn't exactly end the way Sal planned."

Vivi nods. "Thanks to your badass zias." Vivi's mind wanders back to the space she's been floating in for the past thirty-six hours. "Craig is super cute. How did I not notice him in high school?"

I know the answer to that one. "Craig was a skinny little nerd, and you were focused on the jocks."

"Unfortunately, then I graduated from the jocks to the bad boys, and look where that got me. Married to the mob."

I lift my mug to toast Vivi's. "And divorced from the devil."

Vivi's demeanor deflates. "That's the problem. We're divorced, but Sal's in my life even more now than when we were married. He is never going to leave me alone, Gina. He'll probably even haunt me from beyond the grave, but I know for sure I'm never going to have any peace or happiness as long as Sal's among the living."

I try to look on the bright side. "Well, mobsters don't generally have very long lifespans, do they?"

Vivi chuckles. "I've googled it. It's longer than you'd think. Sixty-eight years on average. But most of them don't die of natural causes. Being a mob boss is considered the most dangerous job in the world because one-quarter of them end up murdered."

I'm deadpan. "So there's hope, then."

Vivi and I look at each other then break out laughing, howling until we're snorting.

The distant chime of a text comes from my phone. Then another. And another. And another. I get up to search for my cell in the bedroom.

"It must be an emergency." Vivi is alarmed. "It could be anything after last night. I hope everyone's okay."

I walk back into the kitchen, reading the texts from the aunts, during which time they send four more. Same message resent over and over, telling me to come quickly: *Gina*, vieni velocemente. *The sky she is raining men.* Sbrigati. *We're planting the garlic bulbs.*

I call the aunts repeatedly, but they don't pick up. Their message makes absolutely no sense to me, but no surprise there. The only part I understand is that they need my help pronto.

Vivi had planned to go for a big walk on the beach this morning, so she offers to take Zoe along, which is a huge help for me.

It's Saturday, so Hugh isn't here working on the bunkie today, which feels odd when I dash out to my car to head into town. The aunts have me

183

worried, but in truth, their problem could be a very simple one and is quite likely a nonemergency. Everything is a matter of life and death in my zias' world. I'm a little confused about the raining men part, but that could be autocorrect.

I would think the reunion festivities would be losing a little steam by now, but they're still going full-bore no matter where I look on my drive into town. It's day four and counting. Feels like day forty-four, and I can't be the only one in that camp. Everyone I see is either physically exhausted from drinking more alcohol than they have since prom night, or else they're emotionally exhausted from coming up short after comparing their lives to everyone they ever knew.

I've realized the frightening truth that high school reunions are like physically stepping inside Facebook and being trapped there with the photos of everyone else's Caribbean holidays, their marathon CrossFit training schedules, and endless pitches from old acquaintances to join MLM schemes for essential oil businesses. Tonight is the grand finale with the Halloween costume dance, and tomorrow the clocks will all go forward again to the present time, when everyone will return to their real lives and this reunion weekend will become a storied part of our shared history, just like our high school years.

It's easy to find a parking spot at Happily Napoli this morning since it won't be open for another couple of hours, at which time the lunch crowd will descend en masse.

The front door into the restaurant is locked, so I walk down the alleyway between buildings to reach the back of the aunts', where they keep their garden gate tied up with at least six bike locks and chains. This gives the aunts peace of mind but wouldn't stop anyone from hopping over the four-foot-high rickety old picket fence.

I call out to my aunts, and they appear at the window of their apartment upstairs. Their curtains part, then close quickly, and I know they're on their way down to meet me. I hop over the low part of the peeling fence that encloses their small yard, the same spot I've been climbing over for nearly fifty years.

The aunts bustle outside through their back door, and their tiny whirling dervishes disguised as dogs fly past them, yapping frantically and creating a sand tornado around my legs. The cursed little imps nip at my calves at least a dozen times. The aunts are even wilder than the damn Chihuahuas today. My zias do their limping run toward me, waving tea towels and crossing themselves for protection, clearly alarmed.

Obviously something really is wrong. "Zias, what is it? Tell me what happened."

"Gina, Gina, thank Godda you here." Rosa is hyperventilating.

"We almost die from the heart attacks." Angela fans her overheated face with her tea towel.

I take them both by the arm to try to calm them down. "What's going on? Why are you so upset?"

"Oh, Madonna, there's a dead man in the garden."

Chapter Twenty-Four

T he aunts are speaking English to me, but I just can't comprehend what they're telling me. "You're not making sense, zias."

Now they're getting ticked off with me because I don't understand them, and they hate that. "Are you stupida? We tell you there's a dead man in the garden."

So I'm thinking they've found a man's old shoe. Or, since it's Halloween today, maybe some kids have pranked the aunts and buried one of those rubber legs or a plastic skeleton in their yard. Yeah, that's probably what's going on here. It's a Halloween joke.

My distressed zias lead me to the end of the yard where they have their vegetable garden.

I wish they'd bloody hurry up and get to the point, but that's not how my zias speak. They start from the beginning of the story and tell you the whole thing, and if you interrupt them, they start over from the beginning again, so one learns very quickly not to interrupt the aunts.

Zia Angela starts off. "It's the fall time. We plant the garlic bulbs in the fall."

Rosa interrupts her. They're allowed to interrupt each other. "The garden she's asleep for the winter now except for the garlic. She's got to go in the ground now, so we can pick her in the summer for the tomato sauce. We wake up early and have the espresso this morning so we can do the plantings."

Angela takes over. "Rosa she gets the spades outta the shed, and we start the digging. And we see this thing in the soil like a little sausage, but he got a nail."

Rosa, "Ange she says, 'What's that little sausage?' I say, 'How am I supposed to know?'"

The arguing ensues. "No, I asked you what's that little sausage."

I just can't. "Zias! Just tell me what happened."

They both look at me sternly for disturbing their flow.

Zia Rosa gets them back on track. "Peppita and Peppeto they run over, and they take the sausage outta the garden to eat it and play some games. They do the tug of war with the sausage."

"But then we go down on our knees to plant the garlic bulbs, and we dig up another sausage and another one, and we see it's no sausage. We dig, and we dig. They all got the nails."

"What?" Oh no, please don't start over from the beginning. I won't say anything else.

Zia Angela crosses herself. "It's no sausage. It's fingers. Ten fingers."

Rosa lowers her voice, which is still yelling for a regular person. "We think somebody's buried in our garden, but it can't be so. We been digging up this garden for sixty years, and there's never been no bodies in there."

Angela shrugs. "So we think maybe the fingers they're falling from the sky. Maybe somebody's throwing the *dito* in our garden for the Halloween trick and treat."

I'm desperately trying to take in what the aunts are telling me, but I think the panic rising in my stomach and throat is pushing their words out of my head so that I'm not grasping the concept. I tell myself they must be mistaken. There's no way this is real. "Jesus, Mary, and Joseph. Where are the ten fingers now? They're probably rubber."

The aunts waddle over to their outdoor table. There's a pasta pot sitting on top of it, and they lift the lid off. I look inside it and scream into my closed fist to muffle the sound that I cannot help but make. Fat stubby fingers turned gray and stiff, dried blood at the raw ends of each stare back at me. They do look like little sausages but with personality. They smell like rotting flesh, definitely not rubber. I step back and take a few deep breaths, then pick a stick up from the ground to move the digits around in the pasta pot.

The fingernails are caked with black dirt from being buried in the garden. I count only nine fingers. "Where's the other finger? There's only nine here. You said there were ten."

Zia Rosa has calmed down since I've taken on the duty of panicking. "We told you, Peppita and Peppeto ran off with first one."

Oh my god, I don't know how this can get worse. Immediately after thinking that thought, I wish I could retract it because, whenever I think that, things inevitably do get worse. "Show me where you found them in the garden." I don't want to see, but what else can I do?

The aunts take me to their veggie patch and point to the spots where the appendages were dug up. Of course, all the rest of the body parts belonging to sausage guy could also be buried here.

The two manic dogs whizz past us, one chasing the other, and fly through the air to leap into the garden. One of them has the tenth finger in his mouth, and the other is trying to steal it away.

I run after the dogs and yell at the aunts to try to grab the little devils. They bellow at the dogs in Italian, which surprisingly, causes Peppita to momentarily drop the finger on the grass. I dive on the digit, screaming when I have to snatch the stiff member up in my bare hands before the dogs can run away with it again. I'm nearly crying from the intense level of the gross-out factor from feeling the cold, spongy finger pressing into my palm. I sprint to the pasta pot and drop number ten into it.

The aunts and I stand, staring at each other for a very long time. I'm grateful for the little things right now, mostly for the fact that the aunts seem to be momentarily stunned into a rare silence, which is a blessing I need to be able to process this bizarre event.

Suddenly, the dogs jump back into the vegetable garden and start digging frantically in the dirt, clearly on the scent of something.

Peppita unearths the treasure they're hunting for and picks the thing up in her mouth. She freezes and looks up at us with a massive toothy grin. I think I may have gone into shock—I cannot move. The dog looks like the Chihuahuas I've seen on TicTok with the Mouth Sync filter applied because there's an entire set of human teeth where the dog's muzzle should be.

Rosa yells out, *"Porca vacca!"* Holy cow!

Zia Angela asks, "Rosa are those your dentures?

Zia Rosa shakes her head, smiles at her sister to show her that she's wearing her false teeth. Angela points to her own mouth; she's got hers in, too.

We all scream, and the smiling dog takes off running around the yard again with the teeth still in her mouth. Peppeto gives chase. We go after the pair of them. No luck. The damn dog refuses to give up the chompers, and I can't catch the fleet-footed fleabag.

Zia Angela trots inside, emerging a few minutes later with bowls of actual sausages. The rats jump ship, drop the dentures, and run to their mamas to chow down on some fresher fare.

I take one of the aunts' tea towels to collect the teeth and drop them into the pasta pot with the fingers.

"Let's go inside, zias. We're going to have to call the police."

We sit at a table in the empty restaurant, and the aunts do their best to force-feed me, but the last thing I can think about right now is food. I take out my cell to dial the police station.

Floyd and Lloyd must absolutely dread seeing my name come up on their screens with the next-level dramatic messages I've been sending them over the past three days. However, all of those emails will pale in comparison to the one they're about to get from me now.

Just as I open my phone, a text comes in.

It's from Dick.

Even before I read it, my stomach flips, and a wave of nausea rolls over me. I know the news is going to be very, very bad because nine times out of ten, Dick blows into my life on damaging winds. I brace myself, sure that he's about to deliver a Category 5 cyclone that will rip the roof off my life.

It's a terrible thing that Sal continues to haunt Vivi long after their marriage has ended and makes her life a living nightmare. But I also live under similar circumstances. Dick has been dragging me down with him and his endless debacles for decades. Marrying Dick was like strapping myself to the Titanic, and I have no way to escape his sinking ship even after our divorce.

I read Dick's message with utter dread . . .

Whatever you do, don't call the cops. I'm not asking for my protection. It's to keep you and the kids safe.

WTF?

My response: *What are you talking about? Are you insane? Actually, you don't have to respond to the second question. I already know the answer.*

A few seconds later, Dick replies: *I can't tell you anything over the phone in a call or text. It's not safe. Meet me in person, and I'll explain everything.*

As if. *Nice try, sicko. And please explain to me how you know there is anything going on that I would contact the police over?*

A few seconds later: *I'm sorry. I'm not trying to be creepy, but I've been watching you and the aunts from my apartment because I'm right across the street, and I can see their place clearly. I know what the dogs dug up.*

"Jesus H. Christ." I say that out loud, and the aunts start blessing themselves and kissing their dangling crucifixes.

Once again, Dick leaves me with zero choices. *I'm not going into your apartment, and you're not coming to my cottage. Where do you want to meet that isn't totally sketchy?*

I'll meet you in the aunts' garden shed. Go outside in five minutes.

OMG. So it *was* Dick who I saw skulking around the aunts' garden shed the other day. What in God's name is he up to now? Does this have something to do with the "very bad men" who are allegedly trying to kill him? And has Dick possibly dragged my poor old zias into his life-threatening mess? I don't even want to spend the next five minutes contemplating the possibility because I don't think I could survive that situation.

The aunts assume I've been messaging the police all this time. Zia Angela means business. "You tell the police they not going to be digging up our garden now. We got the garlic bulbs planted."

Zia Rosa is on the same stubborn page. "The police can come back in the springtime after we take out the garlic before we plant the beans and onions and cucumbers. Then they can dig up the garden to look for the rest of the man."

Zia Rosa winks at her sister. "He's probably good for the soil. Maybe we don't have to use the fertilizer this year."

CHAPTER TWENTY-FOUR

Zia Angela winks back. "So many tomatoes for the sauce!"

And the two dark-hearted old biddies cackle like a couple of witches. Happy Halloween.

You're really kicking me while I'm down this year, Universe.

I stand up. "You two stay in here, so the neighbors don't start wondering why we're spending so much time poking around a sleeping garden. I'm going to go look around in the yard for a bit and see if I find any clues."

"That's good you go. We gotta start getting the pizzas ready for lunchtime customers." Both aunts jump up and get right to work with the daily myriad of kitchen duties, chopping peppers and kneading dough.

I head back into the yard, check in all directions before I cross slowly toward the garden shed for my secret meeting with my unpredictable and unstable ex-husband. I pick up a spade that the aunts left by the veggie patch, just in case I need to defend myself.

I can't tell whether Dick is already inside the tiny old shed or not. And I have no idea whether it would be better for me to enter before him or after him. What I do know is people will be able to hear me scream from in there, and that's basically my only comfort right now.

My hands are shaking as I reach for the door. I gingerly turn the old latch to open it silently, but the bugger of a door has hinges that screech like a banshee announcing my entrance: *I'm here. Get your chloroform cloth and the duct tape out.*

Okay, plan B, maybe I can startle him into submission. I quickly throw the door open wide, and it slams against the fence and then flies back, knocking me into the shed. It's dark inside and crowded with old pots and planters, broken tools, and rickety wooden chairs. I smell him before I see him. Dick has always worn way too much cologne.

"Gina, close the door."

Against my better judgment, I do what he asks and close the door behind me, but I stay next to it, keeping my hand on the knob. We stand in silence for a few moments. I haven't been this close to Dick in six years, and it feels so strange. It feels foreign and familiar all at the same time, and that is proving to be a very disorienting concoction. This man is the father of my four children. I did love him truly, madly, and deeply once upon a time, but he destroyed the trust we shared, and I don't believe any relationship can withstand that. Ours certainly couldn't. I wish he weren't such a royal schmuck. I wish we could be friends. I wish I didn't hate him so much. I wish I didn't feel afraid of him now. I do, though.

Once my eyes adjust to the low level of light, I can see that Dick looks totally overwrought. He is beside himself. He has always been a hyperactive, type A bundle of nervous energy. If he is made to sit still, he chews gum, snapping it nonstop because his adrenaline never stops coursing. You could put a picture of Dick in the dictionary under the word *stress* and non-English speakers would understand exactly what the word meant.

The most important question I need answered is…. "Dick, did you bury human remains in my aunts' vegetable garden?"

A very long pause. I suppose even now, when Dick is painted into a corner of his own making, that he is fully aware there is no way out of, he still struggles with whether to tell the truth or to lie.

Today he chooses to tell the truth. Today I wish he had told me a lie.

Dick nods. "I had to."

Chapter Twenty-Five

I take back everything I just said to myself about wishing we could be friends and wishing I didn't hate him. We will never be friends, and I will never stop hating him. "Why, Dick? Why are you involved in this sketchy-ass mess? Did you murder someone, Dick?"

Dick's head shakes like a junkie's. He is an adrenaline junkie, and I guess the body responds in some similar ways when too many chemicals are running through veins. "No, no, of course, I didn't kill anyone. I told you there are these very bad men who are after me."

My patience with Dick ran out a decade ago, and my tolerance level for him is zero—out of one hundred—so my voice is two octaves higher than normal, and my own body is starting to shake. With rage. "That doesn't explain why you're hiding body parts." I may be screaming now. "In my aunts' garden!"

Dick holds his hands up to cover my mouth to keep me quiet, but he could just as easily be reaching to wrap them around my throat. How would I know? I leap against the door, beat against his arms, and try to lift my spade in the cramped space. I only manage to hit myself in the shin with the heavy tool and knock over a couple of terra-cotta planters. "Dammit!"

"Shhhhhhh. Shhhhhhh." Dick puts his hands up in the air to show me that he's not trying to strangle me. "You have to keep your voice down or we could all wind up in jail. Or worse."

I think my vision is going. "Who might end up in jail? And what's worse than jail?" I might pass out.

"Me and you and your aunts could end up in jail." Dick's voice is eerily calm now in contrast to mine. "And you know what's worse than that."

My hysteria is spiraling into delirium. "You're not making any sense. The worst thing I ever did in my life was marry you, and the worst thing the aunts ever did was oversalt the pasta water. Don't you dare try to involve me, and especially not my aunts, in your train wreck of a life."

"It's too late for that, Gina. It's done already."

"What?" Shrieking again. "You already involved us in your nefarious activities?" I take deep breaths and try to slow my heart rate. "Okay, you need to start from the beginning because I am totally lost. Question number one: If you didn't kill anybody, why are you burying a body?"

Dick speaks slowly, quietly. "Because I owe those very bad men I told you about a great deal of money, which with their extremely high interest rates, appears to be doubling every week. And they came around to collect. I do want to repay them, but I don't have that kind of cash at the moment. So they made me an offer I couldn't refuse, literally. Saying no is not an option. They're forcing me to do some small jobs for them—"

"Dirty work. Illegal stuff."

"Yes, as a means of paying off my debt."

"Like burying bodies."

"Yes, like that. Well, not bodies, not yet anyway, but body parts."

"Oh, important distinction, so much better." Not. "Like fingers and teeth, the parts of a body that can serve to identify the human being to whom said body parts belong?"

"Yes, that's correct. But you can rest assured there are no other human remains in your aunts' vegetable garden."

That is so damn specific a statement that, knowing Dick, I have to assume there are other dead things that Dick has disposed of in other places, if not the vegetable garden per se. Could be in the aunts' flower beds. Or in their basement. I'm super glad I'm a vegetarian in case Dick snuck into the Happily Napoli kitchen while picking up takeout and slipped some extra meat into the spezzatino.

"Question number two: Who is the dead man? Did you know him? Maybe he has a family, and they're looking for him. Maybe the police are looking for him. And maybe they're going to gather evidence that will lead them to my aunts' backyard."

Dick manages to keep his composure now. I guess because we can only afford to have one person freaking out at a time in this situation, and I called it first. "No, I didn't know the dead man, but I know he worked for these same people. It's not like he was a nice guy. None of them are good guys, Gina. You don't need to feel guilty about that or sorry for him. The world is probably a safer place with this man off the streets."

"I don't feel guilty because I didn't do anything wrong here, but I wouldn't mind knowing who's pushing up garlic bulbs in the aunts' yard. Question number three: Why did you bury these damn body parts in the aunts' yard? Why did you come anywhere near them or me or Sunset Beach? You could have gone anywhere else in the country, far, far away from us. Please explain this to me because I cannot for the life of me come up with a reasonable answer to that one unless you are purposely trying to harm us."

"I would never purposely hurt you, Gina. You must know that."

"Bull, you've done it a million times. Just answer my question."

Dick always gives way too much detail, as compulsive liars do. "Obviously, time was of the essence. I mean, it's rotting flesh, so I couldn't exactly drive too far out of the city. Also, I didn't want to get caught with the damn things, so I didn't want to keep them on my person any longer than necessary. For those very good reasons, I didn't want to have to travel more than a couple of hours outside the city. So a small town like Sunset Beach was the ideal distance, and after years of spending summer vacations here with you and the kids, I know the town pretty well, so it made sense. Sunset Beach truly is the perfect place to bury secrets. I mean, everyone keeps to themselves around here. Floyd and Lloyd aren't exactly NYPD blue, and nothing bad ever happens in this town."

I beg to differ. "You moved here." My mind is truly boggled by the extent to which Dick is capable of thinking only of himself. Dick is the poster boy for narcissism. He never considers anyone else unless there is something he wants from that person, in which case, he will turn on the charm and pull out all the stops, but it's always a performance, never genuine.

Dick ignores my comment, carries on. "And as far as why I chose your aunts' place, well, think about it. No one would poke around in your Italian aunts' veggie garden."

"Except the aunts. Which is why the identifying features of your departed colleague are currently sitting in a pasta pot on the aunts' patio, waiting for the police to pick them up and identify the poor schmuck they belong to."

"You can't do that, Gina. I'm telling you, you cannot get the police involved. These guys do not fool around."

"Is Sal Fortuna involved in this? Is he the one forcing you to break the law?"

"The less you know, the better. Trust me."

"See, that's the problem, Dick. I can't trust you. I don't trust you, and I never will again."

"I'm trying to keep all of us safe now, Gina."

I blow my stack again. "Question number four: Why Dick? Why? Why are you such a colossal screwup? You do know you're never going to pay off the debt to these people, right? That's how extortion works. They're going to keep you doing their dirty work for as long as they want, which is forever, unless they decide to have your body parts buried in somebody's veggie patch."

Dick shakes his head solemnly. "I'm sorry, Gina, but I have to do what they tell me to do. I don't have a choice."

"Well, I do, and I'm choosing to go to the police." I turn to leave, grab the shed door handle.

Dick reaches out in one quick move and puts his hand over mine, preventing me from turning the doorknob. He stares into my eyes. "No, Gina, I can't let you do that."

This is the first time since I walked into the shed that I've felt truly terrified. My anger was greater than my fear up until now and overshadowed it. But in this moment, I'm immediately flooded with memories of Dick's lying, and his temper, and his physicality, and I am especially reminded of the lengths to which he will go to get what he wants. "How will you stop me?"

"They'll hurt our children."

"Our children are in Europe."

"They know that. They know everything."

I would never take any sort of risk when it comes to my kids, but I remind myself that Dick is a great liar. "I don't believe you."

"They told me you and the kids are planning on going to Iceland for Christmas. They said there are thousands of places in that remote country for people to disappear on cold winter nights."

My blood freezes in my veins, my heart catches in my throat. Dick had no way of knowing about our plans for Iceland. The urge to call my children and make sure they're alright overrides every other thought in my head.

I need to get away from Dick, and I need to protect my kids, which means I need to say yes to everything he asks of me. I take three deep breaths to steel myself. "You can't leave the body parts here. And you can't leave anything else here again. You can't involve the aunts in any way in your illegal activities."

Dick nods, looks extremely relieved. "Okay, I understand. Go get me the fingers. All ten of them. And the teeth. I'll take them somewhere else."

"Why can't you just bury them out in the woods somewhere?"

"Too risky. Animals dig them up all the time. Your aunts' garden was the perfect place."

"Not when it's garlic-planting season."

Dick laughs for a split second only. "I didn't think of that. I thought they'd have put the veggie patch to bed for the winter. Don't worry I'll find somewhere else."

"Wait here." I peek outside the shed door before I head back into the aunts' yard. I cross the lawn to the outdoor table with the creepy pasta pot sitting on top of it. Through the kitchen window, I see my zias working away over their commercial stoves as rising steam from skillets and boiling saucepans clouds the air. I lift the lid on the gruesome pot and double-check the numbers, counting ten digits and one full set of pearly whites. I carry it over to the shed, trying not to scream, which is not easy. I kick at the door.

Dick peeks through a crack. "Anyone around?"

I look up and down the alleyway beside the shed and shake my head. He emerges very slowly, checking in all directions, not trusting my judgment at all. I don't think Dick can trust anybody, least of all himself. I hand him the pot. He lifts the lid and counts the rotting appendages for himself, again not trusting me. And to be fair, he shouldn't. At this moment, I am certain I would give him up to the police in a heartbeat if it weren't that my children's safety might be at stake. I don't know if I've ever felt more disdain for this man than in this exact instant, and that is saying a lot.

Before he departs, I state what I hope is the last thing I ever have to tell him. "Don't contact me or come near me or the aunts again. And pick up your dinner from some other restaurant from now on. Ideally, in another country."

Dick barely glances at me, doesn't take the time to respond. He nervously scans the alleyway once again to make sure the coast is clear before he strides swiftly down it toward the street. I watch him hastily shove the pot with the dead guy parts into the trunk of his car and speed off.

Chapter Twenty-Six

The gala event of the Sunset Beach High 150th Anniversary Reunion is finally upon us, the all-years Halloween costume dance. I am thrilled out of my mind because this means the reunion weekend is almost over. The end can't come soon enough.

I'm back at my cottage just after lunchtime, and I have never been happier to be alone. I probably need a decade on a mountaintop in Tibet with a temple full of Buddhist monks who have taken a vow of silence to be able to process the events of this morning. Never mind the emotional mudslide of last night's bonfire party—so much has occurred in the twelve hours since Team Outcast introduced himself to me on the beach, and Sal threatened to carve his initials into Craig's face with a broken bottle that those happenings seem like ancient history. And compared to this morning, last night feels like a walk in the park. Or to put it into perspective, if last night were a bikini wax, this morning would be a full fricking Brazilian.

Dick and all the fingers and teeth have disappeared from the aunts' property, which is good, but even though I told Dick to stay away from all of us and not to contact me, deep in my gut I know that's not going to happen. After today, I wouldn't be surprised if the next phone call I received from Dick is his one call he's allowed to make from the jailhouse, in which case he will definitely have dialed the wrong number.

Speaking of jailhouses, my friendly neighborhood police chief, Floyd, finally rings me, full of apologies for the delay in updating me on the Team Outcast case and thanking me for all the info I sent him on Cassie Williams's brother. They've been swamped with reunion-related infractions.

199

I so want to tell Floyd about Dick and the buried body parts and the criminals he's got himself mixed up with. The words are on the tip of my tongue, and I have to bite them back to keep them in. But when I call to mind the possible risk to my children, it's easy to keep my mouth shut.

Floyd tells me that they've picked Sean Williams up and are presently questioning him. He was released from a Nova Scotia jail a few weeks ago after doing three years for break and enter. He's got a checkered legal past and a history of mental illness resulting in regular therapy as a parole condition. Floyd says Sean has been meeting those conditions and that he didn't actually break the law with the emails and photos he sent me. But they've applied for a peace bond restricting him from contacting me or the other three girls further, and they've warned him away from us. Floyd tells me that they probably won't be able to hold him all night, but they're going to keep him for a few more hours to make sure Sean's scared enough about the possibility of returning to jail that he won't bother us anymore.

I feel for Sean and for the sister and mother he lost so tragically at a tender age. I shudder at the thought of his two loving female caretakers being replaced by an abusive, alcoholic father. The pain and grief would have scarred him for life. And all of that agony would have been made a thousand times worse by years spent in prison. Bullies aren't born; they're made. The cycle of abuse is a vicious and often lethal one. My heart goes out to Cassie's little brother, whom she loved so much. I truly hope that Sean Williams gets the help he needs and finds some peace.

I give my cat, Spook, loads of cuddles and treats, and I take Zoe on a marathon walk along the beach because we both need it badly. I'm working on exhaling about a thousand pounds of pressure.

When Zoe and I return, Hugh drives up and jogs over to meet me on my porch. He's grinning because he can, since he didn't dig up human remains today and have his family members' lives put in danger, all of which he has to keep top secret so that people don't die. I have to smile and sound like a normal person, which is damn near killing me.

"Happy Halloween." Hugh smiles broadly.

"Is it?" It's Halloween but so far not happy. I force a smile because I must.

Hugh looks mischievous. "So, do you know what you're dressing up as for the costume dance tonight?"

Haven't given it a thought. "What do gravediggers wear? I've got a spade and a dead body, well dead body parts." Not doing so hot at the whole sounding-like-a-normal-person thing.

Hugh looks taken aback, but, again, is now accustomed to the randomness that regularly pours out of my mouth, so is able to take my comment in his stride. "Overalls, maybe? I hope it won't be one of those sexy gravedigger costumes like the sexy nurse and sexy maid outfits that are everywhere on Halloween because those costumes objectify women, and I am not here for that." Hugh smiles. "I'm a feminist. Truly." He means it.

This guy makes me laugh despite my foul mood, and I am aware that is a very good sign and also, at the moment, extremely annoying. "I'm definitely not feeling sexy anything so no danger of that happening. In fact, I'm not feeling like going to the dance at all."

Hugh is sympathetic even though he was also there last night for the narrowly averted bloodbath, and it was he who was about to tango with Big Benny. "I get that after all the weirdness that went down on the beach, but I don't know if Florrie will let you off the hook for tonight's festivities. I'll go with you if that would help?"

I look at Hugh skeptically. "A few days ago, you stood right on this porch and told me that you weren't planning on attending any of the reunion activities because you didn't go to Sunset Beach High."

"That was before you threw me up against the side of the bunkie and sucked my face off, which was, by the way, the best kiss of my life. Well, it's in a tie with the kiss I shared with Posh Spice the following night. So, what do you say? We can dress up as gravediggers and go to the dance together."

My smile is unforced, so that's progress. "Yeah, okay, let's go together. But not as gravediggers. I'm feeling sort of zombie-ish"

Hugh thinks for a moment, then nods. "Sure, I got some ideas for that. Pick you up at eight?"

"Sounds good." Zoe and I step through the door.

Hugh jumps down the porch steps, calls back over his shoulder. "This will be our third date, by the way. So you know, the whole third-date rule thing kicks in."

"Oh my God, that's so much pressure." I hope he's joking.

He is joking. "That's what wine is for. I'll bring lots." He chuckles.

Hugh makes me chuckle, too, which is no small feat. After this morning, I thought I might never laugh again.

I stare out the window with some tea and cookies and let an hour slip by until it's time for me to shower and get my zombie on. I wild up my hair with half a can of mousse and apply sickly-looking pale makeup to my face. I'm not interested in being a sexy zombie, but pretty zombie might be a good compromise just so the pets aren't quite so terrified. Loads of black eyeliner, stitches on my cheeks, and blood on my lips.

The clothing part is easy. I wear a super distressed pair of jeans with my Docs, rip up an old white tee and tear up a plaid flannel shirt that I haven't worn in years. I look in the mirror. I've done a decent job on my costume. Unfortunately, my flesh looks a lot like the gray sausages the aunts dug up in their garden this morning, and I now wish I'd dressed up as something a little less corpse-like.

There's a knock at my door, and Zoe runs to it, barking. I open it, curious to see what kind of getup Hugh has on.

Oh. My. God. I am dead for real now. This guy is clever. And so ridiculously hot. Standing on the porch before me is Negan Smith from *The Walking Dead*. This must be Jeffrey Dean Morgan in the flesh. Hugh is wearing a black leather jacket, low-rider gray jeans, and a red scarf around his neck. He's even carrying Negan's barbwire-wrapped baseball bat. Swoon. And he's smart too. The weapon may come in handy later tonight. Totally wishing I had gone for the sexy zombie look now.

Hugh smiles disarmingly, as if he ever smiles any other way. "I'm the zombie hunter to your zombie."

I definitely didn't think this through. "I'm already regretting what I'm about to say, but I can't let you wreck my makeup."

Hugh laughs, hugs me hello instead of his usual kiss. "That's okay. We've got the whole night."

We tuck the dog and cat into the cottage for the evening, leave all the lights on, and lock it up tight.

The streets are still busy when we drive into town. The sidewalks are jammed with adorable little ghosts, goblins, fairies, and witches, and multitudes of superheroes going door to door for their tricks and treats. Nearly every house has the welcoming, blinking light of a jack-o-lantern on the front porch.

It's not that late when we pull into the high school parking lot, but it's already tough to find a spot. The place is bumping, and all the partygoers are fully decked out in every kind of Halloween costume imaginable.

Fred and Wilma Flintstone take our tickets at the door. The school gymnasium is glowing with hundreds of tiny orange lights, and there are amazing, creatively carved, candlelit pumpkins flickering on every round table for eight, courtesy of the current and extremely talented art students.

I text Vivi and Florrie, and seconds later, they are waving us over to the table where they've held two seats for us.

Florrie is a perfect Velma, and Marty is a barely recognizable Scooby-Doo in a brown turtleneck and corduroys with large black paper spots tacked all over his clothes. He's wearing a bright-green dog collar, pointy cardboard ears glued to a hairband, and a long tail pinned to the butt of his pants. I would have expected more from a theater professor, but he makes me laugh out loud, and I'm glad his costume is a homemade one.

Vivi is a gorgeously elegant-looking vampire complete with fangs, and her sidekick Craig is the world's-goofiest-looking bat. His true inner geek is shining brightly, and I love that. I also love that he ditched his original Moses costume to match up with Vivi. So sweet.

My eyes scan the rest of the room, and most people are unrecognizable in their masks and face paint. I count three Grim Reapers. I'm confident none of them are our Team Outcast, as Floyd and Lloyd probably still have Sean Williams in custody.

I can't help but smile as I look back at our table, take it all in. How truly wonderful our little group looks. We all need a drama-free night of fun, and

I'm hoping against all odds that tonight is going to be it.

Thirty seconds later, my hopes are dashed when Sal and his entourage make a sweeping entrance. All eyes are on the eight of them. They're dressed flamboyantly in matching fuchsia-and-turquoise loose satin shirts—except for Tiffany's, which is knotted at her bare waist and barely contains the contents of her push-up bra. They've come as a bowling team and have the name "Sal's Pin Pricks" embroidered across their shoulders. Sal's shirt has "Kingpin" emblazoned on his chest, and as an accessory, he carries a honking huge gold-colored trophy that he must have won years ago during his heydays as a pro.

Craig looks a little wild-eyed when Sal intimidatingly stares him down as they saunter past. They take an empty table in the corner where Sal has a perfectly clear view of our group.

Vivi is obviously shaken. She leans over to me. "You have to go to the bathroom?"

"Sure, let's go." A gal can always go to the bathroom. I squeeze Jeffrey's, I mean Hugh's, broad shoulders as I get up from the table.

Florrie jumps up, gives Marty a peck on the cheek. "I've got to go get ready for the awards presentation. We're doing those first before everybody's too hammered to tune in."

"There are awards?" I crinkle my nose. I think everyone is going to hate that.

Florrie pleads innocent. "It wasn't my idea. This is all the old Yearbook Club's doing. I haven't even seen the list. I just have to read them out."

Sal keeps his eyes on us as we cut across the middle of the floor to enter the girl's change room door.

When Vivi and I come out of the bathroom cubicles, Tiffany is standing in front of us, arms crossed, looking like a pissed-off toddler.

"FYI, old lady, you're going to sell us your crummy little cottage. I'm already having plans drawn up for the new one Sally and me are going to build there."

Vivi walks around Tiffany to wash her hands in the sink next to me. "I know you were in my cottage with an architect. I talked to him. I told him that you're not the owner, that you were trespassing, and that I might have the cops charge him with break and enter if he ever shows up at my home again. I don't think he wants you as a client anymore."

Tiffany looks completely shocked. "So you're the reason he's not returning my calls. Poor guy, Sal had one of his employees visit him and knock, I mean *talk*, some sense into him. That's on you."

Vivi is livid. "It's not going to happen, you spoiled little bitch. You're never going to own my cottage."

I follow Vivi out the door.

Tiffany calls out after us with a distinctly threatening tone, "Never say never. It's really not safe for you to stay at that cottage, Vivi. Anything could happen to a woman all alone in a secluded place like that."

Chapter Twenty-Seven

Vivi and I link arms, walk purposely back to our table without looking in Sal's direction.

"Tiffany's a psychopath, Vivi. You can't stay at your cottage alone until she and Sal have pulled out of town and are long gone."

Vivi's face falls, and she looks completely beaten down now that she doesn't have to put on a tough façade for Tiffany. "Yeah, long gone and six feet under." She rallies. "I can't let them know they're winning. They'll smell the fear and go for my jugular. Let's have some fun."

Vivi sits down next to Craig and throws back the glass of wine he hands her, then holds her empty cup out right away for a refill.

I hear my name being bellowed from the opposite corner of the room. "Gina, Gina, *vieni qua!*" Come here. I don't know how the aunts recognized me in the dim lighting with my white face and frizzy hair. Must be their finely honed sixth sense. "Gina, Gina." I know they won't stop calling me until I go over to their tarot-card-reading booth, and I don't want them to come to our table in case they mention the human sausages they dug up in their garden this morning, so I fast walk over to them, hoping to succeed at damage control.

The aunts are the biggest celebrities here. Whenever they go anywhere in the gymnasium, they're swarmed by desperate souls seeking answers for how to fix their messed-up lives. I think the reunion has made many people realize just how much time has passed, and how little time there may be left to make their dreams come true. Some of them are in full-on panic mode. Yet another reason to skip your high school reunion. The list just keeps on growing.

The aunts have a long line of customers dying to know whether they married the right person, whether they should quit their job on Bay Street and sail around the world, or whether their spouse is going to find out about the affair they started with their old high school flame in the last forty-eight hours.

When I reach the fortune-telling booth, the aunts are just finishing up a reading with a man dressed as Harry Potter, who is convulsing in tears after hearing the news about his future. This looks like a pattern.

Zia Rosa waves away the next person in line, motioning for them to back off in order to let me squeeze in to talk to them.

The music is already loud. I lean in close so they can hear me. "Zias, why do you have to make everybody cry? Why don't you just tell them the good news? Tonight's supposed to be a fun party."

Zia Rosa scoffs. "We tell them the good news, too, if there is any. That man, he's crying because he's happy. His wife she's going to leave him, and he can't wait."

Zia Angela is speaking using her regular outdoor voice, but thankfully she's mostly drowned out by the music and the hundreds of booming conversations carrying on all around us. "Where are the dead fingers?"

I leap to cover her mouth with my hand. "Shhhhhhhh. Don't talk about that, Zia!"

Zia Rosa leans in. "Did you take the teeth to the police?"

"No, not yet. Keep your voices down. Just leave it with me, and please don't tell anyone anything about this. It's a secret for now, okay?"

The aunts both shrug. They could care less. Their long line of customers is getting antsy with me holding them up. "I've got to go back to my friends, zias. You two be nice, and don't make anybody else cry." I start walking away.

Zia Angela yells out to me. "Bye-bye, Gina. Don't worry about the dead man. We no tell anybody!"

They're going to make me cry. The few people standing closest to them overhear and look at me strangely. I wave at them and smile. "Halloween zombie joke."

I see that the church-sponsored non-alcoholic punch table is set up again and being run by none other than Bible Babe herself, Pious Iris. She's dressed as an angel in a white choir gown with giant feathery wings stapled to her back, and a halo rigged out of coat hangers and silver Christmas garland. She might be the first victim this zombie rips the head off of.

Back at our table, Vivi is already looking a little tipsy, and she's busy videoing absolutely everything with her phone for her Instagram account. The guys have grabbed loads of snacks on paper plates for us to share, and Hugh pours me a glass of pinot.

A high-pitched squeal reverberates through the gymnasium, and everyone covers their ears in pain. Florrie is standing at the mic on the stage, tapping it with her fingers, getting ready to present the awards. "Welcome to Sunset Beach High's final festivity of our reunion weekend. Everyone's costumes look great. And this weekend has been amazing, am I right?"

The entire gym cheers and claps loudly.

We have a few special awards to present, which you all voted on if you returned the ballots that were emailed to you in your reunion welcome package.

I turn to Hugh. "I bet you they could count all the returned ballots in about three seconds flat," I ask everyone at our table. "Did anyone here vote?"

They all shake their heads.

Catwoman lookalike Cordelia arrives late, straight from her part-time job, so she's left her dominatrix attire on for this costume party. So much latex, so little room to breathe. I have no idea how she walks in those four-inch stiletto boots. "I didn't even read the welcome package." She pulls up a chair next to Craig, who is trying hard not to register shock at the sight of her sexy, skin-tight outfit. Cordelia snaps her three-tailed whip at him à la *Fifty Shades of Grey*, and even with his bat mask on, I can see that Craig turns fifty shades of red.

Florrie reads out a list of silly awards and the former students who have been chosen by a handful of their peers to receive them. After a while, most people aren't listening anymore and return to chatting up the people at their table. Florrie calls out awards for Most Enviable Job, Most Dangerous Job, Grayest Hair, Least Hair, Most Marriages, Most Divorces, Most Children, Most Popular (Vivi wins that), Most Famous (they call out my name), Most Likely to Wind Up in Witness Protection (Sal).

And then Florrie announces the next award, and she's read off so many on the very long list already that the words just spill out of her mouth into the mic before she realizes exactly what she's said: "Most Likely to Be Bullied to Death." The whole room turns silent. Florrie stutters, and perhaps because she's somewhat stunned herself, she continues and reads out the name that goes along with the award. "Uh, um, Cassie Williams." There are some gasps, including one from Florrie.

Talk about a buzzkill. There is the longest awkward silence in the history of long awkward silences. Florrie clearly doesn't know what to say next. I look all over the room for Sean Williams. Only he would have slipped this onto the awards list, although I have no idea how. I don't see him anywhere in the crowd.

Moments later, Florrie recovers enough to finish up her emcee duties. "Okay, well, that was fun until it wasn't anymore. But anyway, thank you, everyone, for voting and for being good sports." She raises a half-hearted cheer. "Gooooooooo, Whitecaps! And hey, let's party like it's 1999! See you all on the dance floor!" Florrie cues the DJ, and Prince's song "1999" blasts out of the speakers and gets half the crowd on their feet in seconds, busting out all their best moves. So much dad dancing going on.

I spot the three Grim Reapers that I saw earlier sitting at various tables, and I walk briskly up to each of them and demand that they remove their black hoods in an authoritative costume police voice. They are all confused, but they all comply. None of them are Cassie Williams's brother, Sean.

When I return to our table, Florrie is back sitting with Vivi and Cordelia. All of them look distraught. I pull up a chair across from them. The guys are huddled together, deep in conversation themselves.

Florrie is still stunned and upset with herself. "What the heck was that? How did those words get on the list, and why in God's name did I read them out?"

I squeeze Florrie's hand. "It's not your fault you'd already read fifty award names off the list, and you were on autopilot by then."

Cordelia passes me my glass of wine. "Florrie is worried that she ruined the dance, but I told her to look around. Everyone's already forgotten about it because it wasn't about them. Most people don't expend energy on anything that's not about them. Any luck with the Grim Reaper strip searches?"

I shake my head. "I haven't seen anyone who looks like Sean Williams here tonight, but there's a lot of people wearing masks. Floyd and Lloyd were holding him for part of the evening, but it doesn't mean he's not lurking around somewhere by now. Cassie's brother is the only person who would want to remind everybody that Cassie was bullied and make the point that it caused her death."

Like the rest of us, Vivi is saddened by the whole thing. "It was actually a clever thing to do. I get it. He wanted everyone to remember Cassie, and for a brief moment, everyone did."

Cordelia agrees. "What happened to Cassie, what happens to all victims of bullying is terrible, and it has to be stomped out whenever possible."

I point at Cordelia. "You're basically a professional bully."

Cordelia gives me a side-eye. "Only when my services are requested and paid for in advance."

I wink at her.

Florrie perks up. "Hey, that's what we should do. We should create a fund in Cassie's memory to pay for resources for victims of bullying in town."

Vivi is getting excited, too. "And some monies could go toward educational and outreach programs to teach kids how to identify and help stop bullying."

Cordelia lifts her wineglass in a toast, and we join her. "That's what we should have done a long time ago. But better late than never."

The guys have been listening in. They all agree that it's a brilliant idea, and they're all willing to open up their pocketbooks on the spot.

I give Florrie a little shove. "What are you waiting for? Get up on stage and announce the Cassie Williams Anti-Bullying Fund. Collect donations from everyone here tonight, and you'll be off to a great start."

Florrie is over the moon. She scurries back to the stage, cuts the music, and makes the announcement. The cheers are raucous, and loads of people swarm her, wanting to throw money into the fund. Now I'm hoping that Sean Williams is somewhere in the house. Nothing can bring Cassie back or heal her brother's broken heart, but this small goodwill gesture is something, at least.

Vivi and Craig jump up on the dance floor when MC Hammer sings "U Can't Touch This." It's not long before they notice that Sal and Tiffany have danced right up alongside them. Sal repeatedly bumps into Craig. Hard. And laughs. Tiffany bangs into Vivi's back, almost knocking her over.

Vivi whirls around to face the two of them. "Screw off, Sal. You're the biggest bully there ever was." She grabs Craig by the arm and leads him off the dance floor back to our table.

Hugh and Marty return from the bar with another round of drinks for everybody. We all noticed what was going on.

Our group of seven sits down together, disgusted and feeling so sorry for Vivi. Craig looks shell-shocked. I pick at the cheese and crackers and grapes that the guys loaded up on.

Vivi is furious. "He is such a piece of garbage."

Cordelia's lips curl. "Like attracts like, and that piece of garbage has attracted pure trash. I saw his brainless arm candy purposely banging into you when you were dancing."

Big Benny approaches our table, and all of us freeze. We don't know what's going to happen but we're assuming it's going to hurt.

Hugh stands up to meet the hulking wiseguy to run verbal interference between the goon and Vivi and Craig. "We're not looking for any trouble, buddy."

Benny speaks to him slowly, corrects him. "It's Benny."

Hugh nods, astounded at the low level of intelligence. "We're not looking for any trouble, Benny. Why don't you go back to your boss's table, and everyone can enjoy a nice evening?"

Big Benny looks Hugh up and down, then seems to discount him as a threat out of hand. He sets a magnum of Cristal down on our table in front of Vivi. "With apologies from Sal. He wants me to tell ya he was just joking around."

I'm impressed. "Wow. That's a four-hundred-dollar bottle of champagne."

Hugh is surprised. "They're not selling that up at the school gymnasium bar." He looks at me. "Not that I'd ever buy one anywhere."

I agree. It's a little rich. "Me either, but I wouldn't refuse a glass if it was given."

Hugh sits back down next to me, whispers in my ear, "I guess it's a peace offering. That's a good sign."

I whisper back, "Unless it's a bribe."

Vivi picks the bottle up and reads the label. "Yes, it is. How sweet that Sal remembered that this is my favorite. And he brought it along with him because I suppose he planned on doing something tonight that he knew he'd have to apologize for." She hands the bottle back to Lurch. "No, thank you, I don't want it. Apology not accepted. Return it to your boss, please."

I whisper in Hugh's ear, "I guess I won't be trying Cristal tonight, then."

Big Benny's face is a dark cloud with the large protruding forehead of a Neanderthal. He doesn't bother to peel the foil off the top of the bottle or even untwist the metal cage covering it. In one quick motion and with zero effort, the strength of his giant thumb pops the cork off the bottle with a loud bang that sounds like a gunshot. He aims it straight at Craig. Our whole table jumps, and Florrie screams when the flying cork hits Craig with a bull's eye in the chest, followed by a stream of champagne that soaks his shirt. Craig yells out and recoils as if he's been clipped, and for a split second, none of us know whether that isn't exactly what's happened. Craig rubs his hands over his sternum, checking to see whether he's been hit with a bullet. All seven of us are in total shock.

I look over at Sal, who is laughing so hard at the prank he planned on Craig that tears are springing from his crinkled eyes.

Vivi grabs the now half-empty bottle of very expensive champagne and marches over to Sal's table. I jump up and run along behind her just in case she's about to do something reckless, and I'm able to intervene.

Sal sees Vivi steamrolling toward him, and he sits upright, instantly dons an innocent-looking face, and raises his hands in a proclamation of not guilty. "Hey, hey, hey. Cool off, Vivi. Your boyfriend's okay." Sal is trying really, really hard not to laugh. "What, your *babbo* thought Big Benny came heavy and he got pumped full of lead? Did you tell Batman that Big Benny was only packing a cork?" All the guys at Sal's table chortle.

I grab Vivi's shoulder to hold her back. I'm not certain what she's planning on doing with the bottle, but I know it won't end well. She glances at me, and I'm pretty sure changes her mind about whatever she'd been considering doing. Instead, Vivi slams the half bottle of champagne down on the table with a loud thud. The fast, hard motion makes the bubbly drink fizz up and spill over the open top.

I'm acutely aware that someone may be about to get very badly hurt here, but I can't help thinking, *What a fricking waste of four hundred bucks.*

"I don't want your champagne. I don't want your stupid jokes. I don't want anything from you, Sal. Leave me and my friends alone."

Tiffany's been blowing huge, pink bubbles with her massive wad of chewing gum. She expertly bursts a loud one. "I want your cottage."

Vivi turns to the young woman. "Go to hell, you little gold digger."

Tiffany is unfazed. She's probably been called a lot worse. She shrugs, blows up another big bubble.

Vivi turns back to Sal. "I don't want to see you or hear from you ever again, Sal. I wish you were dead."

Sal is not laughing anymore. Nobody at his table is laughing. That is something you never say to a mob boss. Never. No matter who you are that's a line you don't cross. Vivi knows this, and she doesn't care anymore. She turns on her heel and grabs hold of my arm. I fall in step with her to march back to our table. I look back over my shoulder once to make sure none of them are coming after us and see a dark-eyed Sal pouring himself a glass from what's left of Vivi's Cristal champagne.

When we get to our table, Vivi takes a deep breath, and her whole body starts shaking uncontrollably—her nerves have finally thrown in the towel and lost the battle to remain calm. "It's time for me to go. You don't have to leave, though, Craig. I'll see all you guys, tomorrow or whenever."

Craig jumps up. He's more than ready to book it. This joint is no good for his health. "Oh no, I'm definitely ready to leave, too. Let's get out of here!" Craig obviously feels unsafe with Sal in the vicinity. We all do.

Florrie has done so much over the past weeks preparing for this reunion. I feel bad that some things didn't go as she planned, or worse, in her estimation, some tanked. All high school reunions are filled with their fair share of drama, but I think the Sunset Beach High festivities must have been a box office record-breaker.

Florrie's face is drawn with fatigue. "It's eleven o'clock. My duties here are done, and these soggy crackers and rubbery cheese cubes aren't cutting it. Who wants to hit up my bakery for some real food?"

Marty, probably inadvisably, does his Marlon Brando in *The Godfather* impression about Florrie's offer he can't refuse. The seasoned theater professor has perfected the sound of marbles in his mouth.

He didn't bank on Florrie being a not-too-shabby Don Corleone herself, who loves any opportunity to perform her favorite line from the film about guns and cannoli.

We're all exhausted, and stressed, and completely burned out, and still, we can't help but laugh. That's a hopeful sign.

Cordelia is on board. "I'm starving, and I'd love to attend a private after-party—just the seven of us."

Hugh raises his barbed wire wrapped baseball bat high. "I'm in! Let's blow this pop stand."

I also vote a great big yes. "Music to my ears."

We all stand, collect our purses and coats, and gather up the bits and bobs of our costumes that have fallen off and gone by the wayside during the course of the evening and especially as a result of our exuberant "Rock Lobster" flat on the floor routine.

We're just about to leave when we hear a loud smash, yelling, and a major commotion happening across the room. We all spin around to look.

Sal's table has been flipped over, food and glasses are spilled everywhere. His goons roughly push people out of the way and drop down to help Sal, who is on his back.

Sal gasps for breath, clutching at his chest. We all run toward them. White foam pours from Sal's blue lips, and his black, beady eyes dart around, desperate and wild. He looks at a frozen Vivi, who stands near him, her hands covering her mouth to keep from screaming.

"Someone call 911!" Multiple cell phones are out and dialing emergency services. The entire party has ground to a halt, and most people have gathered around and pushed in as close as possible to Sal and his men to see what's happening. The crowd doesn't look so much worried as overcome with curiosity.

Tiffany can't stop screeching at the top of her lungs. Not helping one bit. Hundreds of cell phones are recording the chaos.

Sal grunts and sputters, frantically flailing his arms about, throwing them into the air in all directions. He convulses on the floor, clutching at his throat, his entire body battling to save itself, twisting and turning, gulping and grasping.

Vivi drops onto her knees next to him, obviously unsure whether she should touch him. Sal grabs the front of her vampire dress. His arms jerk, yanking her toward him. Vivi tries to pull away, but Sal holds onto her tightly, stares into her face as he bucks on the ground. And then his movements slow, soften, and finally cease completely. His eyes roll upward, and his hands drop away from Vivi's clothes and fall to the floor. A completely terrified Vivi scrambles backward in a crab walk away from her ex-husband.

Big Benny reaches across Sal's torso to hold his fingers against Sal's jugular.

The room falls silent.

After a few moments, Big Benny growls like a dog, as if he's in physical pain. "The boss is dead."

Everyone turns to look straight at Vivi.

Tiffany stops her hysterical howling just long enough to point at Vivi and yell bloody murder. "She killed him!"

Chapter Twenty-Eight

loyd and Lloyd are at the high school in less than five minutes with their entire force of six uniformed police officers in tow.

Sal's enraged and vengeful-looking men stand guard around their fallen leader, holding the perimeter, while a serious-looking Floyd and a pensive-looking Lloyd inspect the scene.

I ask Hugh to drive the aunts back to their apartment for me, and he graciously agrees. He can barely lift the cash box from the night's take of their lucrative tarot-card-reading booth. The aunts cross themselves about a hundred and twenty times as they walk through the gym and past Sal's dead body. Lots of novenas being muttered in Italian for Sal and his poor mother. But, also they look a little excited and can hardly wait to get home—they want to check Sal's astrological chart before they go to bed. They proudly and loudly state that they predicted a death would occur at the dance tonight, *attacco di cuore*, heart attack.

The handful of uniformed cops focus on crowd control, and it's not an easy task attempting to funnel five hundred inebriated, costumed rubberneckers out of the gymnasium who do not want to leave and who are trying to snap shots of blue-faced Sal for their Facebook pages. Tonight is, for many of them, the most exciting night of their lives, having never before been this close to deadly action or deadly men.

Floyd and Lloyd take a still hysterical Tiffany over to the far end of the gym to sit her down at a table and take her statement.

The evening has come to an early and unexpected close, but that doesn't stop a few of the very drunk and stubborn celebrants from harassing the DJ to put the music back on so they can keep dancing. A couple of belligerent boozers also yell at the bartender, demanding that he open back up to serve them.

The flashes from phone cameras flare nonstop, and everybody videos everybody else. Cordelia tells us that people have already uploaded the news and footage of the night to every possible platform, and some of it is going viral.

The place is a circus, but the freakiest thing I see is an angel standing near Sal's body, praying, arms outstretched to the heavens. Mobster after mobster shoos Iris away from Sal's corpse, but she persists in trying to get close enough to pray over him and, I suppose, usher his spirit up to the pearly gates. I don't think Bible Babe realizes that Sal is likely headed in the opposite direction.

The seven of us stand off to the side of the room, comforting Vivi, who alternates between mournful crying and flashes of anger, both for her ex-husband.

Vivi sobs heartbreakingly each time she mentions her children. "How am I going to tell my kids that their father is dead?"

I take Vivi's phone out of her pocket and place it in her hands. "You're going to have to call them right now, Vivi. Sal's death is all over social media. I hope they haven't heard about it online already, but they need to hear it from you first, if possible." I'm quite certain that Vivi's two kids have been expecting this call their entire lives, but that won't make the dreaded news any easier to accept. "You should probably call Sal's mom, too."

Vivi nods robotically. Cordelia takes Vivi by the arm, leads her into the girl's changeroom, so she has some privacy and a quiet place from which to make her difficult calls.

The crowd inside the gymnasium is finally starting to thin out.

Floyd and Lloyd walk over to our group, looking extremely somber, even for small-town cops who have a dead body on their hands and very few resources to process it with. Lloyd watches Vivi. "Where's Vivi going?"

He's a little too interested in her, probably thanks to Tiffany's big mouthful of unfounded accusations. My hackles are up. "She's going to the bathroom.

I hope you're only asking about Vivi because you're concerned for her emotional well-being."

Lloyd doesn't respond to me.

I notice two of the uniformed cops directing Sal's men to step away from the body now and cordoning off the area with yellow crime-scene tape. "Why are you having that tape put up? Are you treating this as if it's a crime scene?"

Lloyd won't be telling me anything more than he needs to. "We use crime-scene tape to protect all areas under investigation, whether for an accident or a possible crime."

Florrie clings to Marty for support. The pitch in her voice is smoke alarm high. "You think somebody killed Sal? It looked like he was choking on a cheeseball or something. Maybe a pretzel went down the wrong way."

Lloyd listens to Florrie, expressionless. I don't even think he blinks.

Two police officers wearing latex gloves carefully place the bottle of Cristal champagne into an evidence bag. They're doing the same with all the glasses and food that are now strewn across the floor, but were on Sal's table. After all, Sal was frothing at the mouth.

I speak quietly. "Lloyd, are you thinking that Sal may have been poisoned?"

Something flashes across Lloyd's eyes. I don't know whether it's interest or suspicion.

Lloyd looks at me intently. "Why would you ask that?" Suspicion.

"Because psychopath Tiffany is trying to accuse Vivi of killing Sal. And Vivi did have that champagne bottle in her hands for a couple of minutes, but every mobster sitting at Sal's table, including Tiffany, could have touched that bottle. I mean, you know as well as the rest of us that participating in illegal activities, including murder, is what Sal and his friends do for a living."

Lloyd drops his voice. "A number of witnesses heard Vivi say tonight that she wished Sal dead."

I defend my friend vehemently. "Vivi would have to get in the back of a very long line of people who wished Sal dead. Why do you think Sal always has half a dozen bodyguards surrounding him? It's not to keep the hordes

218

of fans and autograph hounds from his *Bowling for Dollars* days away. I can tell you that."

Vivi and Cordelia emerge from the girl's changeroom, and both of them have red, swollen eyes.

Cordelia nods. "Vivi reached both her kids. They hadn't heard the news about Sal yet, which was good."

Vivi blows her nose into a tissue that Florrie hands her. "They haven't liked their father since they figured out what he did for a living, and neither of them has spoken to him in a couple of years, and I think maybe that makes this news even harder for them to deal with. They both sounded wracked with guilt on top of being grief-stricken and confused. It breaks my heart."

Craig puts a long arm around Vivi to comfort her, and she gladly leans into it.

I think of my own four kids and the nonexistent relationship they have with their father. I know they'd also have feelings of guilt to deal with if Dick were to pass away suddenly and everything between them was left unresolved. I hate it when people find out that you don't speak to a family member, and they tell you that life is short—that's not a reason to continue in a toxic relationship. Life is too short to invest time and energy and to compromise your mental health by staying in toxic relationships. It's just so complicated. My kids don't know how to bridge the enormous gap between them and their father, and they don't think that they want to try. There's no way any healing could ever occur unless Dick got healthy, and he is oceans away from being in that place. Especially in light of his new job disposing of body parts for hitmen he owes money to.

There are so many things that I wish were different, but what keeps my hurting heart from breaking is my eternal optimism. Hope is my drug of choice. It keeps me going when the darkness threatens to overtake. I hope that my children will find peace in their relationship with their father one day because that will be better for everyone—my kids, their future life partners, and future children, and for Dick, if he can ever get his act together.

I hope for Vivi and her two children, too. I hope they can eventually feel peace when they think of Sal instead of the anger and hatred that tortures them now. That doesn't mean they have to forgive him for all the terrible things he did—that can be too tall of an order—but finding peace is different. It's about understanding and acceptance and there's a freedom that comes with it.

Lloyd's voice snaps me back to the present. "We're going to have to get statements from all of you, but we don't have the hands to deal with that for another couple of days. I'm going to ask you lot to remain in Sunset Beach until you hear from us, and please make yourselves available when we contact you."

Nearby, a uniform is telling the exact same thing to Sal's bodyguards and ushering them out the door to leave. I wish the mobsters weren't going to be hanging around in town.

Hugh enters the gymnasium as Tiffany walks out past him. She looks over her shoulder, checking him out appreciatively. She doesn't look all that broken up over her boyfriend's death. Maybe she was crying so hard because now she won't be able to get her mitts on Vivi's lakefront cottage.

Our group is the last of the costumed partygoers left in the school. Everyone else still present is here on official business.

Floyd has joined us now. "Is this true that the seven of you had a row on the beach with Sal and his boys last night? Broken bottles as weapons and all?"

Hugh reaches us just in time to hear what Floyd says, so he responds, "Not true. Sal and his goons were wanting to start something up, and the only person with a broken bottle was Sal. The fight was over before anyone took a swing."

Florrie jumps in. "Gina's aunts threatened to call Sal's mother, and he backed off. I don't think he wanted to disrespect the zias."

Vivi points to Craig. "But the night before, Craig was jumped in the school parking lot here and beaten with a baseball bat. I know Sal sicced his brute, Big Benny, on Craig because he didn't like that Craig and I were dancing together."

Lloyd turns to Craig, looks at him, taking in his black eye and the cuts on his face. "But you didn't report this assault? Why not?"

220

Craig stutters and doesn't seem to want to say.

Vivi isn't holding back anymore. Sal's gone for good, so there's no reason to. "I asked Craig not to report it. I knew it would only make things worse for him with Sal if he got the police involved."

Now Craig finds his voice. "And I thought it might make things worse for Vivi, and she was already putting up with so much irrational and threatening behavior from her ex-husband."

"I told Craig he should skip the rest of the reunion weekend and get out of town in case Sal got even more pissed off, but he didn't leave." Vivi looks at Craig warmly. "Because he's a stand-up guy."

The coroner, Dr. Fischer, arrives. He's an old local physician with training in death investigation. That's how it works in rural Ontario. I think he was present for the births of everyone in our group, and he recognizes us because it's that small a town. Dr. Fischer waves to us, then gets right down to work examining Sal's corpse.

Floyd and Lloyd want to stand next to the doctor to hear every observation he makes, so they're done with us for now. They both wink at our group and tip their hats before they take their leave to join the doc. That's as friendly as our neighborhood police chiefs can allow themselves to be in light of the grave matter before them and the accusations flying around that one or more of us could be involved in Sal's death. There are certainly loads of people with motive to murder this mobster.

Two uniformed officers cross over to escort the seven of us out the door. As we walk past Dr. Fischer, we are all silent and straining to listen to what he's telling Floyd and Lloyd regarding his initial findings. We walk ridiculously slow, and luckily, everyone around us is so busy that nobody seems to notice.

Dr. Fischer is examining Sal's face. "Looks like a possible heart attack, but he also looks to be in good general health, so a heart attack would be a surprise, but perhaps he was under a lot of stress. It's also possible that heart failure was induced by a poisonous substance. We'll have to run toxicology tests on his blood to know for sure. Unfortunately, it takes four to six weeks to get results from toxicology reports. But I can take samples from his urine, hair, and fingernails to test for poison and have those general results to you in a few days."

Floyd writes everything down in his little black notebook. "Well, that's a good start."

Lloyd glances over at us but seems too preoccupied to take the time to move us along. "We're going to need the pathologist to do an autopsy, I guess."

Dr. Fischer nods, labors to pick his stiff bones up off the floor to retrieve his medical bag. "We need to know if he had heart disease or any other pre-existing conditions. If the deceased was poisoned, the one thing I won't be able to tell you is whether the poison was ingested by accident or if someone murdered him. That part of the investigation is your boys' department."

Floyd and Lloyd chuckle at the old doc, their old friend.

Dr. Fischer knows Sal the same way everyone in town knows Sal. "What we can confirm is that our dead guy here was in a dangerous line of work. Very high mortality rate in the car dealership and electronic parts business."

The three men guffaw at the doctor's sarcastic joke.

We've dragged our feet as long as we possibly can without attracting attention to ourselves, so we have to exit the gymnasium now. The last of Dr. Fischer's words trail off out of our earshot, but we all heard enough to keep us in the loop regarding the direction in which the police investigation will focus.

The brisk autumn air feels refreshing after the stuffiness of the gymnasium and the stressfulness of this very long and shocking night. I'm worried about Vivi. This has all been so very much. Everyone is worried about Vivi.

Hugh refers to what we all just overheard the doctor explain. "There's a lot to try to get a handle on, but I think we're too tired to hash through any of it tonight."

All are in agreement on that point.

Marty is surprised. "Gina, I guess your aunts were right with their heart attack prediction. That's amazing. Maybe I should get them to read my future."

Florrie and I yell our warning in unison, "No!"

Marty jumps back, even more surprised.

Cordelia offers her best advice to Vivi. "If the police call you in to talk to them tomorrow, try not to say too much. Retain a good lawyer from the city if you need to, just to err on the side of caution."

Vivi nods but is clearly overwhelmed.

Florrie checks her watch. "It's three a.m. Do we still want to eat food?"

I can't handle a replay of my goat-eating-python episode a second night in a row. "Too late for me. Vivi, you're going to stay at my place tonight, okay?"

Vivi looks grateful for the offer. It's not a night to be alone, even if all she's going to do is sleep.

The main doors of the school open, and a gurney carrying a zipped-up black body bag rolls out and into the parking lot. We all turn to stare at it in silence. Two men in overalls push Sal toward the coroner's van. Sal is taking his last trip through town to the hospital morgue this time.

The coroner's van drives off with Sal in the back, and it seems that we all feel terrible even though some of us didn't know him very well and all of us thought he was a horrible human. It's impossible to believe that a few short hours ago, Sal was living and breathing and laughing and dancing to MC Hammer and stirring up disturbances wherever he could. And now he's just gone. Forever. Sal is over.

Vivi watches the taillights of the van disappear around the corner. "What I'm feeling most of all right now is guilt."

Florrie squeezes Vivi's hand. "It wasn't your fault that he died, Vivi."

Vivi's honesty and internal conflict are real. "Not that. I feel guilty because I'm relieved that he's gone. I'm glad that Sal is finally out of my life. Out of everybody's life. This was the only way that was ever going to happen."

The rest of us exchange concerned looks. I sure hope Vivi doesn't repeat that statement in front of the police.

We're startled when headlights turn on across the street, and we see a big black SUV pull slowly away from the curb. The windows are tinted nearly completely black, making it impossible to see into the vehicle. We know it's Sal's men. There are no other cars like this in town. His crew was probably waiting to watch their boss leave the place where he had the Big Arrivederci.

The SUV stops on the road in front of us, and the driver's window lowers slowly. Big Benny looks straight at us, more menacing than he's ever looked before. He points his index finger at our group, makes his hand into the shape of a gun, and cocks his thumb.

Bang.

Chapter Twenty-Nine

A s if the night wasn't nerve-racking enough already. But it's just way too late, and we're all far too exhausted to be any more freaked out than we already are. We've hit our max. All of us need to sleep and regroup after we've recharged somewhat.

Everyone agrees that we'll meet at my cottage at ten tomorrow morning so we can discuss everything that happened tonight and what we should do or not do moving forward. Also, try to come up with ideas of how to keep everyone alive.

Florrie has promised to bring brunch so nobody could turn that offer down, and eating is one good way to stay alive, so it's on the agenda for tomorrow's meetup.

Big Benny is long gone, and now Floyd and Lloyd, and the six uniformed cops have all spilled out into the high school parking lot and are milling about. The streets of Sunset Beach are safe for now.

We all hug and kiss goodnight. Then, same as last night, Marty and Craig walk Cordelia to her house around the corner and will escort Florrie back to her apartment over the bakery, then they will carry on to crash at their motel up the street. Hugh drops Vivi and me off at mine. He waits until Zoe has done her business outside and makes sure we're all locked up safe and sound in my little cottage before heading back to his own place. Mobsters and dead guys definitely put a damper on sex and romance, and we're all feeling it.

Ten o'clock in the morning feels as if it comes far too early. I'm still washing my face when I hear the cars start pulling up in front of my home.

The gang's all here, albeit looking a little worse for wear. Florrie carries in a Sunday brunch to die for, trays and boxes and bags that all smell divine. Everyone helps schlep and unload. Hugh gets the woodstove roaring, and the little cabin could not possibly be any cozier. Zoe and Spook love all the head scratches and belly rubs they receive.

The coffee is ready, and the first pot is drained within minutes, but the next pot is put on straight away. Florrie sets about warming up her gourmet meal. To keep us going while we wait for the main event, she lays plates of homemade cinnamon rolls with cream cheese icing and slices of marbled sour cream banana bread on the kitchen table for us to pick at. She also sets out bowls of fresh, bright berries, and I indulge in those. The three guys are thrilled with the brunch. Find someone who looks at you the way these men look at Florrie's food.

Everyone sits down around my kitchen table after Florrie shoos us all away from the stove. She needs her elbow room, but she knows we're all ready to leap in to assist whenever she gives us direction. And we'll definitely handle the whole cleanup. The coffee and cakes are heavenly. I warm my hands around my steaming mug of joe. The good company, along with the scents of breakfast mingled with the burning cedar and cherry logs in the fireplace are all the medicine we need.

"Gina, you're off the hook for your author appearance and book reading at the library this afternoon." Cordelia knows she's delivering good news. "It's been canceled. Sal's death put quite the damper on the rest of the reunion weekend, and apparently, a lot of people checked out of their motels and cottages to head home earlier this morning than expected."

"Probably more because they're hungover than traumatized." Marty bites into a perfectly squishy cinnamon roll. "But death is the consummate party pooper."

Cordelia knows I was dreading the author appearance, but I don't want to tell her that I also completely forgot about it. "Can't say I'm not relieved to skip the book reading. Thanks, Sal."

"Told you only good would come from Sal kicking the bucket." Vivi is quiet, looking like she's in her own world, but is also back to recording Florrie and her food and all the coziness of our morning on her phone as she sips her lavender tea.

Florrie asks Vivi, "Did you talk to your kids again? How are they doing?"

Vivi exhales about four cubic feet of stress. "I did. Both of them are equal parts sad and angry. I'm flying out to spend some time with them as soon as the police say I can leave town."

Cordelia fills us in on the latest news. "Sal's passing has actually caused traffic jams in Sunset Beach."

We all look at Cordelia, surprised.

"Oh, wow, is that what the backup of vehicles on High Street was about?" Florrie waves a spatula around. "I thought everyone was heading down to have one last look at the lake before they wrapped up their reunion weekend."

"Nope." Cordelia shakes her head. "All those cars were piling up in front of the estate that Sal rented on the water. Murder tourists are actually a thing now."

I object. I don't want a rumor circulating that could endanger Vivi. "We don't know that Sal was murdered. Dr. Fischer thinks it could have been a heart attack."

Marty talks through a mouthful of banana bread. "Doesn't matter if it was murder or not. That will be the tale told because he's a mafia boss who bit the dust in a cinematic ending in front of hundreds of witnesses."

Craig agrees. "Infamous people who die of natural causes don't sell slippers on Amazon—the websites want headlines that scream murder and mayhem to attract online advertisers. So that's how this story will play out regardless of the facts."

"I heard on the news that the roads heading up here from the city were busy this morning, too." Hugh pours more coffee for himself and tops up everyone else's mugs, too. "People are driving up to Sunset Beach to take selfies in the town where a mob boss died. Reservations for lanes at the Sunset Bowl are booked solid for the next month."

"Gross." Cordelia makes her I hate people face.

"Well, that should be good for business." Florrie looks on the bright side.

"I thought I'd have a break once the reunion was over, but it sounds like the bakery will be booming for a while yet. I guess I should put some cannoli on the menu."

I'm blown away by the whole concept of murder tourists. "What are people doing when they stop at the cottage Sal rented? I can't imagine Sal's crew will want strangers hanging around, and those guys aren't allowed to leave town yet."

Cordelia witnessed the sight firsthand. "I don't think they have a choice except to put up with it. This is the fallout from the whole true crime obsession. Stans videotape each other standing as close to the cottage as they can get. When I drove past, they were climbing over the rocks on the beach to get better shots, and that water is damn cold. Tiffany is definitely loving all the attention, though. I saw her lounging on the front porch and waving to onlookers. She was appropriately dressed in black, but missed the mourning mark a little since it was a black negligee."

"I've read about murder tourists breaking into crime scenes to pose in rooms where murders took place." Florrie passes out mimosas in fluted glasses. "Some of the worst ones call the victim's family members and say cruel things like they're glad the victims were killed or that they were married to the killer or knew him in a past life."

Florrie serves up an amazing brunch, beginning with mushroom, leek, and fontina frittata and breakfast burritos with eggs and avocado. "Vivi, I always wanted to ask you this. Did you know Sal was involved with the mafia when you married him?"

Vivi shrugs. "Yes and no. Everybody knew he was always in trouble and did time in juvie as a teenager. When he moved out of town, he went to live with his cousins in Hamilton, and they got him into the life. I knew he was running with a fast crowd, and it was exciting to me at first. I was young, and there was so much money splashed around and lots of late nights at fun clubs, and I was attracted to his reckless tough-guy bravado, I suppose." She looks over at Craig, who exemplifies the exact opposite qualities, and he knows it. But Vivi knows it, too, and that's what she likes about Craig. "That shiny penny was tarnished very quickly. There's no part of me that wants anything to do with any part of that lifestyle now."

Craig's shoulders relax in obvious relief.

Cordelia's voice is laced with concern when she asks me about my ex. "Have you heard from Dick again since he showed up here asking for your help the other night?"

I want to tell them all about Dick and the fingers and teeth he buried in the aunts' garden, but I know I can't breathe a word of it to a living soul. I can't afford to take any risk that could pose a possible danger to my children. I shake my head no. This is a conversation I can only trust to my late BFF, Siobhan. I tell her all my secrets, and she keeps all my confidences. I'm due for another graveyard coffee klatch.

Florrie dishes out a last course of spinach and harissa shakshuka baked with runny eggs and spicy tomato sauce and serves it with chunks of crusty bread for dipping. It is all ridiculously delicious, and by the time we're finished, none of us can push our plumper bodies away from the table.

Hugh brings up the practical topics that we planned to discuss. "So Floyd and Lloyd want us to stick around town until they have time to take our statements. That's no problem for most of us, but what about you two guys?"

Craig shrugs. "I called into the office and told them I wouldn't be in this week."

Marty is cool with it, too. "It's reading week at my university, so I'm off anyway. It's not a problem to extend our stay at the motel. They're basically empty after reunion week, but maybe these murder tourists will start checking in now."

Hugh feeds scraps off his plate to the massive, black, furry head that's parked on his lap. Zoe is extremely grateful. "As far as what we all need to or should do, I guess the answer is nothing. Wait around, is all. None of us have any information to give the cops other than what we've already told them. And what everybody's really waiting to hear about are the results from Sal's autopsy. Our only real job right now is to stay away from Sal's goons and keep each other safe."

We're all in agreement. There isn't much else to say on the matter.

Vivi turns to me, brings up another topic. "I'm really concerned about

Dick owing money to guys who are pressuring him. I've seen that a lot, and it never ends well. It could easily be Sal or men who are close to Sal that he's in debt to. I'm sure I remember hearing Dick's name kicked around a few times at least."

I'm not going to go there. "I have no idea, and I don't care. I have a feeling Dick's going to be leaving town soon."

Vivi sounds a dire warning. "I hope so. Because guys like Dick who get into trouble with guys like Sal often bring the people around them down with them."

I think my voice is a little snippy. My stress level is rising, and I don't want to discuss Dick. "Well, good thing I don't spend any time around my ex-husband, then."

Everyone knows we've said all that needs saying. We all pitch in on cleanup, and it doesn't take long before the kitchen is sparkling again, leftovers are packed up and parsed out, and everyone is on their way. Craig and Vivi are going for a drive along the lake. Cordelia's off to the library, and Florrie and Marty are going to her place to binge Phoebe Waller-Bridge's *Fleabag*. Netflix and chill.

It's just Hugh and me and the pets left in the cottage. And that feels pretty nice. I've been out so much lately, poor Zoe is desperate for a walk. Hugh comes with me, and we do an hour along the beach. It's chilly but sunny, and we're dressed for it. Hugh holds my hand for most of the way, and I think I've never felt safer.

When we're almost back at the stretch of beach in front of my place, we stop for a few minutes while Hugh throws sticks for Zoe to burn off the last of my playful pup's energy. I turn around to look at my cottage, and my eye catches something moving through the window of my rickety old wooden boathouse that sits at the water's edge. I'm just about to tell Hugh when I see the male figure dart out the boathouse door and scramble into the woods next to my property. If I tell Hugh, I know he'll take off in a sprint to chase after the trespassing man. But I don't say anything because I know who it is.

It's Dick. And he's definitely up to no good.

Chapter Thirty

Back inside my cottage, I'm pretty sure Hugh is hoping we'll Netflix and chill next to the woodstove and pop open the nice bottle of chardonnay he brought over. I had been thinking the same thing up until a few minutes ago.

Now I can't think about anything other than what on earth Dick was doing in my old boathouse, and my mind is leaping to the worst imaginable scenarios. Is it ears and eyeballs today? Tongues and toes this time?

I don't want to get rid of Hugh in case I need him to help me out of a dangerous situation, but I don't want him to stick around if there's Dick damage control that I have to deal with in secret. This is not good. Not good at all. Dick is the absolute bane of my existence and the worst thing that ever happened to my love life, never mind my financial life.

Hugh stokes the fire. Zoe and Spook are already stretched out in front of it.

I stutter, "D-do you mind hanging out in here for a few minutes? I have to go check on something outside."

Hugh looks the slightest bit confused. "Sure. But I can go do whatever it is for you. Or I can go with you. We all still need to be extra careful, right?"

"Yeah, of course." I sound so sketchy. World's worst liar. "I'm good to do it on my own, though. I'll only be a couple of minutes."

"Okay." Hugh's finely tuned crock of crap antennae are up.

I'm pretty sure I am completely devoid of crock of crap antennae, as if they were amputated from my aura at birth. I have always believed way too many people way too often, much to my own detriment. Lacking bullcrap antennae also renders me unable to bullcrap others. It's a major disadvantage in life, especially when there's a possibility that you have dead people's body parts being buried in your boathouse.

I pull my coat and boots back on. "I'll be quick." I'm out the door and sliding down the slippery trail to the water's edge. I look back at the cottage and don't see Hugh watching me out the window, but I know that he probably is. I would be.

I scoot around to the lake side of the dilapidated structure and try to force open the crooked boathouse door. I wonder if Dick is leaning against it to keep me out. I call to him in a loud whisper, "Dick? Dick! Open up if you're in there." No answer.

I have to put my whole shoulder into it and push with my thigh, but the door opens about twelve inches, just enough for me to squeeze through. My heart is racing. It's dark inside, so I flip on the light switch. It doesn't work. The bulb is probably broken. I never come in here. There's an old rowboat lying on the rotting wooden floor and a canoe hanging from the ceiling that I loved to paddle out in as a kid.

It's hard to see in the dimness, so I pull out my phone to use the flashlight, and I search around for dead guy parts. So far, nothing, and I am so frigging relieved. But, also so frigging suspicious. What was Dick doing in here? Maybe hiding out. Maybe the whole Sal dropping dead thing has something to do with Dick, or maybe Sal's goons think Dick is connected somehow to get out of paying off his debt? The possibilities for trouble are endless when my ex-husband is involved.

Okay, no body parts. This is good. I'll go back to Hugh and see whether I can get my brain back into a sexy-time space. Unlikely.

I cross to the door to leave but then think of one last place I didn't check. An involuntary shudder runs up the entire length of my spine. Oh God. Let that hanging canoe be empty, please. I climb up on an old wooden ladder that's missing every other rung. The canoe is still only barely within my reach. Managing to get a few fingers on the rim of it, I bang on the edge to tip the boat toward me so I can see inside it. It rocks back and forth, back and forth, a wider pendulum sway each time. Until I finally make it swing wildly, and the damn thing tips right over, and something huge and heavy flips out of it, crashes on the floor below. I scream and fall backward off the ladder, landing on my ass with a thwack. My cell phone skids away from me.

I can hardly breathe. My whole body shakes. I try to calm down. It's too dark to tell what the big lump on the floor beside me is, but I can think of a few possibilities. It's probably just a musty old camping tent that hasn't been used in decades. Or an extra canvas boat cover rolled up into a huge ball and put into storage years ago.

I reach over to pick up my phone and aim the flashlight at the lump. I lean in close to get a good look.

The lump's glassy eyes stare back at me. Dead as a frigging doornail.

I scream into the sleeve of my coat to muffle the sound and scramble to my feet. I lurch for the door at the same time that it fills with a black shadow.

"Hugh?" No, not Hugh. Damn it.

Dick steps hurriedly into the boathouse, shoves the door closed behind him.

I holler and not into my sleeve this time. Dick grabs me in an instant and holds his strong hand over my mouth to keep me quiet.

His voice is infused with the sound of sheer panic. "I can explain. It's the next job these guys are making me do. I've got to get rid of this body, or I'm going to be the dead guy hanging up in a canoe. Don't worry. I'm not going to leave him here. I just needed somewhere on the lake to stash him for a few hours until I can take him out to his final resting place. I'm bringing a boat around tonight to pick him up, and you won't have to think about it anymore. I'm going to take my hand off your mouth now, but you can't scream. Okay? Promise?"

I nod. He takes his hand away. I have to draw upon the power from every cell in my body to keep from yelling out, but I manage to.

"Did you kill Sal?" My voice is nearly inaudible.

Dick is genuinely shocked. "What? No. I haven't killed anybody. I would never kill anyone. You know me, Gina. Don't be ridiculous."

"Were you involved in Sal's death?"

"Of course not. Do I look suicidal? You think I'm stupid enough to kill a kingpin? I can't say I'm not thrilled that he's dead. Sal's been the one forcing me to do all this dirty work for him. I'm hoping this nightmare will be over now that he's gone, but unfortunately, they'll probably have someone stepping in to replace him ASAP. I'm just trying to stay under the radar and stay alive."

There are so many things I want to yell at my ex-husband, so many questions I want answered, but now is definitely not the time. There's a dead body six feet away from me and a live one waiting for me sixty feet away. I don't know if Sal threatening to hurt our children was leverage that he'd never actually follow through on, but I do know what Sal and his mobster gang are capable of—the evidence is lying on my boathouse floor.

"I've got to go. I've got a friend in the cottage." I step around Dick.

"Hugh?" Dick says the name with a mixture of hurt and unkindness.

"Move out of my way." I speak with pure unkindness.

I pull the door open and scream.

Hugh is standing in front of the door. Dick slips behind the door. There are two inches of wood between their two bodies. I hate my life.

Hugh tilts his head to see around me and inside the dark boathouse. "Is everything okay? What are you doing in here?"

I literally cannot think of a response. It's times like these when a gal's got her ex-husband hiding inches away from her new boyfriend and a murdered man in rigor on the floor beside her that being good at lying would sure come in handy.

"I just needed to think." See what I mean? Cannot lie to save my life. "But the light's broken in here." I press against Hugh to squeeze out through the half-open door.

I start up the path toward the cottage, and luckily, Hugh follows me and doesn't go inside the boathouse to take a look around for himself and trip over a dead body or run into a live one, which is what I was afraid he might do because it's what I would have done.

"You went into that cold, dirty, broken-down boathouse with no lights to *think?*"

I stop walking and turn back to face Hugh. The only strategy that has ever worked for me is being honest. In this situation, I can tell a half-truth, but no more. "No. There's something more going on, and it has to do with Dick, and I'm going to ask you to trust me and give me some time to deal with it. I promise you that when I'm at liberty to discuss it, I will."

Hugh takes a minute to digest my words, then he nods in acceptance, and we walk back to the cottage in silence.

The ordeal with Dick has put a damper on the rest of the afternoon, that's for damn sure. Hugh and I drink the bottle of wine and make out on the couch for a while, but I can't stop seeing the murdered man staring into my face, which isn't great for the libido even when the guy you're with is a Jeffrey Dean Morgan clone, and a hell of a great kisser, and a hell of a great guy who is really, really into you. That's how big of a buzzkill Dick can be. I'm also not comfortable making love with Hugh for the first time, knowing that Dick and his dead buddy are hanging out in my yard, so I can't go there, not today, at least.

Hugh is understanding, but he's definitely thrown. I tell him that I'm staying at Vivi's tonight so that she won't be alone, and he thinks that's the right thing to do, of course.

The plan was for Vivi and Florrie to come to my cottage to spend the night, but I don't want to be here with Dick skulking around the property, and he said he's coming to retrieve the dead guy tonight, so I really don't want to be here for that. Plus, Zoe will very likely hear or smell him and bark her brains out if not chase him down. I text the girls to let them know of the change in plans.

It's after dinner and already dark outside by the time we all arrive at Vivi's. Cordelia is coming later after she's finished whipping a new client into shape.

We're all still stuffed from brunch, so we just graze on little plates of pickies for the evening and sip lovely herbal teas, which is perfect. Florrie and Vivi have loads to share about their budding romances with their two new beaus from our old high school, and it is super sweet to hear them both gush. It's a great distraction from all the heaviness bearing down around us. The gals are anxious for me to fill them in on how things are progressing with Hugh and me, but I'm not in the mood to chat, unfortunately, so I'm not very forthcoming. I've got dead bodies on the brain.

Zoe isn't settling in, which is concerning me. She's been in Vivi's cottage before but not to spend the whole night. It's strange for her, and she's pacing a lot, looking out the windows, and growling and barking at every sound. Every time Zoe barks, Florrie's little Snowflake runs around doing the same. I get up to look for what she might be seeing, and there's nothing noticeable, but it's an extremely dark night, and a powerful wind has whipped up off the lake, drowning out most other sounds.

I wonder how Dick will be able to take the dead guy out in a boat in this weather. I assume he's going to dispose of the body in the water. Lake Huron is the fourth largest lake in the world, and it's extremely deep, but still, you'd have to go a long way out to dump a body and be sure that it wouldn't wash up on shore weeks later. I suppose he'll have to weigh it down. I cannot believe that these are the thoughts running through my mind. Dick, you are such a dick. I dislike you intensely. You have also effectively ruined enjoying swimming in this lake for me for all eternity.

Zoe is pressing her nose against the window on the roadside and barking extremely aggressively at something.

"Maybe it's Cordelia driving up." Florrie parts the curtains to peer out. "No car. Nobody around." She pets the dog. "Zoe, what's the matter, sweetheart?"

Zoe and Snowflake won't stop sounding the alarm, and they're becoming borderline frantic. All three of us look outside, but there's no sign of anyone. It could be Dick. It could be Big Benny. It could be Sean Williams, our Team Outcast.

"Should we call the guys and ask them to come over?" Florrie picks up her phone to start dialing. She's nervous now.

"What's that smell?" Vivi sniffs the air. So do the dogs. "It smells like something's burning."

Florrie struggles to remain calm. "Maybe somebody's got a campfire going on the beach?"

I shake my head. "Not in this wind."

The smell is getting stronger very quickly. We all hurry into the kitchen to check the stove and oven. Nothing's turned on or burning there.

Vivi starts running around, looking in each room. "Check the electrical panel. And the baseboard heaters." We all dash about, searching for signs of smoke. The smell is growing more acute. Then Florrie sprints out of the living room and screams loudly. "There's a fire at the front door!"

We all charge in and see bright orange flames leaping against the wooden frame. This old cottage could go up like a matchstick.

"We need to get out of here."

We rush to the back door on the lake side only to find a tall blaze pressing against that exit, too. Florrie scoops Snowflake up into her arms.

"We have to go out a window." I yank the old kitchen window open and pull the women toward it.

I keep a tight hold of Zoe's collar—I'll be lifting her through that window before I climb out it myself.

We're just about to start scrambling to get outside when we hear sirens wailing and see the flashing red lights of a Sunset Beach fire truck reflecting against the walls.

Moments later, the roar of power hoses blasts against the front and back doors of the wood-framed cottage. Water sprays through the window I opened, and we're wet in mere seconds. We scream, and two firefighters reach through the kitchen window, motioning for us to go toward them. They help pull us and the dogs outside.

The fires at the front and back doors had only just gotten started and were small enough that the flames are out and smoke subdued ten minutes later. There's damage, but a firefighter tells us that we're lucky. This old wooden cottage is a tinderbox, and there would have been nothing left of it in thirty minutes' time. We can smell the gasoline that was poured onto the front and back porches before they were set ablaze. Definitely arson, no question, says the fire chief.

Vivi and Florrie are crying a little, a mixture of fear and relief, but mostly they're in shock. Cordelia arrives and offers much-needed support.

I am just completely perplexed. Not so much with who would attempt to burn Vivi's cottage down—an angry and psychopathic Tiffany is the obvious suspect, although she likely had help from Sal's men, who know how to set fires without getting caught, so proving them guilty is probably impossible. The main questions that I'm racking my brain over are how could the fire department have responded so quickly? And who called them? Those are the real mysteries.

And then I look over and see a figure standing just beyond the fire truck. Maybe I was wrong to blame Tiffany.

Team Outcast stares at me.

Chapter Thirty-One

I have Zoe on her leash at my side, and I storm over to Sean Williams, Cassie's brother. How is he this bold? Or is he this mentally ill?

I am furious with Dick and Sal and Tiffany and Big Benny, and I completely go off on Sean Williams. "Are you totally insane? You could have killed three people and two dogs. And now you're just standing around waiting to get caught? You know you're going to go back to jail for this, right? Don't you care?"

Sean stares at me in silence for a long time. "I came to your cottage tonight to thank you and Florrie and Cordelia and Vivi for setting up the anti-bullying fund in Cassie's memory. It's already raised over ten thousand dollars. It means so much to me, and it would make her really happy. And I wanted to tell you I was sorry for scaring you. I was never going to hurt any of you. I just wanted you to know how Cassie felt being bullied her whole life. I've felt so angry. And so sad. Ever since Cassie died."

My heart breaks for this person regardless of what his anguish has caused him to do. "There are people who can help you deal with those feelings, Sean. Pain from losing someone, from being bullied or watching your loved ones get bullied lasts forever, but there are ways to heal some of those scars some of the time. It's worth trying."

Sean takes a deep breath, then carries on, "When you weren't home tonight, I came over here. And I saw the girlfriend of the mafia guy who died last night and another guy getting ready to light Vivi's place up. I could see you were all inside, so I called the fire department. And the police."

Two patrol cars with sirens on speed up the road toward Vivi's as we

239

speak.

"I believe you, Sean, but I'm afraid the police won't. You're the one standing here. They're probably going to think it was you who set the fires." I am truly concerned for this damaged man who has lived a life of torment because bullies destroyed his family and his world. It's all so unfair.

Sean holds his phone out to me. "I videoed the whole thing."

He plays a few seconds of the video, and Tiffany and Big Benny are completely recognizable, skulking around Vivi's cottage, jerry-cans in hand. Greed and incompetence are a lethal combination.

"The mob guy's girlfriend was here the night I left the newspaper on your porch. I saw her hit your two friends on the back of the head when they were out walking. She was on her own that night."

"Thanks for telling me."

We're quiet for a few moments, and I'm not sure what Sean is thinking, but I step forward to give him a long, tight hug. He doesn't hug me back, but he doesn't pull away, either.

"Thank you, Sean. I'm so sorry you lost your sister. Cassie was a beautiful person, and her death was a tragedy. She didn't deserve any of the bad things that happened to her, and neither did you."

Sean's eyes gleam in the light shining from the police cruisers, and I think they're wet with tears. Mine definitely are.

"I'll see ya." Sean turns to head over to the cops to give them his phone.

I take a few steps after him. "One more question. Did you kill the three boys who did bully Cassie? Tom Lucknow, Jason Bragg, and Ethan Coleman?"

Sean stares into my eyes for a long time, deciding how to answer, and then he chooses the truth. "Accidents happen. That's what all three of those men told me about Cassie being hit by the train." Sean turns and walks away.

And I let him go. His truth will stay with me. I couldn't save Cassie, but I will do this one thing to try to save her brother Sean.

We can't stay at Vivi's after the fire, so we're back to my cottage for the rest of the night.

Zoe was quiet, so I assume that Dick took care of his risky business while we were sleeping. I check the boathouse in the morning, and thankfully, it is corpse-free, which is a relief but on the heels of that is the sickly feeling that I am not Dick-free—I know in my gut this is not the end of my troubles with my ex.

As soon as everyone's awake, Florrie, Vivi, Cordelia, and I all head into town to have breakfast at the bakery, which is lovely. Most of the reunioners have cleared out of Sunset Beach, but High Street is still crawling with a motley crew of murder tourists. I'm sure some of their selfies went viral today when the lucky ones recorded images of Tiffany and Big Benny being arrested for arson. I heard the rest of Sal's crew hightailed it out of town right after, despite the police requesting that they stick around for questioning. Good riddance.

Not surprisingly, two hangers-on who really seem to not want to leave town are Marty and Craig. They must return to their work posts eventually but not without endless promises of many weekend trips back up to Sunset Beach to visit Florrie and Vivi. I guess we'll see in time whether reunion fever wanes or if it actually did reignite old flames that will continue to burn.

As for me and Jeffrey, I mean Hugh, things are as hot as ever, judging by the kiss he gave me when he stopped by this morning, and we're both hoping that one of these days, we'll actually make it past third base without being interrupted by a murderer, stalker, mob boss, or other such mood killers.

When I pop by to check on my zias, who have to be exhausted after feeding hordes of ravenous customers all week long, and single-handedly wrecking multiple marriages with their booming fortune-telling biz, I run into the very last people I want to see.

Sissy Greensplat and Russ Carney are bustling out of Happily Napoli just as I'm heading in. They're arm in arm, and about as lovey-dovey as an about-to-be-divorced couple can be.

Sissy is gushing like a high school cheerleader who's just made captain of the team. "Gina, your aunts are so amazing!"

"They are?"

"They were right about Russ having an affair with that horrible woman who works in accounting at his office. Weren't they, honey?"

Russ looks as if he knows this is TMI but has no way to stop his wife from talking short of strangling her, and from the color of his face, I can see that happening one of these days. He jerks his head, more like a nervous twitch, but Sissy reads it as a nod in the affirmative.

"But now that I know the terrible thing he's done to me, I know how to fix it. We're going to go to counseling, and Russ is going to find a job at a different company, and we're going to be happier than ever, right, honey?"

Another flinch from Russ.

Sissy squeezes his arm. "Maybe we'll even move to another town."

I try to conceal my fear. "Not to Sunset Beach, though, right?"

Sissy shrugs. "Who knows? Anyway, Gina, I'm so grateful to your zias for their fortune-telling talents. They're the real relationship experts. Everyone should be calling them the Ex-Whisperers instead of you."

I flinch and twitch in response about the same way that Russ did.

Sissy trundles off with a very tight grip on her hubby's very short chain.

The media turns out to be worse than the murder tourists when it comes to saturating the internet with stories about Sal's death and speculation about what did him in. One of the most popular theories involves Vivi and a poisoned bottle of Cristal champagne. But the story doesn't stop there. The real juicy part has to do with Florrie and Cordelia and me, The Ex-Whisperer, who, with her gal gang, planned the entire execution of an ex so perfectly that we're sure to get away with killing a kingpin.

Four weeks later, Sal Fortuna's autopsy report comes back from the pathologist. And because it's full of facts, rendering it wholly uninteresting to the general public, and because, as we know, the truth doesn't sell slippers on Amazon, it barely makes the news.

The aunts' tarot cards were right after all, and their gloating that ensues is epic.

Sal Fortuna wasn't poisoned. Sal wasn't murdered. Sal died from severe heart failure resulting from a mixture of alcohol and prescription meds for erectile dysfunction, causing his blood pressure to drop. Sal had a pre-existing heart condition he didn't know about. The report states that although erectile dysfunction medication is intended to work on the arteries in the penis, the effects are systemic, so the medication can trigger vasodilation in other arteries, causing a drop in blood pressure, and in Sal's case, triggering a heart attack. Let that be a lesson to all those fifty-year-old men out there popping penis pills and dating twenty-three-year-old women—hookups half your age can be murder.

The truth of how Sal died should have put all the wild rumors about Vivi, Florrie, Cordelia, and me killing a kingpin to rest for good, but it doesn't stop the raging river of raging females who have sent us tens of thousands of emails from around the world and even snail mail that arrives addressed only to The Ex-Whisperer, Sunset Beach, like Santa Claus, North Pole. Every one of them requesting that we bump off their exes for them or at least help them get rid of them for good. They've nicknamed The Ex-Whisperer "The Ex-Ecutioner." And damn, do they pay well!

Acknowledgements

I am completely aware that I am ridiculously lucky. My days are infused with beauty and magic, and joy is my constant companion (sometimes that takes a bit of work). I am carried and protected by the love and support of my family and friends (my chosen family), and my spiritual family (my beloveds who have left this earthly plane but will never leave my heart). I am the wealthiest person in the world because of them and couldn't write a single word without them.

My dream of being a published author came true thanks to the vision, dedication, and commitment of Verena Rose, Shawn Reilly Simmons, and Harriette Wasserman Sackler at Level Best Books.

I am a better writer thanks to the superlative editor Margaret Morris—The Indie Editor.

Many, many thanks to PatZi (with a Z!) of the Joy On Paper radio program—being awarded Best Novel of the Year for 2021 was truly an honour. Cheers to the multitude of esteemed radio show hosts, podcasters, and bloggers, who champion me and my work, along with so many other creatives—your keenness and generosity are so important.

My fellow Level Best authors, Mally Baumel Becker, Tina deBellegarde, Lori Duffy Foster, Lori Robbins, Cathi Stoler, and Cynthia Tolbert, I am in awe of your talent, and so deeply appreciative of our instant connection and growing friendships. I feel rooted and fortified in the writing world because I know that you fabulous females are there for me. And I am here for you, always.

To my readers, thank you so very much for gifting me with your time and support in taking up my book. I truly do this work for you, above all else.

Thank you to the librarians and the booksellers, the valiant foot soldiers of the publishing arena. Your mission to put books into the hands of readers is why we authors are able to do what we do.

Huge gratitude to the amazing social media mavens who read, review, post about, and promote my work, and that of so many other authors. We would be nowhere without you. Bookstagrammers are the reality stars of the publishing industry. Thank you so much for your sharing and support @bookishkate517 @emilyisoverbooked @beastreader @thriller_chick @wanderlustforbooks @thebookclubcookbook @kristis_literary_corner @suzysbookshelf @boozy.bookstacker @booksandchinooks @olive_reads_books @hollys_book_nook @island_book_reader @mrs._lauras_lit @bookclubbabble @novelgossip @lovemybooks2020 @blue.eyes.and.books @carrie.reads @that.bookmom @ladybug_shirls @pomoevareads @wanderlustforbooks @teachalldaywrite allnight @thenerdaily @cant_put_it_down_reviews @carrie.reads @thegoddessbooks@hollys_book_nook @rozierreadsandwine @readwithme_claire @kristinabookreadah @tays_booknook @lovemybooks2020 @shaleereads via Instagram @kaylasbooklist @theliterateleprechaun @books.and.lommie @thewickedwordie @tams_bookstagram @readingwithramona @dr_shani_reads @Jenny.white.author @beaconbookco @mpls.mystery.reader @readingwithmrsleaf @storiesandwanderlust @booksloveandunderstanding @itsallaboutbooksandmacarons @bibliophiles_bookstagram @readsalatte @maryreadstoomuch @booknerdwatercolor @whimsyreadswithshelby @readingwithmarlow @thrillbythepage_ @reader_mama@bookswithana @mads.read.receipts @toriandbooks @what.susan.reads @simosbooks @jah_reads @notablenovels_ @teatime_with_a_book @kml.books @reading.with.t I'm sure I've forgotten some, but please know that I deeply appreciate you all.

Very special thanks and big love to bookstagram goddess @padfootpuff (Kenzie McCarthy) for her exuberant cheerleading and her expert handling of my cover reveal.

To my great girlfriends who tenderly hold my heart when it's hurting, and remind me that I am never alone, that I can do hard things, and that eventually, almost everything can be laughed at. No matter that life often keeps us from regularly connecting, your energies heal me from afar. You are my soul sisters, Mary Chiovitti, Susan Dollar, Christel Francis, Denise Furlano, Jill Johnson, Diane Kozak, Michelle Mayhew Barnes, Cyndie McOuat, Lori Merritt, Debbie Parker, and Irene Yaychuk-Arabei. And loads of luv to my best guyfriends Edward Bastos, Phil Chiovitti, and Don Parker. I would move mountains for any of you.

My best friend forever, Dee, I miss you every day and am so damn grateful to have had thirty fantastic years with you. I could not have done life without you. Your amazing boys Geordon, Rory, Hadyn, and Tanner are my boys too. I love you all forever.

Thank you, mom, dad, and all my grandparents, for the deep, everlasting love and wise teachings. Your blood runs through me and keeps me strong and grounded always.

To my partner Al, steadfast and true, with the heart and hands of an artist, you turn desires into matter, creating beautiful spaces for me to dream my dreams in. Our kindred spirits never stop conspiring to invent new adventures that keep our flames alight.

My four reasons for being on this earth, my beautiful babies, Coulton, Roegan, Holden, and Arielle, you are the breath in my body, the meaning in my mind, the inspiration in my soul. You are perfect, divine creatures descended from angels and I have no clue as to why you were given to me but I do know you are the greatest gifts I have ever, or will ever receive in this world. My admiration for your genius, for your unlimited capacity for kindness, compassion, joy, humor, and love, is infinite, as is my pride in you and my love for you. My life is filled with magic, but being your mother is the most magical thing of all. Thank you for choosing me. I love you with all my heart forever and ever XXXX.

About the Author

Gabrielle St. George is a Canadian screenwriter and story editor with credits on over 100 produced television shows, both in the USA and Canada. Her feature film scripts have been optioned in Hollywood. She is a member of the Writer's Guild of Canada, Crime Writers of Canada, Sisters in Crime, Mystery Writers of America, and International Thriller Writers.

Ms. St. George writes humorous mysteries and domestic noir about subjects on which she is an expert—mostly failed relationships, hence her debut soft-boiled series, *The Ex-Whisperer Files*, which launched with *How to Murder a Marriage* in 2021. Book #2 in the series *How to Kill a Kingpin* followed in 2022, and Book #3 *How to Bury a Billionaire*, publishes in 2023.

How To Murder a Marriage was a Killer Nashville Silver Falchion Award Finalist for Best Comedy novel of 2021 and won the PatZi Award for Best Novel of 2021 in the USA, from the NPR Radio show, Joy On Paper. She is also the author of the non-fiction Gal Guides which include *How to Say So Long to Mr. Wrong, How to Know if He's Having an Affair, and How to Survive the Love You Hate to Love.* Her first short story, "Cold Ethyl," was published in the Canadian Crime Writers 40th Anniversary Anthology, *Cold Canadian Crime*, in 2022.

Gabrielle St. George lives a wildly magical life on a fairy-tale farm along the Saugeen River and spends weekends at her 1930s cabin on the shores of Lake

Huron with her partner (current coupling still alive and kicking) and their extremely disobedient dogs. When she's not writing, painting, gardening, stargazing, moondancing, and daydreaming, she travels the world to visit her four fabulous children who live abroad.

SOCIAL MEDIA HANDLES:
 Instagram: @gabrielle.st.george
 Facebook: @gabriellestgeorgeauthor

AUTHOR WEBSITE: gabriellestgeorge.com

Also by Gabrielle St. George

How To Murder a Marriage: The Ex-Whisperer Files #1, 2021

The non-fiction **GAL GUIDE** series:

The Gal Guide To Breaking Up Without Breaking Down: How To Say So Long To Mr. Wrong, 2021

The Gal Guide To Cheaters And Liars: *How to Know if He's Having an Affair*, 2021

The Gal Guide To Navigating Narcissism: How to Survive the Love You Hate to Love, 2021

Her first short story, "Cold Ethyl," was published in the Canadian Crime Writers 40th Anniversary Anthology, *Cold Canadian Crime*, in 2022

Lightning Source UK Ltd.
Milton Keynes UK
UKHW011959141122
412213UK00006B/22